PRAISE FOR THE BUTTON COLLECTOR

"The premise is original: a jar of buttons prompts memories, each one revealed in a brief, discrete story; the execution, full of sincerity, caressing details until they combine into a world; the result, a lovely, shifting kaleidoscope of Southern mores and domestic lives which contain some truth for all of us. I'll never again look at an unusual button without imagining its history."

Susan Vreeland, bestselling author of *Girl in Hyacinth Blue* and *Clara and Mr. Tiffany*

"I loved the idea of this from the first, loved it as it progressed from chapter to chapter, and love it even more as a completed book. Beautifully written and deeply moving, these several stories form one story whose center is love—and a woman named Emma."

Ann B. Ross, author of the *Miss Julia* books

"Elizabeth Jennings is a master of story weaving. She leads you seamlessly through time and memory to uncover the secrets, joys and heartaches that linger across one family's lineage, drawing them together and keeping them at odds. *The Button Collector* calls its reader to love, understand and forgive his or her own family even as its own characters struggle to do the same. This book illuminates the simple magic of memory and family and the depths to which those quiet moments haunt us and lift us up . . . It reminds us that every story of family, love and loss—even our own—is worth telling."

Amy Willoughby-Burle, author of *Out Across the Nowhere* and editor of *Blue Lotus Review*

The Button Collector

Elizabeth Jennings

Cup of Tea Books

An Imprint of PageSpring Publishing
www.cupofteabooks.com

"Summer Dance" originally published by *Rose & Thorn Journal*, Summer 2008 issue

Cover art copyright © 2013 by PageSpringPublishing

Published in the United States by Cup of Tea Books, an imprint of PageSpring Publishing
www.cupofteabooks.com

ISBN: 978-1-939403-08-7
Cover design by Britanee Sickles
Illustrations by Sarah Allgire
Interior design by Rebecca Seum

For my parents: Doris, who left me her buttons,

and Pryce, who taught me to read.

And for Melody, whose words will always be with me.

CONTENTS

Part One: Opening the Jar · 1

13 · *A Big Turquoise Button*
16 · Kitty Hawk

31 · *The Baby Button*
33 · Expecting

42 · *The Button from the Madras Shirt*
45 · Summer Dance

50 · *The Fancy One*
53 · After the Ball

Part Two: My Inheritance · 63

65 · *The Button Flower*
68 · This Very Day

80 · *The Cowboy Button*
82 · Ground Control

89 · *Navy Blue*
91 · Sorting Through

100 · *A Leather Button*
102 · Through the Screen

110 · *The Odd One*
112 · The Liberation of Maggie Sommers

118 · *A Plain White Button, One of Many*
121 · Sign Watching

Part Three: Fastening · 131

134 · *Fire Pink*
136 · Nice Things

147 · *Three Buttons on a Small White Card*
149 · Ascending

168 · *Satin Covered*
171 · Commencement Exercise

180 · *The Button from Mom's Old Robe*
182 · Bed of Violets

Part Four: Mending · 193

194 · *Serious, Yet Modern*
199 · Still Water

214 · *My Favorite from College*
220 · Truth or Dare

231 · *The Sophisticate*
235 · The Crazy Quilt Lady

248 · *The Eagle*
251 · The High Untrespassed

263 · *A Silver Heart-Shaped Button*
267 · The Doula

282 · *A Large Purple Button*
285 · Kitty Hawk II

297 · *Victoria's Easter Button*

Part One

Opening the Jar

AS SOON AS I SAW THEM, I knew they were the real reason I had come.

The buttons sparkled in the sun, forming a kaleidoscope of color against the drabness of the surrounding booths. A jar of ochre orange merged into lemon yellow, forest greens led to blues and purples—row upon row rising toward the sky, gleaming like a dragon's hoard.

I had thought I'd come to the Zebulon Flea Market to look for chairs—funky old chairs my husband and I could paint and use in the kitchen. But there I stood, unable to move, staring at jars of buttons.

The woman tending the booth bowed her head slightly as I stopped to look. Beneath the jars were boxes of more buttons, stacks of buttons sewn on to cards, button jewelry, button ornaments, button art. Buttons covered mirror frames, made cheerful flowers, formed intricate mosaics. After a moment, I picked up a card that had an assortment of brightly-colored plastic buttons, some in whimsical shapes—giraffes, tiaras, rockets.

The woman laughed. "You'll never guess who made that card," she said.

I didn't say anything.

"The janitor down at Salem Elementary. He picked all those buttons off the floor when he was sweeping up in the afternoon. Makes a right pretty card, don't you think?"

I just smiled, not really wanting to engage with her, but it was too late.

The woman grabbed another card and gave it to me.

"Now those are what you call glow bubbles. They're celluloid with a piece of foil in them that makes them seem to glow. They were real popular during the twenties and thirties. They're similar to poppers, but poppers are made out of glass."

I looked at the woman again. She was probably about fifty-five, wearing a short, brown leather coat, a beige cashmere turtleneck and dark corduroy pants over low boots. Stylish in a matronly way. She wasn't the kind of person I expected to meet here.

"Do you do this full time?" I asked her.

She laughed again. "I'm in real estate down at Banks and Marshall. I just started collecting buttons about three years ago, after I got divorced. It was a distraction, you know? But I found I couldn't stop. It's an addictive hobby. My problem is that I get too attached. I'd like to keep them all, but it isn't practical. I give some to my clients as mementos, and I come here once a month to buy and sell. It's kind of exciting to see what buttons will show up . . . and lately I've been re-selling some of the items my customers make out of the buttons, too, like this piece."

She pointed to a large canvas with a painted, stark brown tree dotted with warm, jewel-toned buttons. "It's surprising how sophisticated it came out," she said. "It has an almost art deco look to it. But my favorite craft items are definitely the bracelets and earrings." She picked up a bracelet with vintage metal buttons strung on a chain along with a key, gears, and a filigree clasp. Nearby were button hairclips, button earrings, and a whimsical collection of button flowers in tiny vases.

The crafts were all surprising in their own way, but I couldn't keep from looking up again at the jars of buttons on the shelf. Some held big buttons, others square buttons. Some were all metal and others all wood. Many were filled with an assortment, a happy jumble of colors and sizes and shapes.

The woman followed my gaze. "They look pretty up there in the light, don't they?" she said, picking up a multicolored jar and gently shaking the buttons back and forth. "A lot of folks like to buy a few jars just to put in their homes for decoration. They create a nice, cozy atmosphere, I think. If I'm marketing a house that seems to need a little warmth, a jar of buttons is the first thing I suggest. Put it on a windowsill where the sunlight catches the fabulous colors."

I watched in silence as she tilted the jar, rhythmically sifting the buttons in a cascade of color. "This jar comes with a card so you can play a game by finding certain buttons. A little like that Waldo fellow. It's fifteen dollars, but the plain jars are only twelve dollars . . . maybe you'd like one for your house?"

She could sense a sale, but I shook my head. "I have one already," I said quietly. And it was true. I had tried to forget about it, but I did have a jar of buttons myself, a jar not too different from these. It was sitting on the back shelf of my study, behind my old yearbooks.

"You collect buttons?" the woman asked me. I couldn't tell if she sounded surprised or amused.

"Oh, no," I said. "Not me. My mother, though . . . she was a button collector."

The woman gazed at the jar, as if mesmerized. "Each button has a story. That's what's so wonderful about them. Sometimes when it gets quiet around here, I just look at them all and imagine. All those stories." She laughed. "Sorry for getting sentimental. I've just been trying to figure out why they mean so much to me. I'm sure there must be a reason."

She reached for another card of buttons, a long piece of shiny black cardboard lined with six cameos. "This is probably the most valuable card I have here." She smiled, all business again, and handed the card to me. "Those are mother-of-pearl, and if you look closely, you can see that each button is a Shakespearean heroine. Ophelia, Juliet, Lady MacBeth . . . I can't keep them all straight, but the names are imprinted on the side. I got that in last month. It sells for thirty dollars, but I'll give it to you for twenty-five. It's not really my style. I'm not a serious collector. I go more for the foolish buttons, but it would make a nice gift for the right person."

She waited while I looked at the card. It wasn't really my style, either, but it did make me think of someone. Softly, I touched the button named Miranda, feeling its coolness on my fingertips. There was no way I could put it down.

It's funny how a tiny little thing like a button can conjure up a person until there she is, right in front of you, as if days and months and years haven't passed since the last time you saw her.

The button seller had good instincts. She turned around and tidied the shelves, giving me space to stare at the buttons while I tried to sort out what was going on, tried to figure out how all these feelings could come rushing back after I'd become so proficient at keeping them tamped down. I kept looking at the card, the iridescent white circles shining against the black paper, feeling the inevitable becoming stronger and stronger.

The woman turned around and quietly looked at me.

"I'll take it," I heard myself say.

She gave me her best Realtor's smile and put the card in a floral paper bag for me. I walked past rows of grimy booths to the car and began the drive home.

As I negotiated the traffic weaving through the lanes around Research Triangle Park, I felt an unpleasant knot of regret tangle in my stomach. I'm not the sentimental type. At all. I'm a computer programmer, and while my work involves designing games full of spiraling galaxies, ephemeral creatures, and shimmering labyrinths, here in the real world I don't give in to flights of fancy. I dissect things, find out how they work, boil them down to code—digits, dots, and dashes, nothing more. When you look at life like that, a button is nothing more than a device to fasten clothing. Useful. A little decorative maybe.

I would not let them be anything more.

* * * *

The smell of tandoori chicken drifted through the air to welcome me as I walked up the broad steps of our front porch, a delicate and warm smell, a smell of home. The knot in my stomach began to untie. When I was little, it had been fried chicken, green beans with bacon, and freshly brewed tea that made my insides completely melt, but after years of being married to Rishi, who could easily open his own Indian restaurant if he so desired, it was cardamom, turmeric, and the delicate floral tones of fresh basmati rice. "Basmati literally means 'full of aroma,'" he'd told me one of the first times we'd hung out together. I was still getting used to his accent, and the way he said "literally"— both distinctly and extremely fast—made me smile and cast a sunny mood throughout the kitchen. At the time, he was newly divorced from a blond ex-sorority girl, and he had dived into Indian cuisine. I guess it was his way of grounding himself back in his culture. He had his daughter, Victoria, with him on the weekends, and our early days together were often spent in his pathetic apartment kitchen, with me helping him chop basil and crush chickpeas, while Victoria colored fairy tale pages at the bar.

It wasn't a conventional courtship.

Which had been my first clue that it might just be perfect.

Victoria, now fourteen, was with us for this weekend, too, and the thought drove away the last bit of uneasiness I'd been feeling. It was easy to tuck the card of buttons in my backpack pocket, forget about them for a while longer.

"Caroline," she said, as I opened the door of our bungalow. Her skin was the color of creamy mocha, her hair jet black, creating a vibrant contrast with the faded blue of her skinny jeans and T-shirt. I know stepmoms and daughters aren't supposed to get along, but I always felt glad to see her face light up when she saw me. She ran up with her sketchpad and showed me a pencil drawing of moonlit rocks along a foggy lake.

Experience has taught me that her drawings require a deeper look, so I held it while the cats rubbed circles around my ankles and my eyes adjusted to the subtle shade gradations on the paper. After a minute, I saw it—two little girls playing by the rocks along the water's edge. What made the drawing interesting was the contrast between the innocence of the little girls and the ominous rocks and fog.

"Nice," I told her, handing it back. "We'll scan it after supper and see what we can do with it." We were working on a game plot together and had already built up a nice library of artwork.

"Sorry," Victoria said, wrinkling her nose in a sheepish apologetic expression left over from her tween years. "I can't. I'm going to a movie with friends."

"Oh, really? Your esteemed father figure is allowing such shenanigans?"

Victoria laughed while pulling a photograph from between the pages of the pad. "I wanted to show you what I found in the desk stack!" she said. "I used this old picture as a model for the sketch of the girls. It's from that time I went to the beach with your family and I played with that girl . . . what's her name? Melissa?"

In the picture, Victoria was dumping a pail of water into a tidal pool while her companion stood nearby, leaning on a shovel. Their opposite coloring made them appear exotically lovely.

"Miranda," I said softly. "My cousin Gail's daughter."

"Oh yeah . . . like the Shakespeare play. What's up with them?"

"I really don't know," I said, trying to smile. "I haven't talked to them lately."

To be exact, I hadn't talked to Gail in three years. Not in any real sense of the word. There had been occasions when we had to be together, of course, like last fall when my brother, Hank, had hosted an extended family gathering for Thanksgiving. I couldn't stay away without hurting my father, which I didn't want to do. I was perfectly civil to her, but I never talked to her alone. It wasn't that hard. There were a lot of people there, and she was busy with Miranda and her little boy, John. After dinner, I helped clean up, then went for a five-mile run while Gail and Hank's wife, Jennifer, talked in the kitchen. All the guys were watching football, and I just had to get out of there. She came up to me right before we left. I'd forgotten how beautiful she seems when she's looking straight in your eyes like that. "Caroline," she said, holding on to my arm. "Why don't you guys come down to Atlanta for a weekend sometime? The kids love Rishi. We can go to Stone Mountain, ride bikes."

Rishi held out my coat. "Sounds good," he said.

"Oh, I know," Gail added, turning toward him. The slightest hint of her perfume drifted through the air. "You can bring Victoria. She and Miranda really hit it off."

I looked at my hands while I pulled on my gloves. "My schedule's pretty crazy these days."

It was quiet for a few seconds. "Anytime is fine," Gail said quietly. "Just let us know. Okay?"

"Yeah. Okay." I managed to get away without saying what I really thought, about how I'd like to spend a weekend with her about as much as Esau might want to hang out with Jacob. I went outside. Rishi yelled goodbye to everyone and followed me, throwing his arm around my shoulder. Gail came to the door and watched us through the screen, but I didn't turn around. I could feel hot, angry tears trying to get through, and shadowy menacing spirit wolves began whining along the corners of my mind. If I stayed quiet, after a while they would go away. They always did.

I pushed the memory back down. Victoria was putting aside the sketchpad and beckoning me into the kitchen. Rishi stood behind the island cooktop, intently ladling masala sauce into a dish. I rubbed his back, and he leaned toward me for a kiss. "My lovely princess warrior returns," he said with a straight face, making Victoria laugh again.

"Smells positively rejuvenating," I replied, sitting down at the bar, kicking off my shoes, letting everything—the aroma, the warmth, the sunlight streaming through the windows of the back door—drape around me until I knew I really was home.

* * * *

Around two o'clock in the morning, I wake up. Rishi is snoring ever so slightly, and the pendulum clock in the foyer ticks steadily. I do a quick scan of my senses—nothing seems amiss despite the fact that my heart is racing.

More than a year has passed since the last time I woke in the night like this. Normally, I'm the kind of person who might have trouble finding my way to sleep, but once I'm there, I'm there for the count.

Normally, that is. But there have been periods of time in the past few years that weren't normal—days, weeks, months— when I woke and got up in the night, wandered around the house and my mind, sometimes until morning finally sifted its way through the dark.

I get up and tiptoe down the hall to check on Victoria, in case it was a noise that woke me. I hold my breath and glance in her room—she still uses a fairy nightlight, and I can see the outline of her young body gently rising and falling. All is well. The big orange cat sleeping next to her doesn't even bother to look up.

I walk into the study, turn on the small lamp at my computer station, and retrieve my laptop from my backpack. The card of buttons falls out in the process and, as I pick them up, the image of the woman from the flea market pops into my mind. I remember then what I was dreaming just before I woke: the woman was holding the jar of buttons, just as before, swirling it slowly. But this time, as I looked closely into the mix, I saw my own buttons as well. "Each button has a story to tell," she whispered, her dream voice reverberating in my mind. "There must be a reason."

I put the card in a small box on the shelf above my desk and sit down, automatically waking my laptop, surfing for something to occupy my mind. I get a cup of tea, pay some bills online, but sleep comes no closer. Finally, around four o'clock, I walk to the back shelf, push my high school yearbooks out of the way, and retrieve the jar of buttons.

My jar of buttons.

My mother left them to me. I don't know why, since I certainly don't sew or mend or do anything remotely related to those domestic tasks. The jar wasn't the only thing she left me, of course. There were also some nice pieces of jewelry, a wool dress coat, her silver. But somehow, none of those brings back everything—the memories, the feelings, the moments—the way these buttons do.

My mother. Emma Tilghman. With wavy brown hair and blue, blue eyes and a soft dimply smile, known for her home-made cookies and vividly orange daylilies.

My mother is dead.

It's been four years, and it's still impossible for me to believe at times. After all, it shouldn't be possible, should it? It simply should not come to pass that the presence you've known since before your birth just disappears. The person who first held you, the person who got up in the night with you, who knew how to drive you to the edge of crazy and then bring you back to safety again . . . how can a person like that just be gone?

I realize I'm not unique. My experience is utterly and completely common, universal. But knowing this doesn't make the feeling go away. Now, I shift my button jar back and forth the way the woman at the flea market did. It makes a rhythmic sound, like muted percussion for a jazz club. In the lamplight, the colors take on a soothing glow that I find slightly hypnotizing. "There must be a reason," she said. I am beginning to understand.

Surrounded by the quiet in the sleeping house, I decide it's time. I take the jar to my desk, turn on another lamp, clear a space.

I sit down and stare at it.

All these buttons came from clothes ruined beyond repair, their fabric long since used for rags or to make things like pot-holders and aprons. My mother let nothing go to waste. She cut out pockets and used them to hold old screws or rubber bands. Elastic waistbands were used to tie up newspapers. She used zippers, too, but I can't remember how. And the buttons went into this completely ordinary old canning jar, a little scratched up and nicked around the rim.

I suppose other families saved old buttons, but I doubt they did it with such diligence. There are all kinds of buttons in this jar. If I popped a button off my shirt, I could look in the jar and find one that was a close-enough match. (Or, as my mother explained, if it wasn't just right, you could always switch it with the bottom button that was tucked into your skirt and never showed anyway.) And if she was making a new outfit, she could save a little money by checking to see if there were any buttons in the jar that matched her material.

I remember how, as a child, I loved to run my fingers through the cool, flat discs, spreading them into a single layer as I searched for just the right one. The one that wasn't too plain, but wasn't too fancy either. The one that was the right color and the right size. The one that caught my eye and whispered to me, "Choose me! I'm the one." When I was seven or eight years old, my favorite thing to do was to sort them one by one, putting all the plain white buttons and plain black ones together, then organizing the rest into a color chart. The most exotic buttons— the ones with metallic trim or satin fabric or some other distinction—received places of honor at the top of the chart. I would keep my eyes open for ways to use them to their advantage.

Each time I opened the jar and poured the buttons out, they became more familiar to me. As the years went by, I recognized a few that had come from my own discarded clothing. Those bright yellow ones from a summer romper I had when I was two. That clear flower button from a church dress I wore in kindergarten. Three red buttons from a sweater our neighbor knitted for me when I started school.

What I liked most were the buttons that had belonged to other people. Serious brown buttons from my father's jacket. Navy blue buttons from my cousin's school uniform. Buttons with blue swirls from my mother's old robe, the one she wore on bad days. Some of the buttons were almost antiques, having come to the jar via an assortment of hand-me-down garments. My great uncle Walter's long herringbone coat. My grandmother's christening gown. A hand-woven vest my mother found when she helped go through my great-grandmother Maggie's house. There were even buttons we had found on the sidewalk, and there were some buttons that nobody seemed to remember at all.

I tip the jar past horizontal, watch the buttons pour out like stolen jewels.

They bounce in the light as they hit the surface. They make a pattering sound. Circles of color dancing and spinning and calling my name.

A Big Turquoise Button

THE PILE OF BUTTONS forms a misshapen pyramid on the desk. One grabs my attention right away because it's so much larger than the others, probably the largest in the whole jar—a square turquoise button with white swirls and two big holes in the middle. I remember it well. When I was about six or so, I would search for this button, then I would build a pattern around it. In my six-year-old mind, it was sort of like the sun, with all the other buttons surrounding it.

I pick it up and try to remember if I ever saw it on a piece of clothing. I can't, but I know it came from an old cover-up my mother wore. In a box somewhere there's a photograph of my family at the beach, taken when I was two years old. We're in front of an umbrella. My dad is holding me on his hip. He's usually the one who takes the pictures, and his expression is a little funny, as if he's not sure exactly when to smile. Somebody else must have taken this photo—one of my mom's relatives, I guess. Hank is standing beside my dad, squinting, and my mom has her arm across his shoulder. She's wearing the turquoise terrycloth cover-up that this button came from.

A lot of families go to the same beach every year, stay in the same house, take the same pictures. My family was once like that. There are pictures of my parents at the beach with Hank when he was a baby, then a toddler, then a little boy, and one with him sitting in a beach chair holding a bundle that must have been me. They all have this same umbrella in the background.

But the pictures stopped the year I was two. We didn't go to the beach after that.

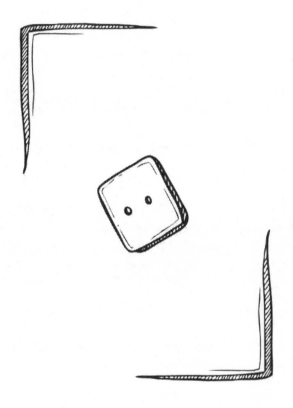

Kitty Hawk

The North Carolina Outer Banks, 1966

THE WET SAND SPREAD OUT like an unbroken sheet of just-made glass, its smoothness reflecting everything in glistening shadows of brownish gray. Seagulls darting through the air. Children running and laughing. Bicycles speeding by. And in the middle of everything, the gleaming brightness that was the sun. Emma sat in the midst of it in a canvas beach chair under a striped umbrella. She put the letter she was writing in her basket and stood up to get Caroline, who had darted out from the circle of shade. There's nothing so delicate as a baby's skin, Emma thought, grabbing Caroline and bringing her, protesting loudly, back under the umbrella. So smooth and thin, it would burn in a matter of moments, and she'd be up all night soothing the baby and not getting a bit of sleep herself. Then, when the little ones were up early wanting their breakfast, she'd snap at them, and everyone's day would be off to a bad start. Back in the shade, she held Caroline firmly on her lap, trying to distract her with the button on her cover-up.

"Aunt Emmy, please don't move. I can't paint your picture when you move." Gail, who turned eight just this week, had been playing with the watercolors all morning, chasing sheets of paper carried off by the wind and trying to keep the sand out of the ovals of color that she dabbed with such earnestness. She had taken fifteen minutes just to get her easel set up so that the morning light was right on Emma, who was trying to write a letter to an old friend in between chasing Caroline and tending to the shivering children running up to get their towels and asking for drinks of lemon-lime Kool-Aid from the thermos.

Emma looked at her watch. Almost eleven o'clock.

"Gail, honey. I have to go in and get lunch ready." Emma pulled her cover-up away from Caroline, who was biting the big shiny buttons. "You can finish your picture this afternoon if you like."

"But Aunt Emmy, it's almost done. Just ten more minutes."

Of course, it had been just ten more minutes twenty minutes ago, but Emma decided to give her a reprieve. She found it hard to deny Gail, the only child of her brother, Mitchell, and his wife, Claire. Every summer when their extended family got together at the beach, Mitchell spent all his time with Emma's son, Hank, and the other boys in the group and let Gail entertain herself. Meanwhile, Claire set herself off a few yards down the beach with a book, dark glasses, and an attitude that clearly said, "Sorry, but I just can't be bothered at the moment."

Emma glanced over at Claire. She wore a black maillot that showed off her long tan legs and tight stomach, and when she went walking down the beach, she didn't wear her cover-up, but carried it flung over one shoulder like a mink. Her bobbed hair was dark black and glinted in the sunlight. She attracted plenty of glances, but somehow always managed to keep her distance. It seemed clear to Emma that no matter how much Mitchell wanted a boy, there was little chance of that happening anytime soon.

"Okay, Gail, I'll tell you what. I'll stay here until the shade from the umbrella moves up to that bucket over there. Then we can go inside and get lunch together. How's that?" Emma was an expert on compromise—this way, Gail would have something visual to note the passage of time and couldn't argue when it happened. The shade was moving inward fast, and the sun was getting stronger by the minute. Emma wanted to get Caroline inside before the glaring light took over everything.

Gail went back to her painting with renewed interest, and Emma returned to her letter. What was it she was wanting to tell Sally? Oh yes, that business about Charles asking if she missed teaching.

I wonder if he thinks I want to go back. I can't imagine. I feel like I'm working all the time as it is. Just yesterday, Caroline made it to the edge of the balcony by herself, knocked over the garbage twice, and got a knife out of the kitchen drawer. And she's just turned two. It's strange, but I don't remember Hank being nearly so active or LOUD. It will be nice when she's a little older and wants to play dress-up and have tea parties and bake cookies with me. I've been doing those things with Gail, and it really is such fun. Boys are fun, too, but there's nothing like a little girl to

"Mama! Mama! Guess what we're doing tomorrow!" Hank ran up to the umbrella, grabbed a towel to wipe off his face, and then dropped it in the sand.

"What's that, sweetheart?"

"Uncle Mitchell is taking us snorkeling. He might even go scuba diving to see the shipwrecks."

"What shipwrecks?"

"Mama, don't you know anything?" Hank looked skyward in exasperation. "There are shipwrecks all along Cape Hatteras. They call it the ghost fleet. Pirate ships and war ships and everything."

"Well, we'll have to talk to your father about this. He hasn't had much time to spend with you yet, since he's had to work in the mornings . . . Hank, Hank, don't run off yet. Please shake off the towel and put it back on the chair."

Hank picked up the towel and gave it a quick fling. "Dad can come, too. It'll be fun. Please?"

"We'll see, Hank. Have you put on Coppertone lately?"

"Yes." He dropped the towel on the chair and ran back to the water, arms extended, swooping and curving like an airplane. Emma noticed how pink his shoulders were getting and how small he looked in his wet bathing suit. He was only ten years old, and she didn't like the idea of sending him off with Mitchell, who would do anything for a moment of fun. In college, he and a fraternity brother had made a pact to swim six miles across Lake Williams in the middle of the night during a thunderstorm. They both made it, but the other boy had to be taken to the infirmary for exhaustion and heat loss, and they were on probation the rest of the semester. Even now that he was an attorney with a respected Atlanta law firm, Mitchell liked to boast about this and other exploits. "You should have seen the lightning coming down all around us," he'd laugh. "I think Benny took a dump in the water!"

Emma looked at the bucket lying in the sand. "Gail, the shade is almost all the way up to the bucket now, so you need to put the finishing touches on your picture."

Gail bit her lip with concentration and carefully selected an oval of color to dip her brush into. She looked at the paper for a minute, then dabbed it once with her brush.

She's beautiful, Emma caught herself thinking. Not for the first time.

The girl looked up at Emma and smiled. "It's finished. Do you want to see?"

"Well, of course I do."

Emma looked at the watercolor, which showed a bright yellow ball hovering over a striped green umbrella. Blue waves of water lapped in the foreground, while a figure in turquoise sat in the middle, surrounded by cool, pastel blendings of color.

"Why, I believe that's one of the nicest watercolors I've seen," Emma said. The odd thing was that the picture really was good. Its symmetry and color combinations were much more sophisticated than most of the children's paintings Emma had been given over the years. It seemed to have a balance, to convey a different kind of perspective.

"We should hang it up on the clothesline so it will dry just right, then we can put it up for everyone to see."

Gail smiled again and carefully carried the watercolor toward the bungalow shared by the two families. Some other relatives, including two of Emma's older sisters and various in-laws and cousins, were in a large three-story house next door. There were always plenty of children running in and out of the two buildings, leaving sand and wet towels everywhere for someone else to pick up. At night, they all ate together, each family taking a turn to host dinner. Breakfast and lunch were supposed to be casual and individual, but somehow Emma always seemed to be preparing these meals for Mitchell's family as well as her own, in addition to the stray cousins who wandered in with Hank. Of course, Claire would help if asked, but Emma always had the feeling that Claire was laughing at her attempts at small talk as they cut carrot sticks, sliced tomatoes, and made Jell-O salad.

Gail, on the other hand, was a willing helper. She was a neat child, cleaning up after herself and performing each task with studied seriousness. Maybe it was because Gail went to a Catholic boarding school. Mitchell had become Catholic when he married Claire—it almost killed their staunchly Methodist parents, but it was out of their hands. At least, the nuns seemed to be doing a good job with Gail. She was a model student and had impeccable manners.

Still, Emma couldn't help but think that Gail's interest in preparing meals and cleaning house had something to do with the fact that she never got to do these things in her own home. She was off at school for most of the year, and then, after the beach trip, she usually spent a month with Emma's family while Claire went on a shopping trip to New York. Emma secretly believed that this shopping trip was Claire's payoff for going on the beach trip at all. Were they really that awful? Emma wondered.

Inside the house, her husband Charles was still at the table, working. His glasses were sliding down his nose, a sign that he had blocked out everything but the papers in front of him.

"Honey, you really should take a break. We are on vacation, you know."

Charles looked up, surprised that anyone else was around. "I've just about finished with this report, and then I'll be out," he said. Charles was a design engineer and was always in the middle of some project that couldn't be left behind, or so he said. Everyone else made fun of him staying inside with his graph paper and slide rule, but Emma found it endearing. She liked the way he tapped his pencil when he was excited about something, and she knew he would be out in the afternoon to watch the children so she could take a break.

"Here, why don't you entertain Caroline while Gail and I get lunch?" Charles' face lit up when he picked up his daughter. He had been delighted to have a girl, but then, he already a boy. Maybe all men still felt they had to have a boy to be happy, Emma thought.

Gail was out on the screened-in porch, hanging her picture up to dry. She placed it deliberately in a spot of sunlight and moved all the wet towels further down out of the way. Then she put her easel and watercolor set in a corner where they would be safe.

21

"Gail, you can set the table and get the pears ready, okay?"

Gail nodded and got to work, making sure each plate was in just the right position, that all the forks and knives matched, and that the napkins were folded into perfect triangles. She found a dried-flower arrangement in the den, dusted it off, and set it in the center of the table. Then she opened a can of pears and arranged them on a plate of lettuce leaves. She put a dollop of mayonnaise in the center and topped that with grated cheese.

The others came in with a burst of confusion—towels and swimsuits and beach bags going everywhere—but eventually, everyone gathered around the table and quieted down enough to eat.

After a few minutes, Mitchell grabbed a pickle from his plate and snapped it in two. "So, Charles, do you think you'll go snorkeling with us tomorrow? I think Glenn and Joe are coming along."

Emma felt her stomach tighten. She had meant to talk to Charles about this, but it had slipped her mind. She didn't want Hank to go.

"I didn't know you were going snorkeling," Charles said. "Where are you going?"

"There's a boat that will take you back into the Sound. It's not like you're on a coral reef or anything, but it's okay. They even have some scuba gear if you want to take a look at the wrecks. You know Blackbeard's treasure is supposed to be down there."

Charles thought about it for a minute and looked at his wife, who had been tapping his shin under the table.

"I don't know, Charles," she said. "There's plenty of activity right here, and the boys haven't spent much time riding waves with you this trip."

"Come on, Emma," Mitchell said. "We've been riding waves all week. Let Hank have some fun. He's a big guy now."

Charles looked at Emma. She felt herself giving in, once again, to her little brother. She nodded, almost imperceptibly, at her husband.

"I guess that would be a good experience," he told Mitchell. "See some nature and history at the same time."

"Great! We can make a day of it. You can snorkel with the boys while I dive among the wrecks." Mitchell gave everyone the thumbs-up signal and got up from the table. He went out on the screened-in porch to smoke a cigarette.

Emma didn't see what happened next, but she knew something was wrong when Gail's lower lip quivered just the slightest bit. She went out on the porch and realized Mitchell had picked up a towel off the floor and flung it over the clothesline.

"Mitchell! You put that dirty, wet towel right on top of Gail's watercolor. She worked on it all morning long."

Emma pulled the towel off, but the picture was ruined, colors smeared together in a meaningless blob. She was trying not to make too big a deal out of this, because she knew it would only embarrass Gail. Still, she had just about had it with Mitchell.

"Well, it was an accident. I didn't even see it." Mitchell seemed unconcerned. "Sorry about your picture, babe," he yelled into Gail.

Gail looked at her lap. "That's okay, Daddy."

Emma felt her blood pressure rise. Stay calm, she told herself. She tidied up the porch a bit and then looked over at her little brother leaning on the rail among the seashells and sand dollars put out to dry. With his dark curls and dimpled chin, he could still pass for a college boy. It had always been hard to stay mad at him.

"Mitchell, I know it doesn't seem like a big deal to you, but Gail was looking forward to showing you and Claire that picture. You should have seen how hard she worked on it this morning, and you know what? It was really good."

There was an uncomfortable silence as Mitchell smoked his cigarette. Emma resisted the urge to pluck it from his hand. Why did she still feel a need to mother him when she had children of her own?

"Anyway, I think it would mean a lot to Gail if you spent just a few minutes with her today. You think she doesn't notice how much time you spend with the boys?"

Mitchell blew a stream of smoke, then turned toward Emma.

"Well Jesus Christ, Mary, and Joseph, what am I supposed to do? Stay inside and have a tea party?"

Emma knew he was using this expression, which he had picked up after he got married, to get under her skin, but she let it pass.

"Well, I don't think that would be the end of the world, but I was thinking of something less drastic, like asking her to paint a picture especially for you and then really looking at it when she does. You could put it up in your office. It might impress your clients to realize you're someone's father, not just a snotty-nosed, prep-school kid still wet behind the ears."

Mitchell ground his cigarette butt into the ashtray and smiled. "Okay, Emmy. You're the child-rearing expert. Hell, I'll even take Gail out to ride the waves this afternoon. But you know, I do believe you are making much ado about nothing."

Emma tried not to smile. Spouting Shakespeare was a trademark of Mitchell's. He used it in a variety of ways—to defuse situations, add humor, and occasionally show emotion he would never otherwise express. Emma didn't know why she found it so endearing, but she did.

They went back inside, where Gail was cleaning off the table. Claire, who had stayed out during lunch, was making herself a salad, while Charles and Hank were getting ready for the afternoon assault on the beach.

"Hey, Gail," Mitchell said. "What are you doing in the kitchen? You should be getting ready to ride the waves with your dad."

Charles walked into the room, wearing baggy plaid swim trunks, white socks, and black sandals. He was blowing up a canvas raft, which made his cheeks turn red. "That's right, Gail," he said, pinching the valve in between puffs. "I'm blowing up this raft for you. Go get your bathing suit on."

Gail carefully put the dishes in the sink and then ran into the bedroom. A few minutes later, she came out wearing a navy blue suit trimmed with a white neckline. She didn't have a lot of clothes, since she wore her uniform at school, but the ones she had always looked just so, Emma thought. She had to give Claire credit for that.

"Did you put your clothes up, Gail?" Claire asked, not looking up from her salad.

"Yes, ma'am." Gail ran out the door to catch up with the others, who were already heading for the beach.

Emma looked out the window while she finished cleaning up the kitchen and saw Mitchell put Gail on the raft as they headed into the water. She felt pleased with herself and began singing a hymn softly as she washed the dishes.

Softly and tenderly
Jesus is calling,
Calling for you and for me . . .

Claire said she had a headache and went into the bedroom, closing the door behind her.

Emma changed to a low humming as she thought about what she would do this afternoon. It wasn't her turn to cook dinner, so if Caroline took a nap, she would be completely free for a few hours. Of course, it would take a minor miracle to get Caroline to sleep, but Emma was optimistic. She would finish the letter to Sally and then maybe work on that cross-stitch piece she wanted to put in the foyer. She might even take a nap herself.

She went over to the table and sat down with her pen and paper. She looked out the window again and saw Hank and Mitchell body surfing with a group of rowdy cousins, while Charles was lifting Gail up and down as the waves came crashing in.

Oh well, she thought. It was a start.

* * * *

The next morning was strangely quiet after the bustle of getting the boys off on their trip. They had left at seven thirty to catch the boat by eight o'clock. Emma had gotten up at six o'clock to make breakfast, pack lunches, and put dry clothes, suntan lotion, and extra towels into a duffel bag for Charles to take along. By the time she had finished all that, Caroline ran into the kitchen with three swimsuits and two bras slipped over her head, a sure sign that she had ransacked the suitcases again.

Gail had gotten up early, too. As soon as the boys left, she put her easel in front of the picture window that overlooked the ocean. She seemed even more serious than usual.

"What are you doing, sweetie?" Emma asked.

"Daddy said he'd like to have a picture of the fishing boats going out for the day with the sun rising behind them," Gail said as she opened a new pack of brushes and set them on the table. The watercolor set had been a present from Gail's maternal grandfather for making all As in school. Mitchell had told Emma how Judge Brennan, as everyone called him, had taken Gail to the biggest toy store in Atlanta and told her she could get anything she wanted. All those toys, and she had chosen a simple watercolor set.

Gail put one of her father's old shirts on over her clothes and pulled a sheet of paper out from the center of the box.

"It's for his law office, so it has to be especially good," she told Emma.

Claire got up and drank a cup of coffee on the porch. Emma took Caroline for a walk on the beach. When she got back, Gail was hard at work in front of the easel. She had created a horizon full of greens, grays, and blues, with a pale yellow glow emerging from the right corner.

Emma took Caroline's playpen on the porch and put her in it with her dolls and a set of blocks. It probably wouldn't work, but it was worth a try. She lay down on the hammock. The morning breeze was still cool, and the sound of the waves crashing and flowing on the sand below was so peaceful . . . so soothing.

When Emma woke it was ten thirty, and Caroline was throwing the blocks against the screening of the playpen. Claire had just come in from walking on the beach and was in the shower. Gail was still painting. By now, the picture showed three shrimp trawlers moving across the water. Wispy gray seagulls followed the boats, and off to the left was a storm-like darkness.

"That's beautiful, Gail." Again, Emma was struck by Gail's use of color. There were only ten colors in her set, but she had blended them to create subtle shade differences—pleasing greens, melancholy yellows, hopeful pinks, and ominous grays.

They both stared at the picture for a moment, considering it from all angles.

"I think it's finished," Gail said.

Claire came back in the room, toweling her hair dry. She looked at the picture. "Yes. You don't want too much color, or it would be tacky."

Emma helped Gail put the picture on top of the refrigerator and surrounded it with cans to prevent another accident. Gail's intentness struck Emma as something powerful and faintly sad. Hank was serious and intent in a way, but he could let loose and act crazy when he was around the guys. Emma had never seen Gail like that. She felt a need to do something to give her some of the lightness most children had.

"I have an idea," she said. "The boys are having an excursion, so why don't we girls go out to lunch? I've heard of place in Manteo where they serve high tea as if you're in England. I can get Margaret to watch Caroline. What do you think?"

Gail looked at Claire, obviously holding her breath.

After a moment, Claire nodded. "Okay," she said, staring out the window. "That sounds nice."

They put on their summer dresses and drove into Manteo for lunch at the Elizabethan Restaurant, with its white linen tablecloths and sterling silver tea sets. Here, Claire seemed perfectly at ease, her poise reminding Emma of Audrey Hepburn in Roman Holiday. Gail quietly emulated Claire's every move, gently picking up the sugar cubes with the tiny tongs, lifting her tea cup with perfectly poised fingers, returning it to the saucer without a sound.

On the way back, they stopped at a dime store to get more suntan lotion. Gail got out the change purse that she kept her allowance in and bought a frame for her picture. They each got an ice cream cone and ate them on a park bench outside. All in all, it had been a good day, Emma thought, a nice change from the long sun-filled days of their vacation.

When they pulled up to the cottage, they noticed that Charles' car was already back and parked along the street.

"I wonder if one of the boys got seasick," Emma said. "They weren't supposed to get back until supper."

She had a vague feeling of regret in her stomach. She pictured Hank huddled on the back of the boat, nauseated and sunburned, trying to be brave while the bigger boys jostled and splashed, oblivious to his distress.

The feeling hardened into panic as Emma noticed a police car behind the station wagon. She glanced at Claire, who said nothing.

When they walked in the door, Hank ran up to Emma and buried his face in her stomach, something he hadn't done in a long time. A wave of fear went through her as she scanned the room for Charles, but subsided when she saw he was here. She had never seen him look this way, but he was here. He was safe.

"Emmy, Claire," Charles started in a rough voice. "Mitchell has been in an accident. We were all snorkeling in Pamlico Sound when he decided he wanted to—" Charles' voice stopped. His face contorted.

"Is he dead?" Claire interrupted. Her face had gone pale, but she stood firm and looked Charles in the eye.

Charles opened his mouth, but only a strange squeaking sound came out. He nodded.

Emma couldn't breathe. She felt that everything about this moment—the pain and guilt on her husband's face, the policeman standing in the corner writing notes, Hank's tight grip around her waist, the humid stillness of the room, even the clothes they all had on—everything was being etched into her soul. She couldn't move. She couldn't speak. All she could do was stand there while this thing pressed through her, burning her like acid.

"I'm so sorry," Charles was saying. "I should have gone with him since the others were there with the boys . . . I should have checked out the guide before we went. He said he knew what he was doing, but I should have gone with—"

"Stupid fool," Claire said, turning toward her bedroom.

Tiny feet pattered across the floor. "Mama! Mama!" Caroline pulled on Emma's dress, demanding to be picked up, but for once, Emma ignored her.

Claire's door slammed, and Emma flinched at the noise. She looked into the kitchen to see Gail pull a chair up to the refrigerator. Emma, Charles, even the policeman, who looked up from his papers, watched Gail climb up on it, shove the cans out of the way, and pick up her picture. Then she ran through the French doors onto the balcony, crumpled it into a ball, and dropped it over the edge.

The Baby Button

I PUT THE TURQUOISE BUTTON DOWN and begin to run my fingers over the pyramid of buttons, smoothing them into a single layer. It's a soothing action that almost makes me sleepy. I'm thinking about going back to bed when a tiny white button pops out from under a cluster, startling me because I recognize it so well. It was the smallest in the jar, and I always called it the baby button. In a way, it's the opposite of the big turquoise button. I showed it to my mother once, and she said it was from a christening gown that had been in her family for years.

"My sisters wore it, and I wore it, and I remember taking it apart—without permission—right before my brother was born," she said. "I altered the gown for you because you were so little. That's why the button is here, but I should probably sew it on the inside hem, so it doesn't get lost. One day, you'll want the gown for your children."

I don't have the gown. I think it went to Gail.

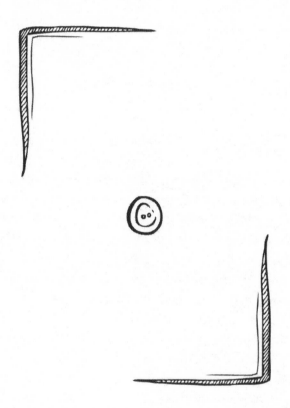

Expecting

Ashton Mill, N.C. 1935

EMMA'S WHOLE FAMILY was gathered around the table for Easter dinner, the girls wearing the new dresses Mama had made. The dresses were simple, but pretty. Emma had been given the job of cutting out pieces of satin from an old dress of Grandma's to make the sashes. They were lucky to have something so fine, since Papa had had nothing but odd jobs for the past two months. Mama had been taking in ironing so there would be enough money to buy a few extra things.

After the family had eaten dinner and was sitting around the table drinking coffee and eating chess pie, Papa looked at his daughters and said, "Well, girls, it looks like you'll have another chance to get a little brother." He hadn't looked proud very often during the last few months, but now his eyes showed some of their old twinkle.

"Or maybe another sister," Mama said quietly.

Margaret and Lorraine, who were just beginning to flirt with the boys in town, blushed and said nothing. Jane, who was studying at the teacher's college in Greensboro, smiled broadly. "This is a surprise," she said. "It will be nice to have a baby, now that Emma's getting so big."

They all turned and stared at Emma. Some children might have been jealous, but she wasn't.

"It will be my baby," she announced to the rest of the family in a sure and steady voice.

The truth was, Emma had been expecting their family would have another baby. For as long as she could remember, she had been "The Baby," and she knew this wasn't right. Babies were comical and carefree. Emma was serious and responsible. Babies needed somebody to fuss over them. Emma needed to fuss over somebody. Somehow, God had made a mistake sending her into the family in last place, and so every night for the past six months, she had been trying to help correct matters, praying as hard as she could for a baby of her own.

In fact, Emma knew that the baby would be a boy because that's what she'd asked God for. A baby boy just for her. Not another girl. A baby girl was little more than a realistic doll, but a boy would be different. Of course, Emma still liked her two dolls, Georgina and Gwendolyn. She still dressed them in clean outfits, took them outside for fresh air, and tucked them in at night, but they didn't require as much attention as she had to give.

A baby boy would be different. Everyone knew boys needed lots of attention. She would spend hours walking him around the house, talking to him, and burping him after he ate. She would wrap him in blankets and take him outside for a stroll on days when the afternoon sun was warm but not hot. She would rock him to sleep at night, singing her favorite lullaby, "Sweet Baby Boy." He would cry with anyone else, but when she took him in her arms, he would smile and coo and fall peacefully asleep.

To Emma, each day of that long, steamy summer hovered as full of anticipation as the moments before a thunderstorm. Papa found a job in Raleigh and was home only on the weekends, when he filled the house with his blustery voice and kept everyone busy washing clothes, cooking and fussing over him. In between, the household settled into a feminine pattern of waiting, a conspiratorial calm permeating the rooms, as if the women had joined a faraway tribe in which the females lived cloistered among themselves. The most excitement came when neighbor women and ladies from church stopped by to have coffee with Mama and share the latest gossip. Emma always felt they were looking for gossip, too, but she wasn't sure why.

"It's a lot harder to have a baby when you're in your forties than when you're in your twenties," Mama told Mrs. Christenberry one afternoon.

"I hear late babies always come fast, too," Mrs. Christenberry said. "Rose Jones barely made it inside the house."

Mama laughed. "I wish I were that lucky. The girls took forever to get here." She lowered her voice. "Each time, I swore that would be it for me."

Mrs. Christenberry delicately placed her coffee cup back on the saucer and leaned toward Mama. "I tell you, Nancy, better you than me. I've had just about as much of that as I care for, if you know what I mean."

Mama cleared her throat and peered over her coffee cup at Emma, who was helping herself to one of the butter cookies Mrs. Christenberry had brought.

Mrs. Christenberry smiled a too-big smile at Mama and mouthed, "Sorry," as Emma sat down in the rocking chair.

Of course, Emma knew that the baby was growing inside Mama's tummy and that after he was born, milk would come out of Mama's nipples for him to drink. The rest of her family acted as if she didn't understand such things, always shushing and giggling when she walked into the room. They didn't know that her twelve-year-old cousin, Mary, had explained pretty much everything to her when Emma spent two weeks with

Mary's family in the country last summer. The mechanics of baby making seemed like an odd and cumbersome way of doing things, but so did eating and drinking and then going to the bathroom, if you really thought about it. She couldn't imagine Mama and Papa doing such things, but she had spent every night for the last six months praying they would. Now it had come to pass. Maybe that's what people meant when they said, "God works in mysterious ways."

Emma felt it was her duty to learn as much as she could about the baby, despite her family's reluctance to discuss it with her.

"Jane will go get Dr. Price and bring him here when it's time for the baby to come," Mama told her when she asked where the baby would be born. "Jane's staying home from college this fall so she can help out."

"How will you know it's time?"

"Well, I've had four babies, so I know the signs."

"What are the signs?"

"They're kind of hard to describe, but don't worry. I'll know when it's time."

"When will you start having milk for the baby?"

"When it's time. Now go on and play outside!"

"If you don't have milk when it's time, can I give it a bottle?"

"Emma!" Mama was mad now. She always looked at the ceiling when she was mad. "There's no need for you to concern yourself with such things. You are just a child, and it's none of your business. If you really want to help, you can wash the dishes. I need to lie down for a few minutes."

As the summer went on, Mama spent more and more time in bed. That was just as well, because when she was up, she spent most of the time looking at the ceiling. Emma knew that couldn't be good for the baby. While Mama slept, Emma quietly went through the baby clothes stacked in a wicker basket. There were a lot of clothes, but most were in bad shape after being worn by four babies over the past seventeen years. Emma worked on the everyday blankets first, learning to mend with the tiniest of stitches. By the time she got to the Sunday outfits, she was an accomplished seamstress and felt confident enough to take a gown apart and remake it like new, only better.

One morning in July, Mama woke up while Emma still had the white christening gown spread across the dining room table in pieces. Leaning against the archway, her housedress thoroughly wet, her skin glistening, Mama looked even more tired than when she'd gone to bed. The day had started off hot and warmed up from there. Nobody had slept well in the heat of the night before.

"What do you think you are doing?" Mama wasn't looking at the ceiling, but Emma sensed that she was madder than she'd been in a long time. Her face was flushed, and her eyes didn't blink as she stared squarely at Emma.

"I'm fixing this gown for the baby," Emma said quietly, as she concentrated on tightening the thread around one of the tiny white buttons she found so adorable.

Moving surprisingly quickly, Mama crossed the room, grabbed her by the arm, and pulled her out of the chair.

"I'll have you know that that gown is a family heirloom," she said as she clamped on to each of Emma's arms. "My father's mother made it for me right before she died. And now you've ruined it. It will never be the same."

"But Mama," Emma began.

"Don't interrupt me!" Mama shouted. She picked up the pieces of the gown and threw them into the basket.

"Do you know how long it will take me to put that back together? And I still have the ironing to do and dinner to make, and your sisters won't be here to help with you until this afternoon. Why do you have to make things so difficult?"

Margaret had been doing the ironing ever since Easter, and Lorraine had prepared most of dinner the night before, but Emma didn't think it was a good time to point this out. Instead, she quietly followed as Mama went into the kitchen and got out the ironing board.

"I'll iron for you, Mama. Margaret's been letting me help her a little bit, so I know how."

"Well, she shouldn't have. You are just a child. You have no business being around irons. I don't know what I'm going to do with a new baby and you, too. A ten-year-old who can't do anything but look for mischief! Now please just go to your room before you make any more trouble."

Emma turned and walked slowly down the hall, her whole face swollen with the tears she'd been holding back. Before she got to her room, she heard Mama gasp. Emma hesitated for a moment, then slowly turned around to see her mother standing perfectly still, her hands resting on the ironing board, body slightly bent, eyes opened wide.

Frozen, transfixed, she observed the elements in the picture before her: the late morning sun making a pattern of light and dark on the plum tree just outside the kitchen window, the scrubbed-white cupboards and yellow walls, the checked blue and white of the dish towels, and, in the middle, her mother's rounded figure, her tousled dark brown hair forming a frame around her contorted face.

It was a beautiful, terrifying picture.

Mama turned her head toward Emma. "Get a towel, quick! My water's broken."

Emma ran to the bathroom and grabbed a towel, which she used to sop up the wetness on the kitchen floor. Her mother still leaned on the ironing board, occasionally making a sound that Emma had never heard before, something in between a moan and a cry.

When Emma had finished, she quickly looked around for the water glass her mother had broken, even though she instinctively knew the water hadn't come from a glass, but somehow from her mother. She wondered how Mary could have left out such an important detail.

"Are you okay, Mama?"

Mama bit her lip, then nodded. "Go next door and get Mrs. Percy right away," she whispered.

Emma flew out the back door, ran across the driveway, and climbed the stairs to Mrs. Percy's kitchen door two at a time. As soon as she got to the door, she knew the house was empty. The kitchen was dark, and the house perfectly still except for her urgent knocking. As she waited to make sure nobody was home, a dry, hot breeze lifted the hair at the base of her neck, seeming to whisper some mysterious message.

Emma ran back home as fast as she could.

Mama no longer leaned on the ironing board. She pressed down as if in a fury.

"They're not home," Emma said.

Her mother seemed to press even harder, and the ironing board creaked at the joints.

"Mama, the ironing board's going to break, and you could fall down."

"I can't help but push," Mama blurted, beginning to pant.

"Well, here, push on the chair," Emma said, pulling one of the kitchen chairs to her mother's side.

Mama didn't say anything, but turned and grabbed the chair.

"I mean I can't help but push the baby out!" she yelled after a few moments of panting. "Help me get to the bed."

They walked down the darkened hall together, stopping once when Mama put her hands along the sides of the wall and pushed outward with all her might. Finally, they made it to the bedroom.

"Pull the covers off and put the pillows against the head-board," Mama said, and Emma did it. Mama then lifted up her dress and pulled her underwear down to her knees before sinking into the bed with a groan. She stared at Emma, then at the underwear.

"Pull them off, so I can get my legs apart."

Emma was amazed that the underwear was not only wet, but covered with clots of blood and mucous. This was something else Mary had neglected to mention.

Settling back against the pillows, Mama seemed to relax a tiny bit. She closed her eyes and turned her head to the side.

"Go get the towels," she said quietly. "All of them."

When Emma came back, her mother was straining against the headboard, the veins in her neck showing prominently, her face as thoroughly soaked as if she were in a rain storm. Emma put the towels over the wet and bloody places on the bed and fanned her mother with an old magazine.

After a moment, Mama let out a deep breath. She stared straight into Emma's eyes.

"Emma, I need you to reach in between my legs and pull this baby out."

Emma stopped fanning and stared at the magazine cover. She began to feel that being the baby wasn't so bad. Having someone to rely on, to take care of you, to be responsible for how things turned out, was really rather nice.

"Emma . . ." Her mother's voice sounded calm and beautiful.

Emma met her mother's eyes.

"Emma, I know you can do it."

Mama leaned against the headboard and yelled. Emma took a deep breath and looked between her mother's legs, at the circle of gooey brown hair separating the shining, rose-colored tissue. She gently reached toward it as her mother strained, as the tissue tore and the baby's head slipped out into her hands.

Her confidence returned; she pulled steadily as the rest of the wet, slimy body popped out.

She held him in her arms, not caring that her dress was dirty, hardly noticing the snakelike gray cord that still attached his body to their mother.

She smiled into his face and looked up at Mama.

"He's just what I've been waiting for."

The Button from the Madras Shirt

DOWN THE HALL, I can hear the clock softly chime the hour. Five o'clock. No point in going back to bed, really, although I'm so tired that I lean my head on my arm, pick up a handful of buttons, and let them fall, gently, through my fingers. For some reason, I wonder if my father is awake, and it makes me sad to think of him all alone in the house, waking up in the darkness without the sound of another person breathing. For a few seconds, I think about calling him, but I don't. Instead, I hold still, willing myself to sense his presence somehow, but all I can sense, besides the sound of the ticking clock, is a vague feeling of unease, a restless stirring of feelings—the wolves pawing and scratching at the edge of my mind. I can almost see them lifting their noses, trying to find a scent of weakness, an angle of attack. The heaviness of night leaves me more vulnerable to them, and I can't help but shiver as I try to shut them out.

A few seconds later, I hear Victoria mumble something in her sleep and roll over. The house is chilly, and she kicks her covers off during the night, so I sneak into her room and pull them back over her. My father used to do this for me. He always thought I stayed asleep, but sometimes I woke up and watched, through slit eyes, as he moved as quietly as he could in the darkness. He probably had the same feeling I have now—a strange combination of awe and fierce protectiveness. The feeling always surprises me, especially considering that Victoria is only with us one weekend a month, plus alternating holidays and two weeks in the summer. But there's something so vulnerable about her, especially as she sleeps in the darkness.

When I get back to the buttons, I'm still thinking about my dad, all alone in the dark, and it makes me feel the same way I feel about Victoria. He and my mother were married for almost forty years. How could he not wake up during the night, missing her? Again, I think about calling, but instead, I poke among the buttons once more, looking for one that belonged to him. It's more difficult, because men's buttons aren't as distinctive as women's, but finally, I find an amber-colored button that I think I remember. I believe it was from a madras shirt that he wore around the house in the summer. The shirt's colors interested me—an interweaving of pale orange, rust, and blue. When I helped fold the laundry, it felt as soft as my flannel pajamas. On Saturday mornings, he would put on that shirt while he did odd jobs, whistling some old big band song while he fixed a faucet or painted a windowsill. The shirt got thinner and thinner over the years, until you could actually see through it. One year we got him a new madras shirt for Father's Day.

He said he liked it, but I wasn't so sure.

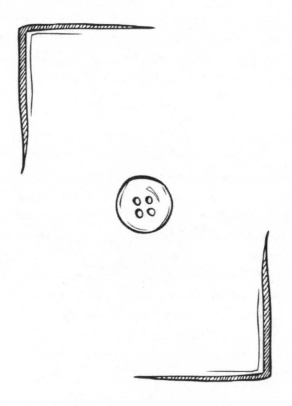

Summer Dance

"FIREFLIES," CHARLES INSISTED. "That's what we always called them."

Emma laughed, leaning her head to one side so that her thick, chestnut-colored hair brushed her bare shoulder, which appeared white in the twilight glow. Sitting next to her on the grass, Charles thought the entire world had softened, had come under a spell, as shapes lost their sharp edges, colors became muted, and the sky darkened. Around them, the silent, synchronized lights swam in dark shadows of the trees, growing brighter and brighter, as if frantic to make the most of their brief time.

"They're lightning bugs," Emma said, glancing at Charles. "Everyone I know calls them lightning bugs. All the children I teach call them lightning bugs. Where did you say you're from, again?"

"Tennessee. Big city of Memphis. My family's lived there since before the Civil War, and we've always called them fireflies."

"Well, now that you're in North Carolina, you should learn to call them lightning bugs. When in Rome . . ."

45

Emma pulled her sweater off the picnic basket and draped it around her, covering the sleeveless cotton blouse she was wearing. The blouse was an unusual shade of blue, and he remembered how pretty she had looked in it when he picked her up to go on the picnic. This was their seventh date. He'd kept track. He had taken her to the Bijou several times, out for ice cream once, and twice to dinner at Palagi's, the nicest restaurant in town. He'd thought about asking her to go dancing, but he'd always turned shy at the last minute.

The picnic had been her idea.

The crickets and frogs were growing louder, the flashing lights more brilliant.

"Let's go for a walk," Emma said, standing up and holding out her hand.

Charles said nothing, afraid of breaking the spell, but stood and gently clasped her hand. He could feel the evening breeze blow through the thin fabric and the gaps between the buttons of the madras shirt he was wearing. They followed the path in silence, watching the lights. Charles wished he had been brave enough to ask her to go dancing. He wanted to hold her body tight against his, to rub on her in a smoke-filled room while saxophones moaned and a drum set kept the rhythm. He didn't know why he hadn't asked her. He loved to dance, had danced with dozens of girls, some of them soft and yielding, others taut and teasing. During the war, he'd gone dancing every chance he got. He could do it all—swing, waltz, slow.

He loved to dance.

It was almost completely dark. In a minute, she would say she had to go home and it would be over. He probably wouldn't see her again until Sunday at church. That's where he had first seen her soon after he moved to Ashton Mill for an engineering job at the Pineridge Textile Plant. In this small town, most of the social activity centered around church. Besides the mill and a small college, there was one movie theater, one drive-through burger joint, a few restaurants, and about a hundred churches. Everybody seemed to know which church everyone else went to. Or didn't. His boss had suggested First Methodist, and so he tied his narrow silk tie, walked through the solid wooden doors, and looked around. She was the first thing he saw, sitting in a broad band of light shining through the massive windows. She was in a pew near the front with her parents—both already gray-headed—and her teenage brother, a notably handsome boy. As the Sundays went by, he learned that she always sat in that same place, her face intent, wearing a hat and tailored suit, not so much beautiful as lovely.

After the service, several young children would run up to show her what they had made in Sunday School. She taught first grade at Ashton Mill Elementary and was clearly a favorite. When Charles thought of her, he always pictured her surrounded by children. He had never envisioned a woman like that before, and he was surprised at the strength of the attraction. There were still things he didn't know about her—what songs she liked, her favorite movie, her old boyfriends—but he knew that he was drawn to her.

He felt that if she did dance with him, it would be altogether different than any dance before.

They stopped by the fountain, shaped like a water lily and lit by a pair of greenish-gray lamps on either side of a plaque that read: "Now folds the lily all her sweetness up, And slips into the bosom of the lake."

"I love these gardens," Emma said. "With the winding paths and flowering bushes, and the cupid statues and the quaint old plaques. There aren't many places anymore where you can go just to watch the evening turn to night."

Charles wondered how it was that he had never noticed the park before; it seemed so wonderful now.

"Look," Emma said. "You can see the moon's reflection in the water. That must be good luck, don't you think?"

"I'm sure of it," Charles replied, staring at their silhouettes wavering below the bright white roundness.

He put his arm around her shoulders and breathed in the cool air.

"I have to go," Emma said, leaning her head against him.

"No. Not yet."

"I have to. I live with my parents, remember? I'm not like those women you knew in the big city of Memphis."

"I know you're not. Please. Stay."

Emma looked at him and smiled. She took his hand, and they headed down the path, a trail of almost total darkness now, broken occasionally by a pale lamplight.

"They're almost gone," Emma said.

"What?"

"The lightning bugs. There's just a few of them left. I guess they've all found each other."

"Oh, the fireflies . . ." Charles looked and saw she was right. There were only a few intermittent flashes that seemed to convey a sad, lost message, as if they had missed out on the only significant thing in their tiny lives.

"I always thought they stayed out all night long," Charles said.

They stopped under a huge sycamore tree, watching the last bit of twilight.

"Most of the flashing is at dusk. My children are studying them in science. The female flashes her light, and the male answers by flashing his. It's a form of courtship."

"Kind of like a dance," Charles said. "The lightning bug dance." He could barely see her now, but he could feel her closeness along his entire body.

"I suppose so . . . the firefly waltz."

He pulled her in toward him, and they swayed ever so slightly. The night creatures, fully awakened, buzzed and sang and flew around them.

The Fancy One

OUTSIDE THE WINDOW, grayness is beginning to overtake the dark, and even though it's Saturday, I can hear more and more cars driving on the road in front of our neighborhood. I've decided that the woman at the flea market, the button purveyor, was right. My jar of buttons should have a visible place in our house. What was it she had said? It would give the place a cozy feel.

Atmosphere. Ambiance. Feng shui. Something like that.

Maybe if I put mementos close at hand instead of hiding them away, I might figure something out, like why I have so many issues about the past. It's not as if I have any deep, dark secrets. My family is Southern, but not Southern Gothic, after all. Why should it feel strange to look at a jar of buttons? I think it's because it makes me remember that feeling of being different, not fitting in, not meeting all the Southern expectations for females. The list is well defined: go to church (First Baptist is best), become a wife and then a mother, work as a teacher or nurse or some other nurturing profession, create a beautiful home filled with fresh baked bread and roses.

Sometimes when the wolves are gathering around, Rishi laughs at them and they run away. He comes behind me and puts his arms around me and rocks me back and forth. "Poor

Caroline," he whispers. "So many WASP hang-ups. You must let them go. Let go and join the river of life, flowing to the ocean of the universe."

He's joking, of course. He's not religious, and besides, he has plenty of his own hang-ups—like the whole vegetarian act when his parents visit, not to mention his Anglophile ex-wife. But he does have a point. Mainly, though, when he puts his arms around me like that and laughs at the wolves, I can forget about them for a while. I love the way his skin is so dark against mine. It appears so exotic and forbidden. I rub his arms and feel the taut muscle and think of a tiger who is tame only for me. I turn to face him, and his eyes are an intense black that a white person's can never be. They draw me in to him, to a safe place where it's just the two of us. Our own creation of saris and jeans, of wind chimes and crystal, of tandoori and fried chicken. A place that is here and now, filled with things of our own choosing.

When I started dating Rishi, Mom's disapproval was almost visible, but I was prepared. I knew she wouldn't like him—he's too different, as she said. What she meant was he's older, he's divorced, he's not Christian, and most of all, he's not white. What surprised me was that after a while—not very long, really—he seemed to get along with her better than I did. By the time we got married, I wouldn't visit my parents without him. He was my mediator.

Yes, I really should put the button jar downstairs. We have beautiful built-in shelves that separate the living room from the dining room—they would be perfect there. I begin to gather up the buttons and drop them into the jar. When only a handful remain on my desk, I notice a magenta-colored button with a ring of silver filigree on the outer edge. Its sparkle catches my eye, and I recognize it as another familiar one, the "fancy one," I always called it.

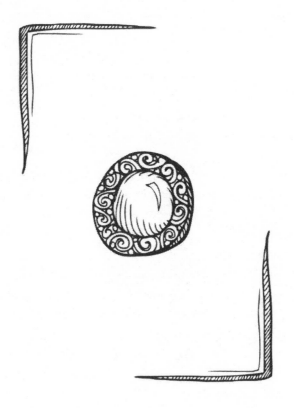

After the Ball

Ashton Mill, N.C. 1957

EMMA HANDED A SOAPY PLATE TO MITCHELL and wondered where the past four years had gone. It seemed as if the last time she had seen him, really *seen* him, he was playing football for Roberts High School and going out with Brenda Armitage from down the street. She remembered how he had looked in his uniform after that last homecoming game—sweaty, grass-stained, hair tousled, and yet so handsome. His eyes got her every time—deep blue and framed by thick long lashes, they seemed to connect to a hidden well of sweetness in his inner being.

His eyes were still the same, only now traces of wrinkles played around their corners. His face was somehow different, too. A tad thinner, perhaps. Or maybe it was something else altogether.

"Come on, Emmy, I thought you'd be happy for me." Mitchell grinned briefly, then looked away. "Get married. Have a family. Isn't that what you're always saying?"

"Oh, I do not."

"Well, you don't exactly say it, but you're always trying to point me in the right direction. Introducing me to nice girls. That sort of thing."

"I don't see what that has to do with anything. The point is, you've only known Claire a few months. What's the rush? Law school is difficult enough without being newly married."

"Oh, it just makes it more exciting." He gave her another one of his quick grins.

They were in their parents' long, rambling kitchen washing dishes after a Sunday dinner for their mother's birthday. They hadn't done this together for a long time, but it felt natural, like they'd slipped back into their old selves. Only now, he didn't need a stepstool to reach the sink. In fact, he was a good half foot taller than she was.

Emma washed a glass, then put it in the rinse water. Mitchell lifted it out and dried it with a white towel. Their mother, who was growing markedly stooped, had begun the cleaning up, but Mitchell had sweet-talked her into going into the living room with their father, who had fallen asleep in the armchair, and the rest of the family. "It's *your* birthday, and Emma and I haven't done the dishes together in years," he'd said, winking at his sister. "I miss it."

Emma had felt proud of him, much as she had when he began recognizing the words she read to him out of their big book of fairy tales that, by the time it got to Mitchell, had a cover worn smooth and soft.

"Mother really liked the scarf you gave her, Mitchell," she said, slipping a plate into the rinse water. "It was nice."

"Claire picked it out."

"Well, she obviously has good taste. I just hope you didn't spend too much on it. Money's going to be tight for the next few years."

"You worry too much. I've got it under control."

Emma turned away and jerked a pot from the counter.

"Whoa, Emma, you're going to scrub right through the metal."

Emma stopped scrubbing and looked at Mitchell. She rubbed her face with the back of her hand, then picked up the scouring pad again. Somehow, she had to get through to him.

"The thing is, Mitchell, you're ambitious. You're smart. You're extremely good looking . . ."

Mitchell laughed and cocked his head to one side. "Thank you," he said in an Elvis impersonation. "Thank you very much."

"Let me finish. The truth is that a lot of women would see you as . . . as a good prospect. I'd hate to see you rush into something you're not ready for, especially with so much at stake. There's your scholarship at Georgia. You'll have to keep your grades up for that. There's your internship. That will take a lot of time. It makes more sense to wait."

"Life is too short to always be worrying about making sense, Emma."

"No. No. That's what *you* want life to be—romantic and carefree, like some bohemian artist's colony or something you see in college. The truth is that life is so short, you've got to make sense of it the first time around. You don't get a second chance."

"Spoken like an expert. As always."

Emma sighed and pushed her hair back. She handed the pot to Mitchell and grabbed another one from the counter.

"Where is Claire anyway?"

"She was tired after meeting all these crazy people so she went back to her room to rest for a few minutes. She isn't used to lots of family crowding around."

"If she's Catholic, I'd think she'd come from a big family."

Mitchell clunked the pot on the counter. "*Don't* bring up the Catholic bit again! I'm sick of hearing about it, or rather *not* hearing about it. There's a deafening silence every time the subject of conversation gets anywhere near religion. All through college, whenever I'd mention a girl, Mother would ask, 'Well, where does she go to church?' Sometimes even before, 'What's her name?' or, 'Where's she from?' I don't understand what the big deal is where a person goes to church."

In the living room, Charles turned on the radio to listen to a football game. "Can you hear that, Mitchell?"

"Yeah! Thanks, Charles."

Emma peered around the doorway. "Don't have it so loud that you wake up Hank. He really needs that nap."

Mitchell and Emma returned to the dishes.

"I don't hold it against her that she's Catholic. I'm really not that kind of person, despite what you believe. I just want you to be happy, and sometimes a person from a different background may seem exotic and exciting as a friend, but it just doesn't work out in a marriage. Like Walter Cox. He married that woman he met in the army. From Persia or somewhere like that? She was nice enough, as far as I could tell, but they weren't happy."

Mitchell began laughing, soft, overflowing chuckles Emma used to call brother bubbles when Mitchell was a boy.

"In the first place, Maria Cox is from Greece," Mitchell said, when his laughter had subsided. "In the second place, I don't know how you can claim to know how happy they are. We barely know them at all. And finally, there's a huge difference between marrying someone from another continent who speaks a different language and marrying a judge's daughter from Atlanta who happens to be Catholic."

"Touchdown! Carolina's ahead, Mitchell."

"I heard it, Charles. Just hold your horses."

Emma let the soapy water out of the sink, her mouth pursed tight.

"Don't pout, Emma. It gives you wrinkles."

Emma stood straight and looked up into Mitchell's eyes. "Listen, you're not too big for me to give a lesson or two, little brother."

"Oh, yeah?"

"Yeah!"

Mitchell bent down, put Emma over his shoulder and began walking toward the back door.

"Mitchell!!" Emma gasped. "Put me down right now. It isn't funny."

"Oh yeah? Then why are you laughing?"

"You're tickling me. Ouch! Mitchell, put me down."

Mitchell carried her outside to a bench in the backyard and set her down. He reached into his pocket. "I need a smoke."

He lit the cigarette, inhaled slowly, then turned his face upward and blew out puffs of smoke.

"Mother would die if she saw you doing that. It's disgusting."

"Helps me keep calm when I'm studying. I'll quit when I get out of school."

Emma straightened her dress, refastened a button that had come loose, and looked around at the sunlight streaming through the green, yellow, and red leaves of trees encircling the back yard. She remembered playing in this very spot as a little girl, having tea parties with her dolls while her older sisters were at school and, later, watching Mitchell play on a blanket in the grass.

"This time of year, I'd like to stay outside all the time," she said.

"So stay outside."

"I have a husband and a baby boy now, in case you haven't noticed. I can't always do what I want to do. Neither can Charles. You might want to give that some thought."

"And the inquisition is on."

"I am *not* as bad you think, Mitchell. I just want to learn a little about your fiancée and your wedding plans. It would be pretty cold if I didn't care at all."

Mitchell drew on the cigarette again and attempted to blow smoke rings into the air.

"Damn!" he whispered when only misshapen wisps came out.

"Why don't you just tell me what you want to about Claire, and I promise not to ask any hard questions."

Mitchell grinned. "Just what I want, huh?"

"Just what you want."

"Well, she's beautiful, as you can see."

"Yes, I noticed that. What else?"

Mitchell looked toward the sky. "Her father is a judge in Atlanta. I did some courier work for him. That's how we met."

"Okay."

"She's kind of quiet, but it's not that she's stuck up at all. That's just the way she is. You know that old saying . . . 'still water runs deep.' It's something like that. There's more to her than meets the eye, even though what meets the eye is pretty wonderful."

Mitchell leaned forward on the bench, and Emma rubbed his back.

"So you like her father?"

"Oh, yeah. He's helped me out a lot, writing letters of recommendation, that kind of thing. He has quite a reputation in Georgia. Pretty tough, but fair."

"What about her mother?"

Mitchell sat up straight. "I haven't met her. She's been sick for a long time and doesn't get out very much. She couldn't take care of Claire, so Claire went to boarding school when she was growing up. She said it wasn't bad. She had a lot of opportunities."

"What's wrong with her mother?"

"I'm not sure. Something happened during the war. Mr. Brennan was on the front, and they didn't hear from him for a long time. The strain made her sick, or something like that." Mitchell turned and looked at Emma. "I thought you weren't asking any questions."

"Sorry . . . sorry. It is a bad habit. I'll admit it." Emma leaned back and smiled at Mitchell. "Tell you what. You interrogate me for a while. Then we'll be even."

"Pshh. You're not nearly as interesting as I am, Emmy. No secrets. Nothing to ask."

Emma sat up straight and glared at Mitchell. "Well, that hurts my feelings. I have plenty of secrets. I am a very mysterious person. Go ahead, ask me something. I bet I'll surprise you."

Mitchell took out another cigarette and grinned. "Okay. Why'd you wait so long to have children?"

Emma was surprised to feel her face blush. "You're not shy, are you, Mitchell?"

"Now you know how it feels. But never mind. You don't need to answer."

Emma was silent for a moment, trying to gather her words. "No. No. Fair is fair. I was just surprised, is all. The truth is I always thought I would get married and have children right away, but I really enjoyed teaching school and we needed the money while Charles was getting started, so we . . . we . . ."

"You took precautions, as they say. Very sensible." Mitchell was using what Emma called his lawyer voice. She always found it annoying because she could never tell just how much he was being serious and how much he was teasing her.

He grinned over at Emma and nudged her with his elbow. "Well, go on. It's really not that unusual."

"Yes, I do know that." Emma was beginning to feel irritated. She tapped her foot, looked at her watch, and thought about going in to check on Hank.

She decided to stay.

She said, "Then after a while when we felt like we were ready to have children, for some reason it didn't happen. I went to three different doctors. I'm not sure if they helped or not, but finally Hank was born, and I've never been happier."

A soft autumn breeze lifted some brown leaves into the air and back down again. Emma felt a mantle of solemnness around her, a sense that she had spoken of something significant.

Mitchell leaned over and tapped the ashes of his cigarette onto the ground. He sat back up and was silent for a few moments.

"That's great, Emma," he finally said. "I hope we're as happy as you and Charles are."

Emma looked at the ground and smiled. "I do, too."

They didn't say anything for several minutes, but sat listening to the leaves rustle and the squirrels chatter.

"I hope we'll have more children one day," Emma said quietly. "But if not, that's okay, too. I wouldn't trade my life for anything."

Mitchell stared into the ring of trees surrounding the back yard, following the progress of a chipmunk casually moving from acorn to acorn. "It's pretty scary to think about sometimes."

"Think about what, Mitchell?"

Mitchell looked at Emma. "Having children," he said in a voice much older than she had heard before. "I don't know anything about it." He laughed. "Hadn't planned to learn for a while either. Too bad I didn't use those precautions we were talking about."

Surely she had heard wrong, Emma thought. She looked around and tried to sort her emotions out, gripping the bench for balance. No, no . . . she had heard right. Deep down, it seemed as if she had known already. Mitchell was looking at the ground, leaning his right elbow on top of his left arm, holding his cigarette up. She tried to keep her face from showing the sadness she felt.

"Do Mama and Papa know?" she asked quietly.

"Of course not. There's no need. We'll get married in a couple of weeks. Then in a month or so, we'll tell them a baby is on the way. We'll be in Georgia, so it won't be obvious. By the time the baby comes, it won't matter so much."

Emma leaned back on the bench and felt the mid-afternoon sun warm her entire body. Sweat started to pop out on her upper lip and brow. "That's probably best. I think parents have an ability to be blind about certain things they don't want to face, anyway."

Mitchell rubbed his hands together. "I'm sorry I've disappointed you, Emma."

"Well, you're doing the right thing now," Emma said briskly. "That's what matters. In a few years, nobody will think about it." She tried to sound cheerful, but it was a struggle. "I am wondering, though, why you decided to tell me. You could have kept it all quiet."

"I meant to. I really did, but I just felt like I had to tell someone . . . and I wanted to ask you something, too."

"What's that?"

Mitchell was quiet for a while, staring straight ahead. "I was wondering if you'd . . . be there for us." He looked at Emma and smiled. "You know, sort of like the fairy godmother in that story you used to read when I was little. The one with the pumpkin and the mice and the bitchy stepmother?"

"You mean Cinderella?"

"That's the one. I have a feeling it's going to be hard for Claire."

They heard a window opening and looked up to see Charles holding baby Hank, who was letting loose a full-throttled cry. "The game's almost over, Mitchell," he yelled down to them. "It's tied 21 to 21! You better get in here." He started to turn around, then came back. "Oh, yeah, Emma, I think the baby's hungry."

"We're coming," Emma yelled back.

Mitchell looked at her. "Well, I guess we better be going in."

Emma could hear Hank's cries becoming more and more insistent, but she stayed on the bench.

Mitchell stood up and held out his hand to her. She smiled and got up.

"I'd love to," she said.

Mitchell looked at her quizzically.

"I'd love to be the fairy godmother. I always did like that part."

Part Two

My Inheritance

ABOUT SIX MONTHS AFTER MOM DIED, Dad began to sort through her things. He was lost for a long time, not doing anything, really, except what had to be done. He always looked tired, and I know he was. I was, too. Then, one weekend I went down to see him, and he'd started making little piles of her stuff throughout the house. Jennifer, Hank's wife, had asked for some of Mom's cookbooks. Dad wanted to know if that was okay with me. The church women were looking for extra Bibles and she had several—would I mind? It took me a while to figure out why he was asking my permission for everything, and then I realized he saw these things as part of my legacy, my responsibility, even. I hadn't thought about that before. I went into her closet and sorted through her clothes, trying to think what she would like done with them. Some of the blouses I thought Jennifer might wear, and Victoria would like to play dress up with the hats. There were a few things—a tailored jacket, a cashmere sweater—that I took for myself. The rest I folded into bags to take to Goodwill.

When I'd finished, I found my dad in the sewing room, looking through her wicker chest where she kept extra fabric, ribbon, patterns, things like that.

"You don't have any use for this, do you?" he asked, pointing to the sewing machine.

I laughed. "As if," I said, trying to lighten the mood.

He smiled a little, then picked up two pieces of cut-out fabric, the makings of a pillow cover. He dropped them back in the chest and laughed. "Do you remember how she would pull the curtains closed when she sewed on Sunday so the neighbors wouldn't see?"

I didn't remember that, but somehow, it made me sad. Dad went over to the sewing machine and looked out the window. "Right now, I can see her sitting here with Gail, teaching her how to sew. She always did enjoy that."

I could see them, too. Their heads bowed together, studying some intricacy of the pattern.

"If it's all right with you," Dad said, almost whispering, "I was thinking about giving the sewing things to Gail."

My throat tightened up, and I could hear the wolves scurrying and digging, but I managed to whisper back, "Of course."

That's when I noticed Dad was holding something. He smiled at me. "I didn't think you'd mind, but then I found this, and I wasn't sure."

He handed me the jar of buttons, and I saw a scrap of paper had been taped to it. On the paper was my mother's unmistakable handwriting: *For Caroline.*

The Button Flower

THE JAR OF BUTTONS does add a nice touch, I have to admit, when I finally put them out one morning. Our house is a Craftsman-style bungalow, and I've always loved how the sun floods the front rooms, streaming in through the large picture window and the small beveled-glass windows along the side walls. The built-in shelves are made from rich maple and set off the button jar's shining glass and assorted colors. Every day, I stop and notice them when I walk by.

I started working from home a few months ago, so I notice a lot of things around the house more than I used to. I'm writing code for a company that makes programs targeted toward pre-adolescent girls. Girls like Victoria—smart and funny and sensitive, standing at a crossroads in their lives. I love it, but sometimes I get stuck. Sometimes I sit at my desk and stare out the window, waiting for my mind to clear. Other times, I get up and wander around the house, noticing little things that I never bothered with before. Domestic things, like how a rooting of rosemary looks in the kitchen windowsill, the way a basket of apples catches the light on the mahogany table, the busy hum that fills the house when the dishwasher is running. And always, it seems, I end up walking by the button jar and looking at it more closely, staring at those colored discs with their hidden stories. They seem not so unlike some of the mystery elements in my game designs. Talismans, labyrinths, secret passageways—things that carry meaning beyond their appearances. In a certain frame of mind, I can even get quite philosophical about them—the circles are symbols of eternity, the pearl of great price, the full moon, Ezekiel's wheel.

See what living with an Eastern sensibility can do to you?

In any case, I've begun to feel at ease with the buttons. Sometimes I take the jar out and pour the buttons onto the Dhurrie rug. I feel their coolness when I smooth them into a single layer with my hand, look at the pattern of colors, stare at the light reflecting on them . . . then I can go back to my work and see it a different way.

A shrink would probably call it therapy. I don't know, but sorting through the buttons does take me back to my childhood in a very gentle way.

Like this button shaped like a flower. It's from a yellow dress I had when I was four or five years old. I wore it to church almost every Sunday, along with white tights and patent leather shoes. I always felt so dressed up when Mom put it on me, but about five minutes later I wanted it off. It itched, and I was ready to climb the pear tree or jump off the retaining wall—things I was not allowed to do in fancy clothes.

The dress didn't last very long. Mom made doll clothes out of it after I tore it playing red rover with Sally Johnson and her friends.

This Very Day

AFTERWARD, WHEN THEY ALL CAME BACK to the house, I was waiting outside between the bushes with my dog, Mustard, beside me. I could see the cars coming down the street. They were shiny from being washed and waxed the night before, and the lights were on even though it was day. Something moved behind me, and I looked up into the living room window. Grandma Nancy's maid, Eula, had pulled back the curtains and was staring at me. Her eyes looked bigger than ever next to her dark brown skin. I stared back until she disappeared. Then I started to run.

"You get inside now!" Eula grabbed my arms so hard it hurt and began pulling me up onto the porch. "You're gonna get that dress dirty, and I ain't got time to mess with you. Not on this day. Law, Law . . . now stand up."

I had gone loose like Raggedy Ann. "No! I want to wait outside with Mustard," I yelled, but she didn't stop until we were back in the kitchen. She grabbed a cold washcloth from the sink and began scrubbing my face and knees. "Now listen here." She pulled a huge pick out of her hair and redid my barrette. "You gotta settle down. That's all there is to it. Otherwise the devil himself might just carry you off this very day."

I heard the front door open. I pushed Eula away and ran toward the living room. It was Aunt Claire and Gail. They were wearing matching black dresses with tiny gold buttons down the front. Claire wore a black hat with a tiny puff of a veil and carried a small black purse covered with beads. Gail's hat had a blue ribbon that was even longer than her hair. I watched from the hall while Claire went to the mirror over the fireplace, took off her gloves, pulled a golden tube out of her purse, and put lipstick on.

"Come here, Gail," she said. She bent down and, using her finger, rubbed lipstick on Gail's lips. "Just a touch to give you a little color. Now wet your lips and nobody will know." Gail looked up at her mother and licked her lips. Claire set her purse on the end table and sat down to smoke a cigarette. Her legs were long and thin, not like Mommy's. "Sit on the couch, Gail, but don't get your dress wrinkled." Gail sat down and folded her hands in her lap. She didn't say anything.

I ran down the hall to the bathroom, climbed up on the tub and looked in the mirror. My dress was yellow with clear buttons and flowers on the scratchy lace collar. My barrette had come loose again, so my hair fell down in my face. My lips looked pale and dry.

The back door opened, and I ran to the kitchen. "Daddy! Daddy!" I grabbed his legs and looked for him to pick me up. "How's my Caroline?" he asked, rubbing me with his rough face as he held me. His Sunday coat scratched my skin. He held the door open for Hank, who was wearing a new suit. Hank wrinkled his nose at me, so I stuck out my tongue.

"Mr. Tilghman, you gotta do something about that child. She had the devil in her all afternoon long, and I still got to set all this food out on the table."

"Okay, Eula. We'll find somebody to watch her now. Come on, baby, I want to talk to you."

We went down the hall to my room and sat in the rocking chair. "Now listen, honey, you've got to be especially nice today because Mommy and Grandma Nancy are very, very sad, and they need you to be nice while all these people are here. Can you do that, please?"

"Pretty please!"

"Okay, pretty please."

The doorbell rang, and I jumped up.

"Wait a minute, honey. You sit in here for a little bit and read a book, okay? Here, look at this one about the bunny rabbit. Okay, just for a minute?"

He walked down the hall, and I could hear him opening the door. "Come in, come in, Mr. Barrett. We're so glad you could make it. It meant so much to the Sommers and Emma . . . no, no . . . they're still at the graveside. They wanted a few minutes alone, but they should be here any time now. You know Claire and Gail, don't you? Yes, can you excuse me for one minute?"

Daddy came back into my room with Hank. "Listen, puppet, your brother's going to watch you while I let people in. You be good." He left. Hank just stood there.

"Your hair is messed up," he said. I ignored him and began dressing Tony Tiger. "That's a doll's dress, Caroline. It doesn't belong on a tiger."

"Does too."

"It looks stupid."

I dropped Tony Tiger and began playing with my tea set. Hank started reading my favorite book, *The Cat in the Hat.*

"I remember reading this when I was a baby like you," he said.

"I am *not* a baby."

"Are too."

"Are not."

"Yes, you are. If you weren't a baby you would have said, 'am not,' but you don't know any better so you said, 'are not.' You were just copying me." He was quiet for a second, then he grinned and said in a low voice, "Baby."

"I'm *not* a baby."

"Are too."

"Are not."

Hank began laughing, rocking back and forth in the chair. Rage overflowed my stomach and spread all the way to my fingertips. I stood up and grabbed the book from Hank. He laughed.

"If you weren't a baby, you could have gone to the funeral today." He began rocking harder and harder, threatening to tip over at any second. "There was a casket and you know what was inside?"

I didn't say anything. I didn't want to know.

"Grandpa Sam. He's dead."

Hank's eyes were getting wider. I stood still.

"Do you know what it means to be dead? It means your skin gets loose and flappy, and you'll never move again, even if worms crawl in your nose." Hank wiggled his finger under his nose, then clasped his arms across his chest.

"You just lie there perfectly still, but sometimes it looks like you might move a little bit when nobody's looking. Like you want to move so bad, even if it's just little jerky moves, but you can't. And people walk by and stare at you. And all the grown-ups are crying, even Uncle Max. And then they shut the casket lid down—BANG! And they put you in a big hole in the ground and cover you up with dirt. And it's all dark and wet, with worms crawling around, but you can't move."

Hank paused for breath.

"Nuh-uh," I said, but I wasn't sure.

"It's true. Ask anyone."

I picked up Teddy and gave him some tea.

"Then at night, when there's a full moon, you turn into a ghost. You know, like at Halloween. And you float out of the graveyard and through the walls of the house."

Hank stopped rocking. He leaned forward, his voice getting quiet. "Then you float above all the people sleeping, and if you're mad at someone, you stop over their bed . . . then BOO! YOU SCARE THEM!"

I jumped, dropping the teacup and Teddy on the floor.

"Shut up, Hank. Shut up!"

Hank was laughing, doubled over in the rocking chair. "You jumped so high!"

"GO AWAY! OUT!"

Hank kept on laughing. I ran over and began hitting him with my fists. "STOP! STOP! MAMA!"

Suddenly, I was being picked up by my armpits. I turned around and saw Daddy's face with its mad look on. I started crying.

"Hank, I specifically asked you to look after your sister. I really needed you to help me today, but you let me down. I'll deal with you later. For now, you can let people in when they come to the door."

"I didn't touch her. She was hitting me."

"I don't want to hear it. Go on . . . now Caroline, you stop acting like a crybaby. Remember you told me you'd be especially nice today?" He put me down, wiped my face with his handkerchief, and tried to fix my hair.

"Come on with me now." He held my hand, and we walked into the dining room where the table was covered with a big white cloth. There were little bitty sandwiches without crust and cookies and pieces of cake. The room smelled like coffee. At one end of the table was a silver pitcher surrounded by china teacups.

Daddy gave me a sandwich. "Go in the kitchen and ask Eula for some juice," he said, but right behind him I could see a huge lady with big blue hair and crumbly skin coming toward me. She looked like the hippopotamus in my alphabet book. I grabbed Daddy's leg.

"Ohhh . . . this must be the baby. She's *so* sweet." Her face was right next to mine. I could see powder caked up in her wrinkles. "She looks so cute with that ragamuffin hair!" She stood up and turned to Daddy. "So how is Emma doing?"

"Oh, as well as can be expected, I suppose. He hadn't been himself for a long time, and I think that was harder, in a way."

"Poor dear soul! I hope he's at peace now."

I went into the hall and stared into the living room, full of grown-ups wearing Sunday clothes. Through the picture window, I could see Hank throwing a football with Jimmy from across the street. Gail was standing on the sidewalk, watching.

Aunt Claire moved about the room, gathering cups and plates.

"Look at her, playing the part of the loyal daughter-in-law," whispered an old cousin sitting on the love seat with another old cousin. "You know she didn't care a thing about poor Sam. She's just here to see what's in the will."

"She wouldn't get a thing if it weren't for Gail," the other aunt whispered. "Sam was always sweet on that girl. Of course, anyone would be. She's such a little lady."

"Lovely, just lovely."

"Of course, she is Catholic, you know. Goes to boarding school and everything." I could barely hear her now. "Claire only sees her a few times a year. Poor dear, with no daddy and a mama who doesn't care."

The first aunt looked around, then whispered again. "Nancy told me that Sam's mother is so distraught she couldn't even come today. Of course, she is very old, but it makes you wonder . . . did you ever hear the rumor that Sam was born on the wrong side of the bed covers?"

"No!"

"That's what I heard."

Aunt Claire walked by with the dishes. She smelled like roses. The cousins got quiet, then they looked at me.

"Well, here's little Caroline!"

"Aren't you a doll baby? Let me look at you."

One of them reached for my hand, but I had seen Mama in the corner of the room talking with Uncle Max and Cousin Vivian. I ran over and grabbed her legs. She absentmindedly ran her fingers through my hair.

"Mama, I want some tea."

"Not now, Caroline." Her eyes were wet, and she had a handkerchief in her hand.

"Please . . . pretty please. Teddy wants to have a real tea party."

"Maybe tomorrow." She looked out the window at the boys playing football. "You know, I don't understand why the children don't seem sad," she said to Uncle Max. "They can just play as if nothing happened, as if they had never had a grandfather."

"Yes, but they didn't know him before he got sick, Emma. They didn't know the same person we grew up with."

"I remember when I was Caroline's age how he would ride me on his shoulders out to the barn to feed the horses . . . Kaiser and King . . . he loved those horses so much. He was sick when they had to be put down." Mama began crying into her handkerchief. "I better go check on Mother," she said and went down the hall to her bedroom.

The dining room was empty now except for two men talking by the window.

"I hear they're planning to bring Coloreds into the county schools next year," one of them said. He was eating cookies, bits of sugar and crumbs collecting in his gray mustache. "Stirring up a hornet's nest, that is."

"I don't know," the other one said, in between slurps of coffee. "I'm just glad I'm not coming up these days. You get to where you don't know what's right and what's not."

Eula came in with another tray of cookies, and the men left. When she closed the kitchen door, I went into the dining room and stared at the china cups. I had only seen them a few times before. They were creamy and had a gold stripe on the rim. I picked one up and turned it over and over, feeling its solid coolness in my hands. I rolled it on my face, my neck, my arms, testing its perfect roundness until it slipped onto the floor, bounced slowly up in the air, and landed on its side.

It broke with a clatter that made me freeze.

Daddy came in from the kitchen. "Caroline, what am I going to do with you?" He began picking up the pieces. "You know you can't buy this china anymore. The pattern was destroyed during the war."

Claire walked in. She had a tiny smile on her face.

Daddy looked up at her from the floor. "Is there any way you could watch her for awhile? I really need to be out there with everyone."

"Of course."

Daddy left the room. I stared at Claire.

"Come here, Caroline, your hair needs fixing."

I stood still. Claire came over to me and redid my barrette. "Let's go outside for a minute," she said, grabbing my hand.

In the front yard, the football game was still going on. Gail and another girl were sitting on the front steps.

"Gail, I need you to watch your cousin for awhile. Don't let her break anything or get in the street." She went back inside.

Gail came over to me. "Caroline, you want to sit down with us?"

"No! I wanna play ball."

I ran into the yard.

"Go away, Caroline," Hank yelled. "You'll get hurt."

Gail grabbed me from behind and pulled me to the edge of the yard. I went limp and flopped down on the grass.

"No, Caroline, you'll get your dress dirty. Now stand up."

Jimmy's basset hound wandered into the yard and began playing with Mustard. "Here Waldo," I yelled. Waldo ran over and put his paws in my lap.

"Caroline, why did you do that? Now you're all muddy."

"I wanted to say hello to Waldo."

"You're all dressed up!"

The other girl—a big redhead with a magazine on her lap—watched from the step. "Well, she's dirty now, Gail, just leave her alone."

Gail stared at me for a minute, then went back to the step. Waldo licked my ear.

"That tickles, Waldo." I was laughing so hard I had to lie down in the grass. Waldo stood over me, licking my face.

"Caroline, get up," Gail said, pushing the dog away. "Don't you want to act like a big girl?"

I looked at Gail's perfect face—her deep blue eyes with thick lashes, her china doll nose, her rosy cheekbones.

"You have lipstick on," I told her.

"Yeah? Well, so what?"

I didn't know what to say, so I walked up the steps and opened the front door. "I have to go pee pee," I told Gail as I ran down the hall to the bathroom. I shut the door, then opened it again. "I can do it myself," I said through the crack. Gail turned around and walked off.

I waited a minute before coming out. This end of the house was dark and quiet, but I could hear soft voices coming from Mama's room. I tiptoed over to the door and peeked in. Grandma Nancy was lying on her side in the bed, with Mama and another lady sitting in chairs beside her. They were looking at pictures.

"This was before we got married," Grandma said. "He was so handsome. I remember how his hair curled just a little above his ears."

I ran back to the living room. Most of the people were outside now. Some big cousins had taken off their coats and were throwing the ball with Hank and Jimmy. The sun shone through the window, sparkling among the beads on Aunt Claire's purse on the coffee table. I stared at it for a minute, then grabbed it and ran back down to the bathroom. I opened the purse and saw the golden tube of lipstick, dazzling me with its beautiful glitter. I took it out and began turning the rich redness up and down the metal sides. I couldn't stop myself until I had climbed on the tub and, looking over to the mirror, put it on my lips.

I stared into the mirror, expecting to see Gail's feminine beauty staring back at me, but something was wrong.

My lips were all crooked. I tried to fill in the lines, but it got worse. I rubbed it in with my finger. I licked my lips. Nothing worked. Now it was on my hands, my face, my dress . . . everyone would know how bad I'd been. I'd get a spanking for sure, a bare-bottom spanking.

Suddenly I couldn't breathe. Maybe Eula was right. Maybe the devil would carry me off today. Maybe he'd try to put me in the dark ground where I couldn't move, where the cold dead people were, and nobody would stop him because of how bad I'd been.

Someone was coming down the hall. Maybe it was the devil now. Maybe Grandpa Sam was with him.

I didn't want to see them. I threw the lipstick down. It hit the floor with a thud, breaking off the tip and leaving a red smudge on the light green linoleum. I climbed in the tub and pulled the shower curtain around me.

The door opened and someone came in. I watched through the curtain as a delicate hand with a gold bracelet and long fingers reached down, picked up the purse and then the lipstick.

"Well damn it all," she said, throwing the tube in the trashcan.

It wasn't the devil; it was Aunt Claire.

A squeaky noise came out of my throat, and Claire turned toward the tub. I squeezed my eyes shut; I held my breath; I wished myself invisible.

Claire pulled the curtain back with a jerk.

"What are you doing in there, you little spy?"

I could tell by the way her nose went open and shut that she was very mad. "Don't you know any better than to go through other people's things?"

She began tapping her fingernails on the tile wall. "This is rich!" she said, pulling her other hand through her shiny hair. "It's bad enough that people don't have anything better to do than talk about me, but now my purse is fair game, too.

"Well, did you find anything interesting? Anything Aunt Edna would like to hear about? Huh? Did you?"

I shook my head, and my barrette fell out of my hair, bouncing off the tub with a ping. Another squeak came from my throat, and I couldn't hold it in anymore. Tears ran down my face and out my nose.

Claire sat down on the toilet and started laughing softly into her hands. "You know," she said after a while. "We actually have a lot in common. Everybody wants to see us and talk about us, but nobody really wants us here today."

She stood up. "Get out of the tub, Caroline. There's nothing to cry about." Her voice was matter of fact, with no room for disobeying.

I got out while Claire wet a washcloth in the sink. She scrubbed the lipstick and dirt off my skin and dress. Then she got a comb and pulled the knots out of my hair.

"Ouch! That hurts."

"Sometimes it hurts to be beautiful." She looked at me for a moment. "Well, that's an improvement anyway."

Claire picked her purse up off the counter. She smiled.

"Here . . . I'll tell you the secret of life."

She pulled a golden tube out of her purse, took off the top, and waved it like a wand in the sunlight. She bent over and gently touched it to my mouth.

"Always carry an extra lipstick."

The Cowboy Button

HERE'S ANOTHER CHILDHOOD BUTTON, but this one is from a shirt Hank wore. He was one of those kids who would wear the same shirt over and over and over, even after it was way too small, and after that, he'd keep it in his closet for several more years. The shirt this button came from had a cowboy style—plaid, long sleeved, with pearl snaps on the pockets and down the front.

He was like that about a lot of things—he'd focus on something and wouldn't let go. Even today, Hank is nothing if not steadfast.

Holding the metal button in my hand, I realize I've taken my brother for granted too often over the years. I've always known that he'll be here for me with his no-drama, engineer's approach to life, even if he sometimes can irritate me until I'm on my last nerve. He gave me a sister when he married Jennifer and a niece and nephew who give us all a reason to continue Mom's traditions now that she's gone. He and Rishi are like brothers, too.

He's been such a stable presence that I've never spent a lot of time thinking about him. I never really stopped to wonder, until now, whether there might be more to him than the image in my mind of my big brother.

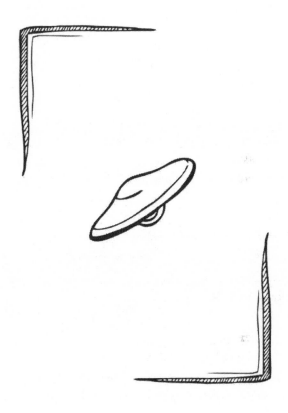

Ground Control

CLICK. The screen went gray except for two lines of white that quickly moved to the center and became one glowing spot, like a star appearing at the end of a telescope. Caroline looked at him and laughed, then ran down the hall.

"Mama!" Hank yelled. "She turned the TV off again." He ran over to the television, pulled the knob back on, then settled back into the couch, waiting for the image to reappear. Before it did, his mother came in the room and turned the television off again.

"You've been glued to the TV all afternoon," she said. "You haven't finished your jobs. Now get up and do something, please."

Indignation filled him from his head, which was a bit disheveled from lying on the vinyl cushions so long, to his toe, which was draped over the end of the couch. "You can't just turn that off," he told his mother, who was still standing in front of the television. "I was watching it."

He got up and went toward the TV, but his mother wouldn't let him by. "It's a beautiful day, and you should be outside raking leaves, not in here, ruining your eyes. I've asked you six times. Now go."

"Mom, I told you. This is really big news. You don't expect me to rake leaves while they're up there in space. Something could happen, and I'd be the only one who missed it."

His mother was unmoved. She bent over and unplugged the TV set. "Go on outside now. If anything happens, it will be on the news tonight."

Hank felt genuinely wronged. He had been following every detail of Apollo 12. He had watched the countdown, the liftoff, and the lunar landing. He had read every article that had been in the newspaper, cutting out the more important ones for a scrapbook he had begun during the summer when Apollo 11 landed on the moon. He had looked up every entry in the encyclopedia that had anything to do with space or the moon or the stars. He had even biked down to the library on Elm Street and checked out all their books on the solar system, filling up the baskets on either side of his rear wheels.

He slammed the door as he went down to the basement to get the rake, and then he slammed the door when he went outside. It just wasn't fair. People didn't recognize the significance of what was going on. Sure, they said things. Things like, "Can you believe those men are really on the moon? What will be next?" Or, "This is the beginning of a new age—things will never be the same." But they didn't mean it—they didn't act any differently at all. They just kept on paying bills or changing lightbulbs as if nothing had happened. Even at school, where you'd think the teachers would want you to witness everything about the space mission, they had only been allowed to watch a few things on TV, like an interview with the astronauts about the importance of science, and then it was back to the same old formulas and essays.

Outside, his neighborhood also seemed strangely unchanged by what was going on overhead. The sky was a calm pale blue, with just a few lazy tufts drifting about. The sun was beginning to set, highlighting the naked tree branches that swayed just the tiniest bit, as if in some hypnotic meditation. Birds scolded the cat from the safety of a telephone line. Down the street, the Johnson twins were playing jump rope.

Hank began raking as fast as he could. Maybe he would get this over and get back inside before anything crucial happened.

Thwack. Something hit him square between the shoulder blades.

"Gotcha! I can't believe you let me get that close to you without seeing me. Good thing I wasn't a spy or something."

It was Bill Allen from across the street. Normally they were good friends, but lately, Bill had become a little annoying. He had been interested in Apollo during the summer and had even started his own scrapbook, but his interest had fizzled out by the time school started.

"Hey, I'm trying to finish this so I can watch Apollo on TV. Why don't you grab a rake and help me."

"No way. I'm done with raking. Besides, they just keep showing the same thing over and over. How many more times do you want to see the moon anyway? Why don't we play catch instead?" Bill's brother had just made the football team, and he was determined not to be left behind.

"Forget it, Bill. I've got to get this done." Hank returned to his raking with renewed determination. Bill shrugged his shoulders and headed down the street to find more interesting company.

It had been a warm day for November, but now the sun was lower in the sky and a chill crept through Hank's soft shirt. He buttoned the top button and began to think about how cold it was on the moon. Minus 155 centigrade at night, they said. It was hard to comprehend how cold that was, how dependent the astronauts were on their space suits. One tear and they'd be left dying in the cold.

Thinking about the Apollo mission always energized Hank, and he began to rake faster and faster. He pictured himself on the moon with Conrad and Gordon, combing the surface for rocks and dirt, taking care not to rip his space suit. He took exaggerated steps and used big arm movements. He spotted a rock in the grass, slowly bent down, picked it up, and inspected it in the sunlight.

"I think this one might be important," he told his imaginary companions as he stuck the rock in his pocket.

Hank returned to raking and once again tried to decide what his favorite part of the Apollo mission was. This was a ritual of his, and he savored going over each phase with its own, unique fascination. There was the anticipation of the countdown, when he waited and waited and waited with breath held for the incredible explosion. Then there was the liftoff's blast of fire followed by billows of white smoke as the rocket rose in slow motion, became smaller and smaller, and finally disappeared at the end of a thin white line. The most unbelievable moment came when the astronauts landed on the moon and stepped out of the module onto the dry, dusty surface, moving slowly but exuberantly, taking small jumps periodically, like children on Christmas morning. Finally, there was the return to earth, with the capsule falling out of the sky into the outstretched ocean below.

He went over each part in his mind and decided that his favorite must still be the landing on the moon. Every night since June 16, he had gone to sleep with that image, with those words. It filled him with a desire to be great and brave. He was no longer afraid of childish things—glowing eyes staring at him from the darkness, snarling beasts, and mournful ghosts that might be watching in the stillness of the night. Now his only fear was that he would be too late, that his chance to blast off to a new and dangerous world would never come.

A great pile of leaves stood before him. A bumpy hill of brown, like something alien to earth, something that wasn't growing and filled with the desire that he felt. He had finished raking and was flushed with the blood that was pulsing into his capillaries. Nobody seemed to be around, so he walked across the yard and then ran and jumped into the pile of leaves.

"I am here!" He lifted his fists high in the air. He didn't know why he did this, except perhaps to make the universe take note of him. He would not be passed by after everyone else had had their chance. He wanted to do something . . . to tame the west, brave the deep, scale the summit, find the pole, or go to the moon. He knew exactly what Kennedy had meant when he said, "We choose to go to the moon in this decade and do the other things, not because they are easy, but because they are hard . . ."

He looked up at the sky, which was now tinged with red toward the west. "O God, please let me do something hard," he whispered, as he sat down in the leaves.

Bang! A car door slammed, and his father walked down the sidewalk. "Hi, sport! I see you've been busy this afternoon. I'm glad you're such a good helper."

"Hi, Dad." Lately it amazed Hank that his father could use words like "sport" and "helper" to describe him. Didn't he know that these were baby words, that Hank found them demeaning? There was no way to tell his father that he was a different person now, that he was ready for something more.

"You better come on in, son. It's getting cold out here." His father walked toward the door, his hat on his head and his briefcase in hand. Hank wondered if he had done anything adventurous in his whole life.

The lights in the house looked warm and cozy. Hank could smell fried chicken and mashed potatoes when his father opened the door. The sweat on his skin felt cold now, and he realized he was tired and hungry.

On the horizon, the moon appeared white against the darkening twilight sky. It did not look like a barren frontier, an unexplored world waiting to be claimed. It looked like something too beautiful to leave a footprint on, something too pure to invade.

The evening air wrapped around Hank and enveloped him in sadness. He trudged to the basement, put the rake up in darkness, then headed upstairs toward where the light of the kitchen poured out in a shaft from under the door.

"Thank you, sweetie," his mother said as she spooned beans into a bowl. She stopped for a moment and gave him a kiss. "You're so cold! Go wash up and we'll eat in a few minutes."

He felt the two cats, Felix and Lucy, rub against his legs, while Mustard, the dog, looked at them with envy. Caroline plopped silverware on the table, deliberately turning the forks upside down. The humid warmth of the kitchen felt delicious, and Hank could barely wait to eat. After supper, he watched the news and worked on his scrapbook.

Later, he burrowed in the softness of his bed, pulling the covers up to his neck. He floated on a cushion of sleep, gently rocking back and forth as shadows of leaves silently fell about him. A pale ray of light touched his cheek, and he ascended slowly, rose through the black asphalt roof, and stopped for a moment on a cloud to look down at the streetlights below.

The stars beckoned with their shining loveliness, but he went toward the pale glow that was now high in the sky. He reached out his hand and was pulled onward until his feet quietly touched the velvet dust.

He did not feel cold. A man in white slowly walked toward him, raising his hand in greeting.

Navy Blue

WHEN I SIFT THROUGH THE BUTTONS, it's always surprising to realize how many belonged to Gail. Like this one from one of her Catholic school uniforms. She had lots of uniforms over the years, but most of them were the same—blue-and-white plaid jumpers. My mom would work on them every summer Gail came to stay with us, taking in the waist, letting out the hem, tightening the buttons. I always thought it was so strange to wear a uniform to school. Sometimes I'd put one on and wear it around the house, pretending to be Gail.

Gail the Perfect was what I called her in my head. Gail, who always wanted to do the things my mom wanted me to do, who kept every little thing in her room as orchestrated as a museum, who loved dolls and babies and playing house, while I was at the end of the gravel driveway, building a stick fort on the edge of a mud puddle. And of course I always forgot to clean off before I came inside. "You're worse than Hank!" my mom would say. Almost every day, it seemed.

Looking back, I realize things now that I couldn't at the time, like how my mom was trying to make life a little more fair for Gail, how she felt that twinge of bittersweet memory when she saw Gail's face turn a certain way. Maybe Mom had her own wolves she had to keep at bay. I guess everyone does.

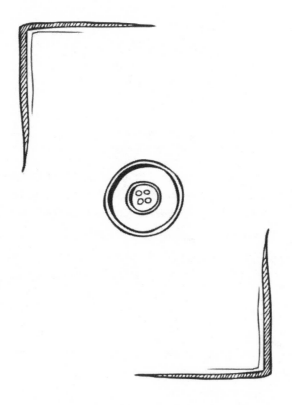

Sorting Through

ON THE FIRST RAINY DAY, Gail pulled out the photo albums and sat at the kitchen table going through the pictures. She did this every summer she stayed with Aunt Emmy, starting with the small, grainy wedding pictures in the yellowing white album. There was one of Aunt Emmy and Uncle Charles looking into the camera with shining faces as they cut the cake. Another one showed the older aunts standing together with arms linked around one another's waists, looking somehow young and old simultaneously. Gail's favorite was a slightly blurred picture that showed her father as a teenager, dressed in an old-fashioned suit, his big grin almost childish in intensity.

After the wedding pictures were baby pictures of Hank, a long, lanky thing with big eyes and outstretched fingers. Then came the pictures of the house. Gail always stared at these a long time, wondering exactly what it was that made this house so different from her own.

The pictures were made right at the time Aunt Emmy and Uncle Charles had bought the house, and the trees lining the street were short and scrawny, offering little shade or cover. It

91

was hard to imagine Hank climbing them, but then, in the pictures, Hank was just a toddler. Caroline wasn't even born.

Now trees towered over the house. There was an oak tree in the back that Uncle Charles had used to hang a tire swing on. Gail felt a catch in her stomach just thinking about it—soaring up toward the branches, stopping for a fraction of a second and then swooping back down. There was a glossy magnolia in the front that filled the air with an almost dizzying smell of perfume on hot summer evenings. There was a big maple tree in the woods bordering the back where Hank had built a BOYS ONLY club. He kept a padlock on it, because Caroline was always trying to sneak in and rummage through the baseball cards, pocket knives, and other private things he and Bill Allen kept up there in an old cardboard box.

If you looked at the house now, you'd swear it had been there forever, nestled among the trees and bushes. You wouldn't guess it had ever sat on raw, violated earth, like the pictures showed, waiting for grass to take root and tiny shrubs to grow. Gail thought it was the prettiest house on all of Mockingbird Lane, although the whole street was nice, lined with rows of live oaks, dogwoods, and maples. Except for the Purcells', whose lawn resembled a golf course, all the yards had a casual, rambling appearance. A little moss on the sidewalks, a few leaves under the bushes, ivy jumping out of the borders. To Gail it seemed as if nature had begun to forgive the earlier intrusion and was taking the neighborhood back.

Gail tried to look critically at the picture of No. 135 when it was brand new. To most people it probably wouldn't seem very impressive. It was a brick rancher, with one picture window and a little wrought ironwork on the front porch serving as the sole adornments. But the picture didn't show the Carolina jasmine that eventually framed the carport or the huge camellia bush hugging the corner. It didn't capture the loveliness the house had grown into.

Right now the house was quiet, which was unusual. Normally, the TV was on in the den, Hank had his radio going in his room, and Caroline seemed to talk constantly. Aunt Emmy would be working in the kitchen, and Uncle Charles would be hammering or sawing in the basement. At least that's what it seemed like to Gail.

She closed her eyes and tried to picture her own home, a new Colonial-style townhouse just outside of Atlanta. It was decorated in clean modern lines, in an art deco variation, her mother had explained. They used to live in a condo right downtown, close to the small art museum where her mother worked, but they had moved when Judge Brennan—her grandfather—retired from his law practice and declared downtown no longer safe for his daughter and granddaughter. Gail missed riding the elevator and talking to the doorman. Sometimes the Thomases, who had lived just above, had let her walk their French poodle, Monique.

Gail hadn't gotten used to the townhouse yet, even though they'd moved in two years ago. It was hard to get used to a place when you were only there for holidays and part of the summer. Most of the year she went to school at St. Mary's, and of course, she spent several weeks in the summer here with Aunt Emmy. In fact, this year she had come here straight from school, so she hadn't been home in almost two months. That wasn't so bad. She had seen her mother the first Sunday of each month during school. They'd go to Mass, then have dinner at The Stillwell House. Unlike most of her classmates, who groaned while getting dressed for family Sundays, Gail enjoyed these lunches immensely. She loved her mother. She loved watching her beautiful hands that looked so delicate against the wide gold-and-diamond wedding band that she still wore, so graceful as she held the marble rosary beads. She loved her shining black hair that turned to perfection around her chin. She loved the crisp clothes she wore and the slight hint of perfume that lingered for a second after she kissed her goodbye.

When Gail's mother entered a room—any room, it didn't matter if it was at the restaurant or even at church—everyone seemed to pause and take a breath, as if there were subliminal music announcing her arrival. Gail had noticed this for a long time. At first, she had assumed it was because her mother was so beautiful, and this was definitely part of it, but there was something more. Something about the way she moved. Or maybe it was the way she looked at you, or the way she waited a moment before speaking. Gail had often compared her—in her mind—to a Siamese cat. Graceful and mysterious, the cat gave you a thrill of privilege on those rare occasions when it brushed its head against your outstretched hand. There had to be something magical about a person who could make you feel special just by being there.

Gail put down the album and looked at Felix, an ancient orange cat sitting on the kitchen chair beside her, on top of her crumpled school uniform that Aunt Emmy was sewing buttons on. She laughed and scratched it behind the ears. The cat began purring immediately, then stretched and yawned and looked adoringly at Gail. Maybe it wasn't the trees after all, Gail thought. Maybe it was the presence of the animals—two fat cats and an ugly but loveable dog—that made Emmy's house seem different. They were always close by, jumping on your lap or sneaking in the bed or looking for a handout. Gail had no pets at home, not even a fish. They were gone too much, her mother had explained once. Then too, pets shed.

This was definitely true. There were dog and cat hairs all over Gail's clothes. She had tried brushing them off, but it didn't work, and after a few days, she didn't notice anymore.

It always took her a few days to get used to how casual life was here. Emmy was always working on the place, beating the rugs or washing the curtains or making new slipcovers, but still there was a lot of clutter—a week's worth of newspapers stacked in a pile on the den floor, Hank's chemistry set spread out on the dining room table, Caroline's toys and books stuffed here and there throughout the house.

They acted differently, too. "Less hushed" was the only way Gail could explain it in her mind. They said blessing before dinner, but not in any ordered sense, not at all like at school. True, sometimes they recited words: *Bless this food to the nourishment of our bodies and us to thy service, in Jesus' name, Amen.* But in a casual, not ritual, way. It was always different, depending on who was saying it. When it was Hank's turn, he always rushed through the words in a mumbled rush to get to the Amen. When Charles asked Gail to say the blessing, she also chose those words. She didn't know what else to do. She didn't cross herself because it didn't seem like a real prayer to her. Emma would say something about the day—the rain that watered the garden, or the first lily of the summer—before concluding with the rest. Charles usually said something funny, like, "Good bread, good meat. Good Lord, let's eat!" Caroline always made a big production out of her turn, thanking God for the grass, the sky, the candy she got at the store, and anything else she could think of, until Hank finally gave up and started eating. Then, of course, Caroline complained to Emma. "I'm not finished!" Gail couldn't imagine doing that with her mother.

Gail opened another album and looked at Caroline's baby pictures. Hank was six years old when his little sister was born, and he didn't appear very happy about it. Peering over Emmy's shoulder at the dark-haired, wailing baby, he had a look of deep concern on his face. Gail wondered what it would have been like if she had a baby brother or sister or even, like Mary Delisle, six brothers and sisters. What if her father hadn't died and he had brought them toys every time he went on a business trip? This was one of the earliest memories Gail had of her father—him walking in the door, holding a brown paper bag, then bending down and pulling out a big white teddy bear and a box of chocolates. "Sweets for the sweet!" he had said, mussing her hair before he went down the hall.

Gail went through the baby album quickly. She had learned over the years that no matter how hard she tried to picture what life might have been like with siblings and a father, in the end, she just couldn't imagine it. Thinking about it made her feel guilty, as if she were trying to mess up the symmetry of her mother's life.

The rest of the pictures hadn't been put in albums, but were kept haphazardly in old shoeboxes. They weren't in any particular order, either, so you might see last year's color picture of Caroline's Brownie troop and then pick up a black-and-white portrait of Hank in first grade. Gail was surprised at how many pictures there were of her. One showed her standing in front of the giant holly bush with arms linked with Marcia Johnson, who lived at No. 204, the blue Cape Cod. They were smiling big, fake smiles, and had their hair pulled up in matching pigtails. There was one from long ago, a picture of her painting with a set of watercolors, which she passed over quickly. In another, Hank, Caroline, and Gail sat posed on a bench in front of a fountain at the horticultural gardens. Then Gail saw her school picture from last year. She picked it up and looked at it a long time. It was one of her favorite pictures of herself, maybe because it looked eerily like her mother's fifth-grade picture, one of many that sat on a shelf in Judge Brennan's library, dusted dutifully every week by Lucille, the aging housemaid. Gail didn't remember giving the picture to Emmy. She turned it over and felt a little jab of shock at the sight of her mother's flowing Catholic-school-perfect handwriting. *Gail Sommers, 1969.* Then, like an after-thought: *Thanks for all your help, Claire.*

It shouldn't have seemed remarkable, Gail knew that, but she had never imagined her mother cutting out school pictures and sending them to relatives. The thought of her mother writing Aunt Emmy something as personal as a note, even a note jotted down on the back of picture, struck her as incongruous. Of course, Emmy and her mother exchanged Christmas cards and discussed details of Gail's visits on the phone and even managed to carry on brief periods of small talk during family gatherings, but Gail had always assumed they didn't *communicate* in the real sense of the word. They didn't chat or write rambling letters or have coffee together just for fun. To be honest, Gail didn't know of anyone her mother did these things with. She occasionally had lunch with some of the other people at the museum, but that was about it.

Gail picked up another picture, a group shot of Emmy, Hank, Caroline, and Gail on a picnic at the lake. Charles' crumpled straw hat lay on the bench. It had come to be a joke, how he was never in the family pictures because he was the one taking them, but he always left some personal item—a hat, a sweater, or even a shoe—to represent himself. He made Gail laugh.

In the picnic picture, Hank and Gail sat on the far side of the table, leaning their elbows on top of a huge watermelon. Aunt Emmy held Caroline on her lap. Gail remembered how wild Caroline had been that day, how just moments before the picture was taken, Emmy had grabbed her as she ran around the table. "Now settle down!" she'd said as Caroline looked up at the sky. "Look how nicely Gail is sitting. Why don't you do that?" Out of the corners of her eyes, Caroline had given Gail a potent glare. Gail wished Emmy wouldn't say things like that.

Gail liked almost everything else about Emmy. She liked the way she spent the whole day around the house, going from making breakfast to dusting to making lunch to sewing matching dresses for Caroline and Gail. She let Gail help with everything, even with the most elaborate projects, like making jam. She spent several hours preparing dinner, always serving at least five different things, several of them from the garden in the back yard. Green beans cooked with bacon drippings and onion. Squash casserole sprinkled with seasoned breadcrumbs. Cucumber salad. Often, she'd stay up late at night canning and freezing and doing various other things in the kitchen. Gail would go to sleep to the sounds of drawers opening and closing and pots and pans being washed.

Looking at Emmy's picture, Gail realized that she already knew the real reason this house felt so different from her own. It wasn't the trees or even the pets. Everything could be traced back to Emmy and her constant busyness about the place. This home was Emmy's life's work, and her being permeated each corner of the house, from the prolific garden to the homemade curtains to the crowded kitchen. It wasn't as beautiful as Gail's real home. It wasn't as organized or balanced or peaceful, but Gail knew a part of her would always come from here.

Gail heard the back door open and looked up as Aunt Emmy walked in with bags of groceries. Caroline came in behind, her hair wet from the rain. She went tearing through the kitchen, yelling her personal rendition of an Indian war call as she went down the hall.

"Caroline, take your muddy shoes off!" Aunt Emmy called as she took off her raincoat and bonnet.

Gail got up and began putting up the groceries. Felix jumped down and rubbed against Aunt Emmy's legs.

"Did you have a nice morning, dear?" Emmy asked. She looked at the pictures on the table. "I really do need to get those things organized. Maybe we can do that later this week."

Inside, Gail smiled. Aunt Emmy said that exact same thing every summer.

A Leather Button

SOMETIMES I WONDER if the buttons move around in the jar during the night, because each time I look at them, it seems that another one has popped into view. Like this large, crinkled brown leather button. To be honest, I have no idea what it came from, but it makes me think of a man's tan cardigan sweater, the kind my neighbor, Mr. Reed, used to wear all the time.

Mr. and Mrs. Reed lived across the street from us in a brick house underneath a canopy of tall oak trees. They were very old even when I was very young. She had thick white hair she wore in a bun on top of her head, and he was tall and skinny with horn-rimmed glasses. In the summer, they'd stay out on the screened-in porch a lot. He'd read the paper and, in the cool of the early morning, she'd knit. I'd go over there sometimes. She'd give me a piece of cake or pie, show me what she was knitting, let me play with the scraps and the buttons. They had this really cool round fan. You could put a piece of paper over it and the paper would stay in the air, spinning around and around and around like magic.

Through the Screen

Ashton Mill, N.C. 1971

THE FAN ON THE SCREENED-IN PORCH whirred steadily from its round metal box on the floor, sending gentle circles of air upward, stirring the corners of the newspaper Frank Reed held in his lap. He had a blanket around his legs and wore a brown sweater his wife, Mary, had knit for him. Mary sat in the glider beside him, finishing the last of the morning's coffee. She never said, "Don't you want the fan off?" when he wore the sweater and pulled the blanket over his legs. She knew that the sound of the fan was soothing, and its breeze made it cool enough to wear the sweater, even though it was mid-morning in June. At one time, she may have thought it was silly to turn on the fan when he was wearing a sweater—why not just take the sweater off and he wouldn't need the fan at all? But she had never said it, and she no longer even thought it.

Mary looked at Frank and knew he was dozing, even though he still held the newspaper as if he were working the crossword. His pose reminded her of a picture she had seen of Ulysses S. Grant when he was in debt and dying of throat cancer. He forced himself to live long enough to complete his memoirs, so his family would have enough money to live on. He spent the last months of his life in a rocking chair on the porch of the cottage at Mount McGregor, wrapped in a blanket, writing, writing, writing. Mary wondered if his wife had asked him, "Don't you want to lie down? Aren't you tired of sitting and writing?" or if she knew that completing this last campaign was all that mattered to him now, was all that gave him comfort.

When Mary and Frank first moved to North Carolina twenty years ago, the screened-in porch had seemed like their own private paradise. They spent as much time out there as possible, sweeping and wiping it clean in April for springtime lunches on the round glass table. On summer evenings, they turned on the lamps and sat together listening to the crickets, which were loud enough to be heard over the fan. Mary knitted and Frank read his magazines. Sometimes, they just sat.

It was so different from Buffalo, where the summers were wonderful, but the cold came so soon and lasted so long. Mary remembered one winter during the war when heating oil was scarce and Frank was gone and the baby, Julie, was crying, crying all the time because of the cold. She had sat in the rocker holding her tight, crying too. That was the winter she learned how to knit. She knitted blanket after blanket, sweater after sweater. At first they were all thick, heavy garments designed just to keep the cold at bay, but over the years she had learned to knit intricate Fair Isle patterns, lace in delicate yarns, tapestries of mitered squares, and whimsical bobbles. She had won several national contests and was the president of the New York Stitching Society for seven years.

Out on the street, Mary could see Hank Tilghman and Bill Allen throwing a baseball back and forth. The two boys ran a yard service during the summer and would come by later that day to mow the grass. Mary knew Frank would watch them the whole time, wistful but not envious. The sound of the ball hitting the boys' gloves had a powerful rhythm to Mary, a well-grounded, solid sound that seemed to issue from their youth. There was nothing ephemeral in their natures—they were all in the here and now, so different from her Frank, who lately seemed to exist more beyond than here.

Behind the boys, Mary could see the Tilghman's yard, shaded by oaks and dogwoods, with clematis climbing up the mailbox post and patches of impatiens along the sidewalk. Caroline Tilghman was playing in a rain puddle at the edge of their driveway, gathering rocks in piles, pushing the sand around, watching the older boys. Mary remembered when Caroline was born—could it really be eight years ago? She had knitted a pale yellow sweater with a single cable of white on each side.

"It's beautiful," Emma said when she opened the box. "It reminds me a little bit of a blanket my grandmother sent." And she led Mary back to the nursery where the tiny girl slept wrapped in a luminous patch of blue and silver.

"I think it's really unusual," Emma whispered. "My grandmother has always been a weaver, but lately she's been doing more artistic things."

Mary touched the silken blanket softly, sensing the impulse that had created it. It did not surprise her that folklore was full of magic garments—the protective red mantle, the sweaters of thistle that turned swans into brothers, the coat that made its wearer invisible. Isn't that what she did when she knitted? Tried to transfer her love into a garment that would protect from cold, danger, misfortune?

With Julie, it had seemed to work, to a degree. Setting off to school for the first time, she had worn a short-sleeved sweater set of lavender and white. All day long, Mary imagined her surrounded by sunshine and happiness. In winter, Julie had three pairs of mittens—one red, one blue, and one white with green edges. When she left for college, she had a trunk full of sweaters and vests and blankets. Now she had children of her own, bridge club, and a part-time job at the bookstore. Her husband was an orthodontist, and they drove a BMW. She called from Rochester once a month and brought the children down every July. She seemed happy enough.

With Frank, it was a different story. Earlier in their life together, he hadn't seemed to need much protecting and now, no matter what Mary did, he seemed to be slipping away. She stopped volunteering at the library, even going to church, so she could stay with him. She'd knitted scarves and sweaters and even crocheted an afghan, which she hated to do. She took him to Dr. Abbott, but he had hardly helped at all.

"He hasn't had a stroke. He's just getting old. He's eighty-two, and his body is starting to slow down."

As if she didn't know that.

"You need to make sure you're taking care of yourself, too," Dr. Abbott continued. "Your blood pressure is high, and you look exhausted."

"I'm fine. I just worry, that's all."

"Well, why don't you take some time for yourself? Come back next month, and let's see how your blood pressure is then. We might need to start you on medication."

That had been six months ago. She hadn't seen much point in going back.

Mary got up and put a pillow behind Frank's head. She picked up the paper, which had fallen to the floor, and put it back in the center of his lap. She had come to a type of peace with the situation. She was glad she was the one to take care of him and not the other way around, like her friend Liz, who had multiple sclerosis. She was glad Julie didn't have to deal with it. She was glad, after a time, to find that the slow, quiet rhythms of their life, no matter how ephemeral, still had value. Watching life go on through this screen on the porch . . . things could be a lot worse.

She heard the tree leaves rustle and a thump as the baseball landed in the mossy yard. Hank ran over, a sheepish look on his face.

"Sorry," he said, glancing toward the porch. "My sister wanted a turn, but she's terrible."

"It's fine," Mary said. "We enjoy seeing you play."

"Me and Bill'll be over after lunch to mow the lawn."

"We'll be here."

Hank ran back to the street. Caroline was standing barefoot with a too-large baseball mitt on her hand, her hair falling out from a ponytail. The Tilghman's dog, Mustard, an aging, sandy-colored mutt, stood by her side as if for protection.

"Let me try again, Hank."

"No way. You're going to break something."

"Hank!" Bill yelled from down the street. "Over here."

Hank pulled the mitt off Caroline, and the two boys moved down the street in front of the Hammonds' house. Caroline watched for a moment, then picked up a rock and threw it toward them.

"Caroline!"

So Emma was out after all. Mary hadn't seen her there behind the Japanese maple, dividing candy tuft, it looked like. She spent most spring and summer mornings working in the yard, which had a pleasing balance of color and green, of light and shade. She was working alone this morning, since her niece, Gail, hadn't arrived yet. Gail came to stay with the Tilghmans every summer and shadowed Emma about the yard like a Greek initiate learning temple secrets. Mary had only met Gail one or two times, but she could sense the girl's closeness to Emma. Mary had stopped being surprised by what she could learn by sitting back and watching through the screen.

Emma looked at her watch and began gathering her things together. "Come along, Caroline," she called. "Let's get lunch together."

The dog trotted a few feet toward the house, then stopped and looked back at Caroline. Caroline stood indecisively a few moments, then ran toward the house, stopping only to jump in the puddle.

Mary laughed and stood enjoying the moment, letting it renew her being. Behind her she heard the paper drop to the floor again. She walked over to Frank and pulled the blanket closer. He opened his eyes and looked around.

"Guess I dozed off."

"That's okay," Mary said, patting his hand. "What would you like for lunch?"

He stared at her a few moments, a look close to bewilderment on his face.

"Is it lunch time already?" His voice had taken on a shaky quality that hadn't been there just weeks ago.

"It's almost noon. Would you like some of that cantaloupe Emma gave us? Maybe an egg salad sandwich? Strawberries for dessert?"

Frank looked around the porch. "I can't believe it's lunch already."

"It is, and the boys will be here a little after one, so I better hurry."

She pulled the blanket around him again and walked into the house, through the den and to the powder room off the foyer to wash her hands. She rubbed her hands under the warming water and lathered them with the soft, lime green soap Julie had sent for Mother's Day. It matched the green of the tile perfectly.

As she stood quietly at the sink, a sudden searing strangeness ran from Mary's scalp to her feet, chasing away the fragrance of the soap, the warmth of the water, replaced by a heaviness that pulled her down. She tried to grab on to the sink, but her slippery hands would not hold and she fell, hard, onto the cold floor.

For several minutes, she couldn't seem to do anything, then she managed to get out a quiet, "Help! Frank, please help me." It took all her strength and she closed her eyes, hearing the steady ticking of the kitchen clock, the birds fussing outside. She tried again, "Frank! Frank!" But she knew he couldn't hear. He was probably asleep. She could do nothing but lie there and try, every once and awhile, to get up.

She waited and waited, listening to the clock. One hundred ticks. A thousand. How much time had gone by? Surely Frank would get up before too long, surely he would notice that she wasn't in the kitchen, surely he would look for her. And when he found her? He could still call for help, couldn't he? When was the last time he had used the phone to call somebody? Three months ago? A year? But he could walk next door and get help. Certainly he could do that. She tried to call again, "Frank! Help!" But her voice sounded little more than a whisper. She lay still.

After a while, she heard the sound of something rolling down the driveway. "Mr. Reed, we're here to do the lawn."

There was no answer.

"Mr. Reed! Is it okay to mow the grass now?"

"But we haven't had lunch yet," Frank finally muttered. "We were supposed to have lunch, and I don't know where my wife is." There was silence for several moments. "Do you know where she is?"

Mary could almost see the boys in the front yard, looking at each other, wondering what to do.

"No, sir. Maybe she's gone inside. I'll ring the bell."

Their loud boys' feet tromped up the porch stairs, and they rang the bell.

Mary saw shadows through the side windows of the front door. She summoned all her strength. "Help! Help!"

Hank peered in the window, putting his hand next to his eyes to adjust for the light.

"Help!" she whispered once more.

Hank tried the door, but it was locked. He looked at Bill and said something. The boys turned and ran down the steps. Mary felt a rising panic fill her throat. She couldn't speak at all.

In a moment, Hank was there. "Mrs. Reed, my mom's on her way. Just stay where you are."

Mary looked up and saw Frank standing in the door. He had taken the sweater off and held it out toward Mary. Hank stared at it for a moment before taking it from him and draping it gently over her. Its warmth and smell made her feel safe enough to close her eyes and wait.

The Odd One

NEXT TO THE LEATHER BUTTON is another large button that seems to have appeared during the night. This one I do remember as coming from a coat my great-grandmother, Maggie, wore. I didn't know her well, except that she lived on a farm in Virginia and had become what people call "odd" in her last years. When she died, my mother and I helped go through her house. She had been a weaver and had a loom in the corner of her living room, along with her spools of thread and other sewing supplies.

"Would you like to learn to weave, Caroline?" Mom asked me in a hushed, hopeful voice.

I looked at the interlacing strings held firmly by the wooden frame. I stared up at the spools of thread hanging on the wall in a grid of color. I felt the sadness of the still shuttle. I admired these things, but they did not call to me.

Mom telephoned a folk arts school in the mountains, and a few weeks later, a young student and her boyfriend met us at the farmhouse to get the loom. After they left, my mom picked up the coat, Maggie's old sewing kit, and a few other things before driving home.

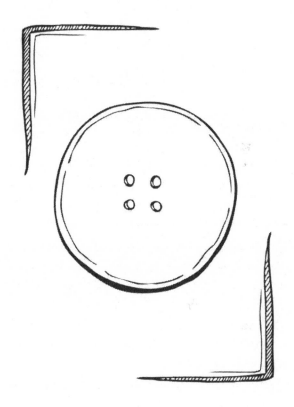

The Liberation of Maggie Sommers

Danville County, Virginia 1964

MAGGIE PULLED HER THICK, grayish-green coat close. The weather was causing this, she told herself. Everything was in between—it was no wonder her mind had wandered. It was neither day nor night, but that too-beautiful mixture of both. Overhead, bare tree branches were silhouetted against gray clouds lit from behind by the very last moments of light. On the eastern horizon, the moon appeared in a patch of blue sky. It wasn't raining, but the November breeze carried a fine mist that sweetened the atmosphere with a smell of wet leaves. Even the air was confused—warm and balmy in places, chilly and breezy in others.

His face appeared before her again, black eyes staring intently. He was about to tell a joke; she knew by the way his lips were just beginning to curl at the edges. She put her hand out to touch his smooth, young cheek, and he was gone.

"Now, Maggie, enough of this foolishness," she said aloud, pushing the mailbox shut. She looked over the field to her solid farmhouse outlined against the trees and clouds and muted light. The lamp in the front room blazed, showing the no-nonsense furniture, the over-stuffed bookshelves, and the spools of thread hanging on the wall behind her loom. She stood still for a moment, centering herself in the tangible here and now.

Suddenly Maggie heard the calls of geese coming from the north. She waited, scanning the horizon, as the calls grew louder and louder. Clearing the border of the woods, a flock appeared, its V formation slightly skewed as the leader dropped back and allowed another to take its place. Then, driven by the urgency of their beating wings, the geese disappeared.

"Beautiful . . . so beautiful," she whispered into the twilight. Hurriedly, she pulled off her coat so the air could surround her more closely. A button popped off, and as she bent down to pick it up, she noticed her shoes—bulky brown things, black laces, wide toes—and began laughing. She was laughing still when her neighbor drove by in his green pick-up truck.

Maggie waved briefly, hoping her face was hidden in the dusk. She hugged the pieces of mail to her and began walking to the house.

He was waiting for her inside, the joke still on his lips.

"I know, I know," Maggie said. "These are the ugliest shoes you've ever seen. Uglier than the ones Miss Humphries used to wear to school. But that never stopped her from being a good teacher. Do you remember that Keats poem we read our junior year? The one about the young couple painted on a Grecian vase? 'For ever warm and still to be enjoy'd, / For ever panting, and for ever young'? That poem is just like you."

Out of habit, Maggie began sorting through the mail. There were a few bills, as always, and a manila envelope from her lawyer. She opened it and looked over the final papers from the estate of her late husband, Paul, a sensible man who had reviewed the farm's assets with her as he lay on his deathbed, a man who had never seemed young. Maggie filed the papers in the desk drawer and locked it with a small key.

When she looked up again, he was gone.

Maggie sighed and walked over to the picture table, as her grandchildren called it—an old oak table draped in hand-woven burgundy cloth and covered with photographs of the family. There was one ancient picture of her parents, the black and white fading to brown, the solemn stares and decorous poses frozen forever. There was another of her aunt, Emma—the one who taught her to weave, the one her granddaughter was named for—sitting, reading in front of the fireplace. And there were many pictures of her own children stairstepping through the years, as well as her grandchildren and even great-grandchildren. Seven great-grandchildren. No . . . eight now, with Emma's brand-new girl, Caroline.

How was it possible to have eight great-grandchildren, Maggie wondered, when she felt like little more than a girl herself?

There were only a couple pictures of Paul on the table. He had been the family photographer, taking on that duty with the same seriousness he brought to everything in life. She remembered how he would count the pictures, making sure there was an equal number for each child. "No, Maggie," he'd said one time when she wanted to photograph their oldest daughter going off to school. "We have four photographs of Sarah already. If we took another, then we'd have to do the same for the others, and we can't afford that."

Her favorite picture of Paul wasn't their wedding picture, where he looked so stiff and uncomfortable, but a later photo of him with Maxfield, Sam, and Sarah on the front porch. He was holding Maxfield on his lap, Sam hugged him from behind, and Sarah had her head on his knee. He was smiling that quiet smile of contentment that was his one luxury in life.

"You know Paul really was a kind man," Maggie said aloud. "He loved the children and the farm. He didn't even complain when my brother came to live with us."

Maggie put the picture down and looked up, but she was still alone.

She went over to her weaving corner and dropped the button into a jar of buttons she kept on the shelf. She strummed her fingers gently across the gold-and-blue threads of the loom. A familiar feeling of comfort and possibility filled her as she sat down and began pulling the shuttle back and forth, back and forth, gold and blue, gold and blue, gold and blue.

Of course Paul had never understood about her weaving. At first he liked it because it saved money, but later he seemed a little jealous of the time she spent at her loom. She remembered the year he gave her some ready-made fabric for Christmas. "So you won't have to work so hard," he said. It was still at the bottom of the cedar chest, fading, unused.

Maggie hummed softly.

She did not see, but strongly felt that he had returned.

She spoke aloud: "Remember this? 'There she weaves by night and day / A magic web with colours gay.'?" Maggie laughed. "Remember what you said to me? 'Surely you don't like Tennyson!' But I did. I do. I like that poem." She kept moving the shuttle back and forth, back and forth, gold and blue, gold and blue, gold and blue. "'But in her web she still delights / To weave the mirror's magic sights.' I like it. It sounds like a song in my head."

Several minutes went by as Maggie hummed with her shuttle. "This is a blanket for the new baby, Caroline," she said. "Sam's wife, Nancy, wanted me to make it pink and white, can you believe it?" She looked up at him and they laughed together. "Just like every other baby-girl blanket in the world. Why do people want to be so ordinary?"

He was standing by the bookshelf, silently calling her. He was still smiling, but there was something serious in his eyes.

Maggie slowly walked to him. She started to reach out her hand, but stopped herself.

"Don't leave me again," she whispered, feeling the same rise of panic she'd felt as a seventeen-year-old girl. Then, reaching into the iron strength the last four decades had given her, she stood up straighter and stared directly into his eyes. A feeling of clarity settled over her, and she was able to see her life as a story. For a few seconds, it bothered her that it had started out so predictably—the stolen moments, the day he left for Europe while she stayed behind, the sickening realization she was pregnant . . . it was all like a Dickens novel, wasn't it? Too true. Too true.

Looking at him, she laughed. "When Sam was born, I decided I would hate you, but you know I didn't. Still, I wish you could have seen him as a baby. He was so beautiful, everybody loved him. And you know what? Paul might have loved him more than anyone. That's how good a man he was. Tame and predictable, but good."

She looked at her loom. "This is what kept me going all those years. Every evening, no matter how tired I was, no matter how late, I would sit down at my loom and dream of all the beautiful things in the world."

Maggie turned back around. He was still there, but his face was growing sadder.

"That's all right, that's all right," she said. "I know you don't know how to handle the difficult times. That's just who you are, someone made for beauty only, for sunshine streaming through stained-glass windows, not for rain oozing under the cellar door and babies crying and people growing old."

He was looking at a book of Shakespeare's sonnets. Maggie picked it up and read. "To me, fair friend, you never can be old, / For as you were when first your eye I ey'd, / Such seems your beauty still."

Maggie smiled. "That's very sweet. You always were a sweet boy."

She looked out the window. Scallops of clouds framed the moon and two bright stars. She looked at her shoes and began laughing again. "I know what to do with these," she said as she pulled them off and threw them in the trash.

"The farm is paid for. I have money enough to spare. My family is close, but not too close. I can do whatever I please."

Barefoot, Maggie walked to her loom. "Here, sit beside me," she said, patting the wooden chair her grandchildren sat in while they watched her weave.

"Let's make a pact," she said, her eyes brightening.

"From now on, everything in our lives will be beautiful."

His face seemed to glow with pleasure.

She began moving the shuttle back and forth, back and forth, gold and blue, gold and blue, gold and blue. Outside, the moon shone on the tin roof, casting a silver haze into the ink-black sky.

A Plain White Button, One of Many

IT'S EASY TO NOTICE BUTTONS that stand out, the ones that are especially large or small, that have an interesting shape or color. It's easy to overlook the plain black ones or plain white ones that form the background so the others can shine.

Take this small white button. It's probably from one of my father's shirts. He wore the same type of shirt to work every day. Long-sleeved, blue or white or gray, with plain white buttons. My mother would iron them on Sunday evening while we watched The Wonderful World of Disney and ate popcorn. She'd sprinkle the shirts with water, put them in a plastic bag in the refrigerator for a few minutes, then iron them with steam. They had to be just so. She used an ironing ham, so there were no creases in the sleeves. She'd finish one, hang it in the closet, then do another one, until there were five crisp shirts in a row. She seemed to have a rhythm to it, knowing just when to pick up the iron and release the steam.

I remember that smell—warm and moist and clean, the smell of somebody taking care of you.

Not long ago, I believed ironing was a waste of time. Even today, I iron maybe three times a year, only when it's absolutely unavoidable. But when I go to the trouble to do it—to pull the board down, pour water in the iron, wait for it to heat up—the process takes me back. The repetitive strokes, the hiss of the steam, the smoothing of the cloth are inescapably meditative. For a few moments, I'm back in the circle of my mother's protection, and it seems that I'm close to discovering the secret of how to stay there, but I never do. The moment disappears just like the steam, and I'm left with a feeling of loss.

Sometimes I wonder if surviving loss is the same thing as growing up. If the only true mark of maturity is realizing you could lose everything.

Rishi, Victoria, our life in our safe little house . . . the fragility is almost unbearable.

I think that's the real reason I don't iron.

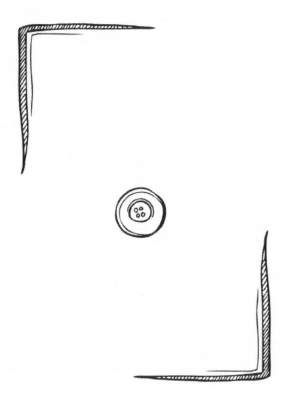

Sign Watching

Mecklenburg County, N.C. 1972

THE AIR RUSHING INTO THE CAR felt more and more humid. Charles envisioned the pressure pushing into the barometer, forcing the liquid down further, an act of atmospheric violence. He knew it was really the opposite—the pressure was falling, and the liquid merely falling with it—but to him, it seemed as if the pressure was increasing, had been increasing for a long time. He stared at the lines on the road, thinking of a way to lighten the mood. Suddenly, a church came into view, and he smiled.

"There's another one!" he said, reaching toward the passenger seat and nudging his son's shoulder. "Hank, write it down."

Charles pointed out the window of the car and read aloud, "'What's missing in CH—CH?'" He stopped for emphasis before completing it.

"'U R.'"

His Adam's apple bobbed up and down as he laughed.

"U R. Get it? U R! That's pretty good, don't you think?"

Hank, who had taken to speaking only when necessary during the past few weeks, moaned as he got the red spiral notebook out of the glove compartment and began writing.

121

"Now be sure you get the identifying information. Let's see, that's Ebenezer Baptist Church . . . May 17, 1972 . . . Old Durham Road . . . The Reverend Gary Mullinax, Pastor."

"Daddy," Caroline said from the back. "You shouldn't make fun of the Baptists. Mom said."

Charles felt the laughter start to leave him for a moment, but he managed to regain it.

"Oh, honey," he said with a small smile. "I am most definitely not making fun. I'm planning your college education. I'm going to compile all these words of wisdom, take photographs of the signs with the churches in the background—you know how people love to look at pictures of churches—and put together a fine coffee-table book. Years from now, it will probably be an important archive about life in small Southern towns in the twentieth century. Sort of like that Foxfire book that's all the rage."

"Well, if you're not making fun, then why are you laughing?"

"I laugh because . . . because I like them, is why. Besides, they aren't all Baptist. There's plenty of Church of God or Christ or whatever that is and Pentecostal and AME and even a few Methodists and Presbyterians. Why should the Baptists have all the fun?"

"What about Lutherans or Episcopalians?" Hank asked.

"Well, I believe I saw a Lutheran sign once out toward Hickory, but to the best of my knowledge I've *never* seen a sign at an Episcopal church. Bonus points to anyone who finds one."

He turned around and winked at Caroline, who was building a tower with an Erector set.

"Can I have the blueprint for that when you're done, sweet?"

Hank turned around, too. "Caroline, I told you to leave that alone! You're going to lose all the pieces."

"I am not either. Besides, it was in the basement. You never play with it so why do you care?"

"Because it was in my part of the basement and it's mine, that's why."

Charles gripped the steering wheel tighter, pushing back the biting words that lately were always threatening to rise into his throat and spew out, no matter where he was. From the corner of his eye, he caught sight of a small sign in front of a church on a hill: "The Rapture—Be Right or Be Left." The sharp words left him as he let out a small chortle and made a mental note to add the sign to the notebook later. He didn't feel up to Caroline's questions now.

Hank began crawling over the seat, trying to get the Erector set. Caroline screamed.

"Hey, hey, hey," Charles said. He was quiet for a moment then repeated, "Hey, hey, hey," tilting his head from side to side with each word. "Hey, hey, hey . . . it's Fat Albert! You know, I haven't seen that show in a long time. Does it still come on?"

"Dad, that's my Erector set. She doesn't know how to use it."

Charles sighed, feeling the heaviness settle over him again. "Hank, it won't kill you to share, and Caroline does know how to use it. I've seen some of her work. Pretty impressive, if I do say so myself."

Hank turned back toward the front and crossed his arms.

"I know what," Charles said. "Read back all the entries we've made so far. Let's see if we have enough for a book yet."

"There's only six pages, Dad," said Hank. "You'll need a lot more than that for a book."

"Yeah, but we're going to have the photographs, too, and maybe some commentary from the preacher about how he came up with the sign, plus the type will be real big so we won't—"

"There's one!" Caroline yelled from the back.

"'The devil is not afraid of a Bible with dust on it,'" Charles read in a deep, solemn tone.

"Good catch, Caroline. Let's see . . . that's the Word of Life Bible Church, 'Where the Living Lord is Proclaimed.' Did you get that, Hank?"

"I got it."

"Put a note that your sister found that one, and keep your eyes open. I'll bet we see a lot more before we get to Charlotte."

Caroline continued to work on the tower. Charles and Hank stared ahead silently.

Usually, Charles enjoyed driving in the country. He liked the way he felt bonded to the car, the ripples of the steering wheel sliding beneath his hands, the engine responding to his touch, the wind flowing over his arm and the sun heating his skin as he seemed to fly past pastures and cows and houses and churches, totally in control. Today, even though the car stayed obediently in the correct lane, he felt as if it were about to spin out and speed away. What he really wanted to do was get on the interstate and keep driving. Where, he wasn't sure—until he got to the ocean, maybe, or perhaps the desert. He'd never been to Utah, for example, and from the pictures he'd seen, he thought it must be a whole different world. He wondered if Mormon churches had signs.

He forced himself to speak. "Go on, Hank. Read what we've gotten so far."

Hank stared at him for a few moments with that teenage glare he'd been perfecting. Charles felt tired. He wasn't up to a challenge right now. He almost sighed with relief when Hank reluctantly opened up the notebook and cleared his throat.

"Okay. Here goes."

Caroline leaned on the front seat to hear better.

"Number One: 'No One Will Know of Your Love Unless You Give Out Samples.'

"Two: 'The Bible doesn't need to be re-written, just re-read.'"

Charles nodded his head. "That's a good one," he said.

"Three: 'The best way to exercise your heart is to lift up others.'"

"Very admirable," Charles said. Caroline laughed.

"Four: 'The greatest ability is DEPENDability.'"

Charles turned toward Hank, who was actually grinning. "Hey, you left out my favorite."

"If you have them memorized, then why do we need to read them?"

"For the experience, Hank. It's a different experience to hear them out loud."

"That's crazy," Hank said.

"Here, I'll do them," Caroline grabbed the notebook and began reading. She was trying to make her voice sound grown-up, Charles knew, but it still sounded completely like a little girl. He loved it.

"Four: 'Sign Broken—Come Inside for Message.'"

"Isn't that great?" Charles asked. "Come inside for message. Ha ha."

Caroline was enjoying the captive audience. "Five—well, Hank already did it. Six: 'A Good Name is Better than Precious Ointment.' I think that one's weird. What kind of ointment are they talking about?"

"Preparation H," Hank muttered.

Charles smiled. "Maybe Ben-Gay."

"Tinactin," Hank said. "Gets rid of jock itch. Must be pretty precious."

"That's gross," Caroline said, making a face.

"Actually, Honey, I think they're talking about some kind of perfume-type balm. It was very valuable in Biblical times."

"Then why didn't they say perfume?" Caroline asked.

"I don't know. Keep reading."

"'Anger is just one letter away from Danger.' 'Character is what you are in the dark.' 'God Car s for You.' What does that mean?"

"I think they ran out of the letter 'e.' It should be 'God Cares for You,' but I thought it was more interesting that way. I wonder what kind of car God drives."

"A Cadillac," Hank said. "White, of course."

"I was kind of thinking of a red 1957 Bel Air convertible," Charles said. "That's what I'd drive if I were God."

"There's another one!" Caroline yelled, straining to read, "'Believe and Receive. Doubt and Do Without.'"

Without warning, Charles felt as if he'd been slugged in the chest. Things just weren't going the way he'd planned. "It has good rhyming," he managed to get out after a few seconds.

Hank looked over at him. "Check this one out," he said with a conspiratorial smile. "'Fight Truth Decay. Read the Bible Daily.' Can you believe that? How corny can they get?"

Charles smiled back in relief.

For several minutes, Caroline wrote diligently in the notebook, recording the church name, pastor, date, location, and seriously confirming the spellings. Finally, she closed it and set it on the seat. "I'm going to look for more," she said, gazing intently out the window.

Quiet filled the car again as the road went on and on and on. Charles felt an ache travel through the muscles in the back of his neck. He wished this day were over. The silence was unbearable. Why weren't there any damn signs?

Miles and miles went by. After a while, Caroline leaned forward, resting her chin on the middle of the front seat. Charles knew she had something brewing.

"Daddy, what does disfigured mean?" she asked.

Charles ran his fingers through what remained of his hair and wrinkled his forehead. "Well, it just means that something doesn't look quite the same anymore. Where did you hear that?"

"Mrs. Thomas said Mom would be disfigured after the operation."

Hank began kicking the floorboard. "Caroline! What were you doing, eavesdropping or something?"

"I wasn't eavesdropping. Mrs. Johnson had come over to the Thomases' for tea, and I was helping them bring the cups into the living room. Mrs. Reed said it was a good thing they'd found it so early, but Mrs. Thomas said Mom would be disfigured. She said that would be horrible."

"Old biddy!" Hank muttered under his breath.

"Henry," Charles said. "That's enough. The Thomases have been very kind to let you and your sister stay with them this week."

The three of them were silent for a few moments before Caroline asked, "Will it be horrible, Daddy?"

"No, Caroline, of course it won't. People just say things like that without thinking. Your mom will be the same as she's always been. You'll see."

Charles continued to drive silently, even when they passed Salem Baptist Church, Tommy Siler, Pastor, which admonished passers-by to, "Keep on trying in trying times." Just down the road, the New Hope Assembly declared, "The man who keeps his eyes on God always gets to his destination."

He sighed and leaned his head back on the headrest, but the tightness in his neck remained. A brand-new sign in front of the tiny Union Spring Free-Will Baptist church stated boldly, even brazenly: "Never Put a Question Mark Where God Puts a Period."

"Yeah, right," Charles muttered to himself, feeling the ache creep around his left temple.

Gradually, the road became bigger as they entered the heavier traffic that surrounded Charlotte. The knot in his stomach tightened even more. He had given it a good run, he thought, but the tension of the last few weeks was about to catch him. He could feel it like a living thing bearing down on him, its hot breath touching him. He was tired. Tired of being the strong one, of thinking what questions to ask, of reaching out, when all Emma seemed able to do was turn inward. Tired of being there, of trying to keep their world together while Emma was gone. He would think he was managing just fine and then *poof!* something—some little thing—would topple his careful construction.

Like this morning, when he had actually gotten the kids dressed and fed and to the bus stop on time, then, as he was heading out the door himself, a button popped off the cuff of his last clean shirt. It bounced on the floor, then skittered under the sofa. Alone in the house, he let out a groan that turned into a wordless yell, sending the cat scrambling down the hall. He picked up a pillow from the sofa and threw it across the room, where it hit the wall with a futile-sounding thump and slid silently to the floor. He sank into the chair and buried his face in his hands. "Christ! What else?" he whispered, then he rolled up his sleeves and walked out the door.

Through the windshield, he saw heavy clouds creeping toward them from the horizon. We'd all feel better if it would just rain and get it over with, Charles thought.

He glanced in the rearview mirror. Caroline had put the Erector set pieces back in the box and now lay across the seat, eyes closed, her hands tucked carefully under her head. Charles took his sweater from the seat and draped it across Hank, who had fallen asleep leaning against the door.

All the awkwardness of their ages disappeared while they slept. To Charles, they seemed much the same as they had in those first few days of life. Innocent. Fragile. In desperate need of protection. For a moment, an incredible sense of responsibility filled him to the point he felt he could not bear it. Hazards were as commonplace as the pieces of broken line going down the middle of the highway. He remembered reading of a freak accident in which a car had swerved on the road, causing a defective door to fly open and tossing the passenger over a bridge. What was to stop something like that from happening to this car on this day? Hank could be gone in seconds. Or Caroline.

My God, Charles thought. Caroline. Was it even possible to protect a daughter enough? Could such a thing be done? Maybe those medieval towers weren't totally unreasonable. At least the view would be good.

Charles merged on to the interstate and began looking for the hospital exit. In the past, he had enjoyed going into the city, taking Emma to the newest restaurant, seeing a movie or play, going to the museum with the kids.

Now it was different. The asphalt and tall buildings appeared unfriendly, hostile to all living things. He noticed the trash along the side of the road—cigarette butts, crushed aluminum cans, bits of paper torn and blown about. Nobody else seemed to care.

As the car slowly curved around the exit ramp, Hank and Caroline woke up. They had that sullen expression they always had when they first woke up, as if leaving their dreams were too unpleasant a task. Their hair was messed up and strange red marks lined their faces. They were both quiet.

Charles felt he should say something to lessen their anxiety, but he couldn't make his voice work. What was there to say, anyway? *Your mother's own flesh turned against her. It began mutating into something so alien and deadly it had to be cut out. She is disfigured. It is horrible. There was nothing I could do. I can't help the way I feel. Everything's different.*

An image from when Hank was an infant played itself over and over in his mind: Emma sat in the rocking chair on the front porch of their little rental house downtown, nursing the baby, still a wrinkled red creature with a cap of fine, dark hair. She sat easily, comfortably, the floral print of her blouse open, her white skin revealed, spots of sunshine lighting her as the wind blew through the old oak. Charles had been coming home from work and had stopped cold on the sidewalk, as if he had stumbled upon an ancient ritual. He had stayed there, simply watching for as long as he could, until Emma finally looked up at him and smiled.

He drove through the dungeon-maze of the parking garage until he reached the top outdoor level. He parked the car in the middle of several open parking places and turned the engine off.

"Here we are," he said to Hank and Caroline, who were putting on their shoes and coats.

Off to the left, a bolt of lightning flashed down. Charles stared after it, waiting for the thunder to rumble through. More lightning descended, seeming to dance around the steeple of a church a few blocks away. The corner of a sign caught Charles's eye. Its sturdy whiteness was outlined against the dark turmoil of the sky.

He got out of the car and stood, straining to read what it said, but the rain came down in torrents and he couldn't see.

Part Three

Fastening

THIS MORNING, MARIE, my neighbor, knocks on my front door. She's in her seventies and has lived in the same house for forty years, long enough to see the neighborhood move to the gritty side and back again. She has a classic Piedmont accent—Southern, but in a pleasingly, soft way, not the drawl of the coast or the tough twang of the mountains. Her hair is curled short, and she wears a lot of denim jackets embroidered with things like cardinals and sunflowers, leftovers from her days as a teacher, she once told me.

She reminds me a lot of my mom.

Yesterday, she borrowed an egg to make cookies for her grandchildren, so today she's being a good neighbor by bringing us some cookies to enjoy as well. "They're oatmeal bars," she tells me as she hands me the plate of goodies. "And I put some chocolate chips in there, too. They were in the freezer, but they're still good, especially if you warm them up in the microwave for a few seconds."

It's about ten in the morning and I'm working, but I invite her in and offer coffee. After her requisite, "Oh, I don't want to be a bother . . ." and my, "Oh no, I insist," she comes in.

"I haven't been in this house since the Tinsleys lived here," she says, slowly walking around the living room. "That was a good ten years ago at least. It's changed a lot. You've done a wonderful job with it."

"We don't get the credit. The people we bought it from did most of the work," I say as I walk to the kitchen to get coffee mugs. "They were practically architectural historians. I think they spent all their free time on it. I'm not that domestically inclined."

When I get back with the coffee, Marie is looking at the bookshelves. "These are just gorgeous. The wood was painted before—can you imagine? And now they're like a work of art."

I'm starting to get a little uncomfortable, wondering what she might think about the Ganesh, Shiva, and Nataraja figures that are placed among various gadgets made from old circuit boards, a stack of *Wired* magazines, and *The Joshua Tree* album cover.

"I love that jar of buttons," she says, taking a mug from the tray and sitting on the loveseat. "It adds a nice balance to your other pieces. Now tell me, what grade is your daughter in this year?"

"Victoria is a freshman in high school—I can't believe she's that old already—but she's not my daughter. She's my stepdaughter."

"Really? I thought she was your own. She looks like you a bit."

I don't know how to reply to that. I've never thought of Victoria looking like me at all. In fact, she doesn't look much like her own mother either, who is as fair as Rishi is dark.

"She's a lovely girl from what I see of her," Marie continues. "She reminds me of my daughter at that age—confident, vivacious. It's such a pivotal age, don't you think?"

I think of Victoria, who can go from watching a Disney movie and holding her stuffed unicorn one minute to getting in the driver's seat beside Rishi the next. She will be following her own path soon, which is a disquieting thought when I let myself think about it.

I nod and take a sip of coffee. We talk a few more minutes, and then Marie gets up to leave. She pauses by the shelves again. "You know, I think I'm going to put a jar of buttons out myself. I have a huge collection. I was an art teacher, you know, and I used buttons in lots of projects. They're great for children. Plus, I like their symbolism. They fasten things together, make them whole, but they do it with beauty."

After she is gone, I get the jar down, take it into the kitchen, and slowly pour the buttons out again, watching them spread across the copper-colored placemat on the table.

And even though in the distance I can sense a lone wolf sniffing and pawing, what Marie said is true. They fasten things together.

Fire Pink

As I sort through the buttons, I notice one that is hot pink. I inherited it from Gail. I don't think I've ever bought anything pink in my life, except once, as a joke, when I gave Hank a pink oxford shirt for his birthday. Some of the clothes I got from Gail were pink, though. Every summer Gail stayed with us, she'd leave a bag of clothes, folded neatly, still smelling faintly of the lavender she kept in the drawer. They were nice clothes, and my mother was excited to get them for me. Somehow, though, even after I'd grown into them, they never fit me quite the way they did Gail. Like the shorts this button came from.

I find it disorienting to think of Gail the child. I've grown so accustomed to thinking of her as an adult, someone who should be held accountable, that it's hard to remember how I felt about her when we were both children.

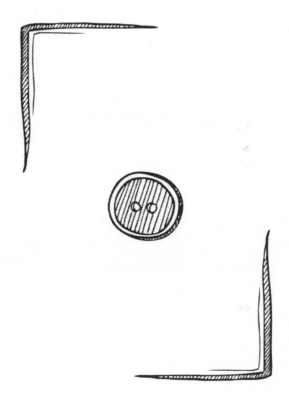

Nice Things

Ashton Mill, N.C. 1974

THE LAST SUMMER GAIL CAME TO STAY WITH US, she was sixteen and beautiful. I was ten.

Since Gail's father was dead and she spent most of the year in a boarding school in Savannah, she didn't have a regular family life, my mother said. That's why we had to be especially nice to her.

Well, maybe Mom hadn't said those exact words, but that's what I understood.

Things always changed when Gail arrived. Mom began organizing elaborate domestic projects. One day it might be hosting a tea for the girls in the neighborhood. Another time we'd make matching dresses with ribbon trim. Or we'd stencil window boxes and plant flowers, or make homemade ice cream, or decoupage a vase.

Gail ate it all up, and my mother loved it. As for me, it was fine for a while, but eventually I'd grow restless and want to go fishing with Hank or hang around with the gang in the neighborhood. I mean, cooking and sewing and stuff are fine, but how many days in a row would you want to do nice things?

That's what my mother called them, "nice things." She'd say, "Caroline, don't you want to stay here and do nice things with us?" Like playing softball or roaming through the woods wasn't nice.

That's another thing that changed when Gail arrived. Hank and Dad started doing more things together without me. Sometimes it was with Hank's Boy Scout troop. Other times it was just the two of them. They'd go backpacking in the Smokies and come back dirty and sweaty, their sleeping bags smelling of wood smoke, their boots wet, their backpacks leaving a trail of crumpled leaves. I watched, silently envious, as they unpacked and complained about how sore or tired or hungry they were.

This division of the sexes happened every summer, but it was even more extreme that last year Gail came to stay. In my mind, that summer retains an almost tangible sensuality . . . the startling reds and yellows of the garden, the hot raw feeling of fresh sunburn, the tangy coldness of lemon in iced tea, the deafening evening song of crickets mingled with the sweet, sweet smell of honeysuckle. And intertwined with them all is my memory of Gail at sixteen. Any time is a hard time to be sixteen, but 1974 was even harder, especially for someone who looked like Gail. Distractingly feminine, with pale skin, dark shining hair, and rounded breasts, she reminded me of one of those dolls Mom would never let me play with.

I remember I went with my father and brother to pick up Gail at the Charlotte airport. As soon as she walked out of the gate, I knew that Gail had come to a turning point and left me behind.

My father and Hank watched her walk through the crowd for a few moments before Dad finally held up his hand and said, "Over here, Gail." He hugged her, but it was more of a sideways pat-on-the-back type hug, not the big bear hugs he usually gives family. Hank just looked at her.

"Hi, Caroline," she said when it was my turn for her attention. "I can't believe it. You're as tall as I am now. I think I've stopped growing."

I may have been as tall as she was, but I felt like a different sort of creature altogether. There I was in my tank top and cut-offs. She was wearing a floral miniskirt and top with wedge sandals and a transparent scarf around her neck. As we walked through the terminal, I realized that people were looking at her. Not staring, exactly, but noticing. Noticing everything.

That night, with Gail in the room with me, I couldn't go to sleep. Her very presence distracted me, although it never had before. Through the darkness, I could hear my parents talking. I sat up and put my ear to the wall when I heard her name.

"Well, she's definitely not a little girl anymore," my father said, laughing the way he did when talking to my mother alone. "We'll have teenagers hanging around the house like those dogs were when Mustard was in heat."

"I don't think it's funny, Charles." I pressed my ear closer. My mother's voice was much harder to hear. "We're responsible for her while she's here. What if . . . what if she got in trouble or something? I would just die."

"Well, if you're really worried, we can call Claire and explain that it isn't going to work out this year. Tell her things are too hectic now that the kids are older, you know, something like that."

"You're not serious."

"I don't want you worrying for eight weeks about something beyond your control. Gail has gotten more attention here than anywhere, more than she would have even if Mitchell were still around. We've done our share already."

Mother mumbled something I couldn't hear. Then I heard my father laugh.

"Of course she's a good girl. That's beside the point. Sometimes when you're a teenager, it's just like spring coming. You can't stop it."

"That's ridiculous."

"As I recall, most people thought you were a good girl."

"That was totally different."

"That's right." My father's voice was growing quieter. They whispered some things I couldn't hear. My father was laughing again. I pulled my ear away from the wall and tried to go to sleep.

* * * *

Now that I think about it, I was wrong when I said the division of the sexes was more extreme that summer. In a way, just the opposite happened. Like my father had predicted, teenage boys began hanging around the house. Neighbors, friends, friends of friends, acquaintances . . . they all found an excuse to come by, sit on the porch with Gail, go on walks, whatever. Sometimes they came to see Hank, but before long he would leave to play baseball or mow lawns and they stayed, politely venturing into the kitchen or the garden or even the sewing room . . . wherever it was that my mother was trying to occupy Gail.

Perhaps it wasn't the division between male and female, but the distinction between the two that became more extreme. The lightning bugs, the crickets, the bright flowers . . . everything seemed to shout, "I am female!" or, "I am male!"

Mom made heroic attempts to engage us in domestic activities, but Gail was easily distracted. John would ask her to go get ice cream, or Allen would ask her to the movies, or Joe would want to show her his dog's new puppies.

You could tell by the look on Gail's face that she wasn't thinking about nice things anymore.

"Is that okay, Aunt Emmy?" she'd ask my mother. Gail's voice had a new quality to it, not quite adult, but close enough that Mother had no choice but to nod her head and watch as Gail and her current admirer walked down the sidewalk, oblivious to everything except each other's presence.

I felt so sorry for Mom that I cross-stitched two pillows and made three dresses that summer. I never wore the dresses much, but I still have the pillows.

* * * *

After a while, one boy began hanging around more than the others. His name was Mike Hunnicutt and he was on Hank's baseball team. A pitcher, I think. He had brown eyes and dark, thick, curly hair. He wasn't thin like Hank, but he wasn't at all fat either. He seemed to be on the verge of sweating all the time.

I thought my mother would like it when the others stopped coming by, but she didn't. She stopped her special projects, concentrating on cleaning the house with a vengeance. Sometimes, I'd find her sitting at the kitchen table, staring at the garden but not seeming to see it.

I felt a sinking feeling in my stomach, seeing her like that. Before her surgery two years ago, she'd never look like that, no matter what was happening. Before, she would always look on the bright side, just like she told us to do. She'd expect the best, not cry over spilt milk, accentuate the positive and all that stuff. It used to drive me crazy, but after her surgery, on those times when she would look so sad, I'd do anything to give her that cheerfulness back.

I never knew what to do, so I'd usually walk away, but one day I got up my courage. I pulled a chair out and sat down beside her, leaned my chin on my hand and said, just the way she used to, "Why the long face?"

I didn't think it would work, and at first it didn't. She just sat there, still staring. I sat there, too. After a while, she laughed a little and leaned back.

"It's just that I realize that Gail is growing up," she said. "I remember when she was your age. She'd be my little shadow all summer long, but now she's interested in other things."

She stopped for a moment and looked straight at me. "You know how when girls get to be Gail's age they like to go out with boys, hold hands, things like that?"

I nodded my head, bit my tongue so I wouldn't say, "Geez, Mom, give me a little credit."

"You will, too," she said, patting my hand. "It's only natural, but I do worry about Gail. Sometimes girls who grow up without fathers or brothers try to please boys too much."

This didn't seem right to me. "She spends the summers with us," I said, not knowing why I felt angry. "Daddy and Hank are here all the time."

Mom smiled, but she still looked sad. "That's still not the same as having your very own Daddy who loves you and worries about you and watches out for you. It makes me sad that my brother isn't here for Gail. It's hard to watch her grow up and not think about him."

Mom looked at me again and brushed back my hair. "Oh well, before long, you'll be grown up, too, so I better get used to it."

"I'm not holding hands with anybody," I said as I pulled my foot up toward my mouth and began biting my big toenail.

"Caroline, stop that! What a horrible thing to do."

"I had a hangnail. What's the big deal?"

"Have you heard of nail clippers?" She stood up and put on her apron. The moment had passed. "Now, do you want to help shuck the corn? Wash your hands first."

* * * *

There's more to the story of that summer, including some things that aren't so nice.

The truth is that I started spying on Gail and Mike whenever I got the chance. It wasn't even my idea. One afternoon, I saw Hank peering in the basement window. He held his finger up to his mouth when he saw me.

"What are you doing?" I asked.

"Nothing!" he whispered. "Go away."

"Tell me!" I said, raising my voice ever so slightly.

Hank was annoyed, but I could see that part of him wanted to tell. "Gail and Mike are in there," he said. "I wanted to see if there's any action."

I balanced myself on the doghouse and peeked in the window. I could see them sitting on the ping-pong table, paddles off to the side, their bodies leaning together, looking into each other's eyes.

"They're not playing ping-pong," I whispered.

Hank looked at me the way only an older brother can, then raised his eyes toward the sky. "You are so stupid you don't even know what's going on." He began walking away. "You better not get caught," he yelled over his shoulder.

After that, I was on the lookout for opportunities to watch Mike and Gail alone. I was about to grow bored with the game when one day, my mother went to Charlotte with some friends. Hank was at the lake. I told Gail I was going over to Sally's house, and I did go to Sally's, but I kept watching for Mike to walk by. It didn't take long. I could see Gail and Mike take a blanket and a picnic basket into the backyard and disappear in the shade of the trees.

I left Sally's house and followed them. I knew all the hiding places in the woods behind our house, and it wasn't hard to find a dark shadow where I could see them, but they couldn't see me.

It hadn't rained in weeks, so the fallen leaves crunched underneath me at the slightest move, making my heart pound with fear they would hear me. I could feel tiny ants and other insects crawling on my legs before I brushed them off. It was still, but from time to time a soft breeze would blow, a crow would caw, and the cicadas would cycle from soft to loud to soft again.

Maybe I noticed such details because a part of me didn't want to pay attention to what was happening. A part of me didn't want to see Mike's thick fingers unbuttoning Gail's shorts with such urgency that a button flew off and landed with a rustle in the leaves. With one hand he reached into her panties, while the other hand held the back of her head as he put his mouth on top of hers. He had taken off his shirt, and Gail's hands were clasped around his back, appearing still and pale against his tan skin. Occasionally he released her mouth to whisper things in her ear, but he kept holding her head as if he were afraid to let go. Her eyes were closed, and when she answered his whispers, it was with a single word.

Over the years, I had often thought of Gail as a type of doll. A china doll with perfect complexion. A Barbie doll dressed to a tee. Now she reminded me of a rag doll. A well-used rag doll—disheveled, limp, lifeless. It was as if she had given herself up.

They were leaning against a huge oak tree, but after a while, Mike said something to Gail and she lay down on his shirt. He knelt over her and began pushing up her top.

That's when I turned away.

I thought about sneaking off, but I'd lost my nerve. The thought of them finding me after what I'd seen was more than I could bear. I felt as if I'd had the breath knocked out of me, like when you're running to catch a fly ball and then you trip and fall on the rock-hard ground. For a minute or two, it takes all your concentration just to remember how to breathe.

And so I sat in the shade of the bushes trying to figure it all out. My parents' whispers in the room next door. The action Hank wanted to see. The transformation that had turned my perfect, graceful cousin into this creature who let a boy touch her in the most private of places. Half-forgotten memories, images, and words raced through my mind, but the more I tried to sort them out, the more confused I became. After a while, I got tired and leaned against a moss-covered log. Its coolness felt soothing, like my mother's hand when I had a fever.

* * * *

When I woke up, it was late in the afternoon. My father was in the driveway, calling my name. I brushed myself off and walked over to where Gail and Mike had been. The only trace of them was Gail's pink button halfway hidden by the leaves. I quickly bent down to pick it up, then ran out of the woods.

"Caroline, where have you been?" Dad said, as I stepped onto the cool grass of the back lawn. "I've been looking for you for half an hour."

"I was working on the fort and fell asleep. Sorry."

He seemed to be debating whether or not to say something else. I walked past him into the kitchen.

My mother was at the stove. Gail was setting the table. She had on a new outfit, I noticed.

"Caroline, you told me you were going to Sally's," Gail said, folding a yellow napkin into a triangle. Her voice sounded a little tight.

"I did, but then I decided to come home," I answered, opening my hand in front of Gail's face. "I was in the woods. I found your button."

Gail stopped folding the napkins and stood still for a moment. Her face began to flush.

The pressure cooker whistled and my mother took it over to the sink. "Well, next time let Gail know where you are, honey. We were worried." She turned on the cold water. "I'll sew that button on after supper."

Gail took the button and slipped it in her pocket. I thought of a lot of things to say. Like how I couldn't tell Gail where I was because she wasn't in the house. Or how it was wrong for everyone to be picking on me when she was the one who had snuck in the woods and let a boy take off her clothes. All of her clothes, I might add. Maybe it wasn't nice of me to spy on her, I would admit that, but next to what she had done, it wasn't bad at all.

Only I didn't say anything. Gail went back to folding the napkins, slowly, carefully, her eyes glued to the task. I couldn't stop staring at her. Right then she had become the enemy, and part of me couldn't understand how she could still look so beautiful and pure.

"Caroline, is something wrong?" my mother asked, as she spooned bacon drippings into the green beans.

Gail looked at me like she never had before, with that begging look our dog used to get when we had roast beef on Sunday. It was the first time that I could remember her asking a favor from me.

I turned my back on her and washed my hands.

"Caroline?" my mother asked as I got the plates down from the cabinet.

I looked at Gail again. Her head was bowed, but I sensed that she was about to cry. An unbidden thought crept into my mind. It must be hard to be nice all the time. Despite myself, I felt my anger starting to melt.

After all, it was always me who gave in and slipped a piece of meat under the table to the dog.

"Nothing's wrong, Mom," I said as I took the napkins from Gail.

Three Buttons on a Small White Card

AMONG THE BUTTONS ON THE TABLE is a small card with three mottled gray buttons sewn on to it. I've thought about taking it out several times because it doesn't seem to go with the others, but I haven't because I remember how it came to be.

When Hank was a junior in high school, he decided he just had to hike the Appalachian Trail. It was a big deal at the time because my mom didn't want him to go, but once he'd decided on something you couldn't talk him out of it.

So he went.

All summer long, we'd send packages for him to pick up. They were full of freeze-dried food, clean socks, homemade cookies. Each time we packed a box, my mom would include a little sewing kit she'd put together, with a needle, thread, and buttons. I don't know what she thought he was going to do with all those buttons, but it seemed to make her feel better.

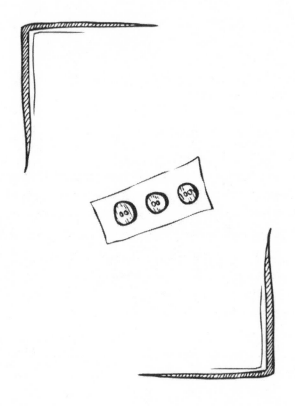

Ascending

Along the Appalachian Trail, 1973

THE FIRST THREE WEEKS had gone well. Mostly clear weather—nippy in the morning, but warm enough to break a sweat by noon. Sunsets pouring crimson over the tops of the mountains. Solitude broken only by briefly meeting other quiet souls at a shelter or a pure spring. For a while, Hank worried that things were too easy, that he wouldn't find out how far he could press himself, that his triumph would be hollow. He felt almost fraudulent when he walked into way stations to mail the postcards he had promised to send.

"Hi! Everything's fine. I should be out of Maine in two days."

That was to his mother.

"Last night I saw a shooting star and wished you were here. Every day I think how many more miles closer I am to you."

That was to Jennifer.

He had known they wouldn't want him to go. On one level, he had counted on it. If anything, Jennifer hadn't seemed worried enough. After all, he had been talking about it for almost as long as they had known each other. What he hadn't counted on was the vehemence of his mother's refusal.

"Absolutely not, Hank," Emma had said. "The idea is simply foolish. What if you got hurt? We'd have no idea how to find you. And you don't know what kind of people you'd meet. They could be, well . . . anything. You just don't understand."

"You don't understand. I've planned this for years. I'll let you know where I am. You can send me packages along the way."

"No."

"But I've gone backpacking by myself before. How is this different?"

She just looked at him.

"It *isn't* different. I've saved my own money to fly to Maine. I've bought everything I'll need. I've arranged to take my exams early. I've done it all."

"Hank, if you think you're getting out of school three weeks early, you have another think coming. That's ridiculous. I don't even want to talk about it anymore."

She'd really left him no choice. He went to his father.

"I've thought of everything," he explained. "I have phone numbers of people we know along the way—Uncle James in New York, The Palmers in Maryland. I've packed up boxes you can send me to pick up—they're all ready to go. I've been working on this all year."

Hank knew he'd made a good case. He knew his father would agree, but there were a few seconds when he began to panic.

"Your mother has been through a lot in the last couple of years with the surgery and everything." His father's voice sounded more serious than usual. His eyes were unreadable. "She doesn't want you to go. She worries."

"I know that, Dad, but she doesn't have a good reason. By the time I leave, I'll be seventeen. Isn't that how old your brother was when he joined the Army? You always talk about what guts he had. You never say he was stupid, and going to war is a lot more dangerous than hiking the Appalachian Trail. Nobody's going to be shooting at me."

His father laughed. "Let's hope not."

"Okay, then."

"Wait a minute, Hank. There's a difference between going to war during desperate times and doing something for a lark."

"This is not a lark. This is something I need to do. If I don't do it this summer then I'll do it next year when I'm eighteen, but then I'll be getting ready for college. I'm all ready for it now."

His father looked off to the left and sighed. "You'll have to be extremely careful. You'll have to send postcards and call every chance you get."

"I will. I promise."

"Your mother's going to kill me."

And, to be honest, the strain between his parents did put a bit of a damper on his excitement. For several days, his mother refused to look at his father, and spent her time organizing and then cleaning room after room in the house. When Hank got home late in the afternoon, she would be scrubbing the baseboards with Lysol or pounding pillows together out the back door.

"Thanks a lot, Hank," his sister growled at him one day when he retreated to the kitchen. "You know what she does whenever she gets upset. She decides it's time I learned how to cook while she tears the house apart looking for germs."

Caroline's hair, which tended to be unruly anyway, was plastered to her head, and her clothes were splattered with some sort of yellow paste. A collection of pots towered out of the sink.

"So what's for supper?"

"Macaroni and cheese, green beans, apple sauce, and corn-bread." She rubbed her hands on her apron. "Did you know macaroni and cheese comes in a box? I know it does. I saw it in the grocery store. You just add milk and stir. But do we have any of it? No. We have to make the sauce from scratch."

Caroline stood over the stove, trying to break apart clumps of cooked macaroni. "I heard them talking last night. She said you're just like her brother Mitchell was and she's not going through that again and if anything happens to you on this trip she'll never speak to Dad again."

"I'm not like Mitchell. He did things without thinking. Nothing will happen."

"It better not. She's driving me crazy already, and you're not even gone yet."

Hank stood still, smelling something acrid.

"I think something's burning," he said.

"Oh no!" Caroline grabbed an oven mitt, pulled a smoking iron skillet out of the oven, and dropped it into the sink. She looked up at him. "It's not funny, Hank!"

She took off the apron and walked out the back door. Hank poured the oil in the trash. He wiped the skillet clean and poured in new oil, spreading it around. He beat the lumps out of the batter and poured it in the skillet. The macaroni seemed al-most salvageable—you could forget the sauce if you just stirred in enough butter and salt and some grated cheese. At least the beans and applesauce were from the shelves of canned goods his mother had put up last year. Even Caroline couldn't ruin them.

"Caroline!" His mother yelled from the guest bedroom. "You know that's dry mustard that goes in the cheese sauce. Not regular mustard."

So that's what all the yellow was.

"She went outside," Hank yelled back. "It's okay. Everything's nearly ready."

He heard his mother come down the hall.

"What on earth!"

"It's okay, Mom. I'll clean it up while the cornbread is cooking."

Emma stood still, her eyes filling with tears. Hank couldn't remember her looking so fragile.

He walked over beside her and rubbed her arm.

"It's okay, Mom. I promise. Everything will be okay. I know what I'm doing."

They stood together awkwardly for a few moments, then Emma looked into his face. "I just want my family to be happy and safe," she whispered, brushing his bangs back from his forehead. "What's wrong with that?"

"Nothing, Mom. Nothing."

"Be careful, Hank."

"I will. I promise."

He thought she smiled a little bit. "You're so tall now. I have to look up at you." She touched his chin briefly. "Here, I'll set the table while you wash."

He had passed his first trial.

* * * *

On the shuttle flight from Boston to Bangor, Hank had sat next to a girl who lived twenty miles from where the trail started. She was a senior and had been to look at Tufts. Her parents had gone, too, but they stayed on for the weekend.

"I had to come back for a field hockey meet," she said, tossing her ash blond hair over her shoulder. Her name was Margo and she was, in some respects, prettier than Jennifer. She had clear, blue-gray eyes and muscular calves and arms that suggested something hard and powerful at her core.

"I've never known anyone who played field hockey," Hank said. "I thought that was just in old movies."

"Well, I've never known anyone from North Carolina." She seemed to be sizing him up. "The game is at four tomorrow. You should come. It will be a learning experience."

"I can't. I have to stick to the plan or I won't make it."

"What's a few hours? You can stay at our place. I've got the car and my parents won't be back until Sunday night."

Hank couldn't tell if she was serious or not. With a Southern girl, it would be easy. If it were a game, some sort of flirtatious dare, there would be that laughing sideways glance, the set mouth holding back a smile, the almost-visible tease hanging in the air between them. Jennifer did it often, suggesting something wildly erotic in the safety of the broad daylight. "Let's go skinny dipping down at Atkins Pond after school," she'd whisper in his ear as they walked down the hall, then she'd slip into her next class, glancing at him over her shoulder, safely knowing he was leaving early for a track meet and she would be at her job at the drug store until seven at night.

Margo, on the other hand, seemed completely serious. Her lips, touched with a hint of pale lipstick, were relaxed. Her eyes simply had a questioning look as she waited for his answer.

"I can't," he finally said. "I've got to get to the outfitter's and then head straight for the trail to get a good start on tomorrow." He didn't know why he felt the need to explain. "I've been planning this all year, and if I start out from behind I'll never make it."

Margo shrugged a little. "Okay. I'll give you my number in case you change your mind and want to spend one last night in bed."

Hank was mortified to feel his face grow warm. He wondered what it would be like to be in bed with this girl. He didn't think she would giggle the way Jennifer did when he started to touch her in the darkened car on Friday nights. She'd grab his hand, whispering, "That tickles, Hank," while his kisses became more and more urgent, until he pushed away her hands and slipped his inside her sweater, inside her blouse, inside her bra. "Please, Jennifer," he whispered into the darkness, and she finally eased back against the seat, letting him touch her softness, even her wetness, even touching him a little, but always stopping when he opened the glove compartment and began feeling for the foil circle he had taped to the back. "Not yet," she whispered, pulling him back to her. It was the same always: "Not yet."

He didn't think Margo would be like that at all.

She was still looking at him. He couldn't think what to do but laugh and then, fortunately, the pilot's sturdy voice came over the speaker to announce the descent.

Margo reached in her brown leather purse and got a piece of paper. She quickly wrote on it and handed it to Hank.

"It's your choice. Call if you need anything."

"Thanks." He stared at the row of numbers written in tight, straight pencil marks. "I'll keep that in mind."

The plane landed and they stood up. Margo was almost as tall as Hank.

"Good luck with the hike," she said as they stepped into the airport.

"Good luck with your game," he said.

She smiled and was gone. Hank pulled his pack off the conveyer belt and walked to the bus stop. He got the number out of his pocket, stared at it again, then dropped it in the metal trash can.

He'd passed another trial.

* * * *

Hank felt invigorated by turning away from Margo; he practically ran up Mt. Katahdin, breathed in the clear air and set out into the limitless wilderness of lake and forest. For the first three weeks, he easily met his goals for each day. He had no trouble finding water and slept well at night dreaming of Jennifer's face and the sunrise. He was doing it—he was living his desire as he had known he would. Some people muddled around life skipping out from one dream to another, but Hank wasn't like that. He chose his goals carefully and stuck by them. He had met Jennifer when he was ten and she was eight. Her father was a math professor and her mother a librarian at the college, and the family had just moved to town. She was somewhat quiet, but not shy and had no qualms about joining the other children as they played around the neighborhood. She laughed easily and knew how to joke, but not at someone else's expense. They had been friends for four years when Hank gradually realized she shared the same steadfastness as he. When he was fifteen, he knew he would marry her. They never talked about it, but he knew she expected this as well.

It would be a while, though, because Hank also knew he would one day become a pilot. He would go to NC State, join the Air Force ROTC, get a degree in engineering, start the pilot's program. When he had been younger, he dreamed of the NASA program, but he realized being selected for the space program depended more on luck than his own ability. He preferred to rely on himself.

He had achieved other goals—running a five-minute mile, reading *The Odyssey*, beating his dad at chess—but hiking the AT was the first goal that he considered truly adult. A stepping stone to all the rest. Proof that he had what it took, despite the obstacles set in his path.

He wasn't surprised when things suddenly got harder. It started raining, the kind of drenching, violent rain that only comes in spring and summer. He covered his pack, put on a poncho, and kept on moving. The water ran down his legs and crept into his socks. Sometimes he could barely discern his way among the many trails of muddy leaves branching off in front of him. He didn't see anyone for three days. The fourth night, when he made it to the shelter, three other men were there. They didn't have backpacks, just clumsily-filled bags strewn about. They were drinking beer by the light of a lantern and watched Hank as he said hello and set up his sleeping bag in the corner. He knew he would meet non-hikers at times, but hadn't expected it in this weather. He considered leaving, not because he thought they were dangerous, but because they disturbed the dual sense of solitude and camaraderie he felt with thru hikers. But the rain was heavy, and he didn't want to risk getting his sleeping bag wet in the tent. He ate jerky and crackers and nuts for supper, then turned his back to the men and willed himself to sleep.

In the morning, the men were gone, but his sense of uneasiness lingered. The rain had slackened, but there was no sun, just fog covering everything. Even the birds sounded dazed, as if they were calling by force of habit, not instinct. The pack was heavy and cut into his shoulders as he stepped back onto the trail. As he walked, his mind kept creeping back to Margo's face, and he realized he had dreamed of her during the night. Dreamed he had gone with her to the house, had let her do whatever she wanted to do to him. Had let her keep him there.

Hank shook his head and kept walking, looking always for the white blaze against the wet, black bark.

* * * *

The rain cleared when he came to Mount Washington. Hank went into the observatory, ate at the cafe, picked up his package. Along with the packages of dried food, there were some extra socks, a roll of stamps, and a tiny sewing kit with thread and three buttons. His mother's handwriting delicately looped across a piece of pink stationery: "We love you. Be careful." There was a handmade card from Caroline. "NEWS FLASH: Black bears scour AT, searching for lone hikers." Inside there was a drawing of a bearish shape grinning beside a pair of hiking boots and a quickly scrawled note: "Mom gave up on cooking lessons. We're SEWING now. Come home soon!" At the bottom of the box was a bag made of blue-and-gold plaid fabric. Hank opened it slowly and pulled out a plastic bag of star-shaped cookies and a note: "Hope you're still watching the stars. I am. I caught these for you. XX OO XX. Jennifer."

He bought a bottle of Coke and ate the cookies slowly, looking around him at the ring of peaks stretching out from the barren top.

* * * *

By mid-June, Hank regained his rhythm and held it through Massachusetts, Connecticut, New York, and Pennsylvania. He met fellow hikers and learned their trail names—Sailor, Bugman, Kirk. Sometimes they hiked together and shared the shelters, but often he walked alone. He quickly came to prefer his tent to a shelter or even a hut. He went into towns less than most— only when he was scheduled to pick up a package or when he absolutely had to buy something. In Maryland, biting flies swarmed around him and he descended from the wilderness into the frontiers of suburbia, stopping in fast food restaurants and convenience stores where people stared at him and kept their distance. He knew this would be the most miserable part of the experience. Soon he would ascend back into the hills and leave behind the lure of squalid mediocrity.

In Virginia he began climbing again, but he still felt dirty, as if smog had penetrated the layer of sweat and dirt that covered his skin and transformed it from something natural and protective into something offensive. He wanted to be clean. Not a civilized clean. A true clean. When he came to a stream, he poured water over his head. During a midnight thunderstorm, he took off his clothes and walked in the rain. It was no use. It had been weeks since he had seen wildlife other than squirrels and birds. The vistas and valleys, streams and shelters changed, but a pervasive monotony seemed to overshadow everything. One day blurred into another. The stars at night seemed ordinary.

Fatigue settled over him, creeping deep inside his being.

The last of the four ridges was the most difficult. The cool morning quickly burned into an almost visible heat. Occasionally, through the trees, Hank could see the ridgeline looming above him, always seeming the same distance away. Gnats crept into his eyes and flies swarmed around his hair. Fat, lazy flies, like the ones that swarm public garbage cans. He stopped to get a bandana out of his pack and caught himself feeling dizzy as he stood up. Disgust filled him, and he began to retch.

Tonight I will sleep on the summit, he told himself. *I will lie under the stars. I will watch lightning dance around the horizon and feel a cool breeze. I will lean my head upon a rock and see angels ascending and descending a ladder. And at the top . . .*

Hank heard footsteps behind him, fairly far away, but coming on strong and steady. More than one person, maybe three. He felt paralyzed and sat down by his pack, holding on to the frayed border of the front flap, willing himself invisible.

"Hey, man, it's Moonwalker." Bones, the first of the three, came into view, followed by Medicine Man and Snake. They had finished medical school in May and were hiking as much of the trail as they could get in before their internships started. Hank had hiked with them a few days back in New England. He lifted his hand to greet them, but didn't say anything.

"You must be booking." Medicine Man smiled the same genuine smile he'd had the first time Hank met him. His angular face exuded confidence and goodwill. "We hopped a bus. Thought we could bypass all that road walking. We figured we would have passed you, but here you are. What are you averaging? Twenty? Twenty-two?"

"Something like that." Hank was surprised to hear his voice sounding as if he were speaking from deep within a cave.

"That bites, man! I never thought a skinny kid like you could do it in four months, but you're going to prove me wrong. I wish I'd had the balls to do that when I was your age. Just think what I'd be doing now."

Snake, the quiet one, laughed softly. "Working off your college loan, most likely."

Bones stared at Hank. "You okay, kid?"

"Yeah, fine," Hank said through the echo. "Just sick of this funk and the heat."

"It doesn't seem as hot as it has been. There's a hostel with showers down in the next town. That's where we're heading. You staying there tonight?"

"No. I don't want a shower anyway. I'll go swimming in the next river."

"That's pretty far off."

Bones seemed to be contemplating taking his pack off. "You sure you're all right? There's been some crud going around at some of the shelters. That's another reason we hopped the bus."

"I don't usually stay in shelters, especially when they're crowded."

Snake grinned. "He's a real man. No hostels. No showers. No problems."

Bones looked at Hank a moment longer, then stared up the path. "Okay. See ya later, Moonwalker."

The three steadily headed up the incline without talking. Fifteen minutes later, Hank sensed he could still hear their boots on the dry leaves. He waited a little longer, trying to summon enough energy to hoist his pack back on. When he finally did, he had to lean against a tree. It took another five minutes before he could get going. The straps cut into his collarbone. His boots rubbed a sore on his heel. His knees throbbed with each step and his heart raced. When he swallowed, a stabbing pain pierced into the soft tissue of his throat. The realization that he was sick filled him with a sense of relief. Another trial, that's all, he told himself. Everything would be okay if he could just make it to the top. He would sleep under the stars and wake up okay. Not well, maybe, but okay. Ready to go on.

He knew that if he stopped, if he put his pack down, he wouldn't make it, so he rested against trees. He drank water from his canteen and ate GORP from a side pouch. He forced his mind to think only of the top, but other images forced their way in. His mother, peering anxiously out the window. Jennifer walking down the sidewalk with another boy. The news report of the Mercury disaster. Margo walking out of the airport, looking over her shoulder, saying, "It's your choice."

The sun began descending, but Hank was still enveloped by heat. He could no longer guess how close he was to the top, how slowly he was walking. Finally, he stepped through the tree line onto the rocky bald and saw a row of cairns leading to the summit like silent, holy watchers. No one else was there.

The heat of the stone came through the soles of his shoes, and a dry breeze traced around his face. When he got to the summit, he sank down and rested on his pack. His sweat no longer tasted salty and a headache throbbed against his temples, but that didn't matter now. He opened up his pack and pulled out his second canteen of water, began drinking, and waited for the sunset. When it came, there was no orange ball, just haze slowly losing the light. He lay back, resting his head on a flat rock, and looked for Venus. He knew he should eat, but he didn't have enough energy to move. He felt his fever cleansing him as he drifted into sleep, fitful at first, then deep and dreamless.

When he woke up, the first thing he noticed was heat lightning crossing the sky, then he felt wind and dampness and remembered a sound that had entered his sleep. He looked around, then felt carefully with his hands and found his canteen overturned, almost empty. He screwed the top on quickly before he was tempted to drink the last. A gust of wind raced across the bald and he shivered. He sat up, trying to melt his being into the mountain, but more and more he felt he did not belong there. There were no animal sounds—just wind and darkness below and streaks of light above. No words, no angels, no ladder to the heavens, just incomprehensible quiet.

At the first hint of dawn, Hank set out again, not waiting for the sunrise. He would make himself wait two hours before drinking the last of the water. His guidebooks said there was a spring about eight miles ahead, not far off the trail, but when he got there, it was dried up. His thirst was almost unbearable. He drained the last of the water from his canteen, rubbed cooking oil on his lips, ate raisins for the moisture. With each step, a shot of self-doubt shot through him: *you won't do it, you won't do it.* He remembered the books he'd read about hiking the trail, about Grandma Gatewood, an old woman who'd hiked the whole thing wearing tennis shoes and carrying a knapsack. Had done it not once, but multiple times. *I'm stronger than some grandmother,* Hank told himself, but the thoughts kept coming. At one point, Hank looked up and thought he saw the outline of a woman going ahead of him, disappearing in the distance. The image turned and changed until he saw the strange street lady who used to tend the flowers on Mason Street. She stood facing him, wearing a flowing yellow gown and wisdom in her eyes. "*There are worse things than being crazy*," she whispered.

Hank shook his head and stomped his feet down hard, banishing every thought that tried to crawl into his mind, feeling the pain in his toes and the force of the air entering his lungs. He went on, vowing not to stop until he fell and couldn't rise.

By ten o'clock, he finally made it to the next shelter. The cistern was empty, completely dry. A scrawled note above it said "Seeping stream app. one mile down, toward rock outcropping."

Hank considered his options. The downward slope was steep and covered with leaves. He would have to leave his pack to find the spring, and when he got there, it could be dry.

If he waited at the shelter, before long there should be some northward hikers who could probably spare some water. That would be easy enough.

He pushed the temptation aside, hid his pack in a thicket of rhododendron behind the shelter, and headed toward the water. Before long, he saw the group of rocks and went toward them, but then he saw another group. He kept going toward the first, but when he got there he couldn't find a spring. He rested a moment against the rocks, remembering stories of diviners and witchers, willing himself to sense the water's presence. He forced himself to go on toward the next group of rocks. The undergrowth grew thick, and he slipped on the leaves, falling to the ground. As he lay there, he felt the coolness of nearby water. Crawling on his hands and knees, he followed it until he came to a dribble oozing out from the rocks. He lay under it and let it drip into his mouth, then filled his canteen, slowly, luxuriously, as if it were holy oil.

On the climb back up, Hank's heart leapt. He had done it on his own. Then he began to consider how far behind he had gotten. A whole day at least. The delay would stop now, he told himself, pushing harder, tearing through the underbrush, pulling himself upward on branches, bearing down on roots. He was at the edge of the rhododendrons where he'd left his pack. He pushed forward into them and a branch snapped back, whipping across his face, carving a ragged scrape through his cheek.

His eye watered and stung so that he wondered if he had stumbled into a bees' nest. He poured a little water out of the canteen and tried to wash it off, then he hoisted his pack on and headed down the trail.

At first he was okay. His eye still stung, but that should go away. Only it didn't. After a while, Hank was convinced a piece of bark had lodged in it. He dribbled some of the water into it and blinked. Then he decided to ignore it. He kept walking, forcing himself to quicken the pace. The sunlight began to bother him, and he was getting a headache from trying to squint his left eye shut. He stopped to wrap a bandana around it and kept going.

He stopped briefly for lunch at the next shelter. A family was there from the side trail that went down to a town. He couldn't remember how far it was to the town; maybe they could give him a ride from the trailhead. He could get some ointment, wash up, even see a doctor. They seemed nice. They had a picnic basket and two clean-scrubbed children who kept staring at him.

Hank drained the last of his water, remembering how he'd found it on his own. *His own . . . his own . . .* an echo bouncing around his brain. He'd come too far to give that up now. He wouldn't ride into town. Trials of temptation, sickness, craziness had tempered him for this moment.

The cisterns were full and he replenished both canteens, then set off down the trail.

During the night, camped under some hemlocks a ways off the trail, he slept but never escaped the burning in his eye. In the morning when he forced it open, everything seemed overcast.

He was scheduled to go for a mail drop about ten miles up anyway. He'd see about it then. By mid-afternoon, his pace had slowed drastically. Even covered, his left eye seemed pained by the sunlight. He could only squint with his right eye and lean on his hiking stick, concentrating on the next step, looking out for signs of the upcoming town. He didn't even hear Bones and his group until they were right on him.

"Moonwalker! I didn't expect to see you so soon." Bones' strong voice almost literally jostled Hank, who turned in slow motion and saw the shadowy outline of three men walking toward him.

"Shit! What happened to you?"

"I just scratched my eye. It's no big deal." The words sounded feeble even to Hank.

"Well, take the bandana off. I'll look at it."

He didn't even have it in him to refuse, but slowly started fumbling with the bandana. Bones took his arm and led him to a rock to sit on, then gently finished unwrapping his eye. Hank had never known light could be painful.

Bones stared into Hank's eyes. "This needs to be seen right away."

"Well, you're seeing it." Hank attempted a smile, but Bones remained serious.

"You need to go to an emergency room or a clinic, somewhere they'd have the right equipment and could give you some antibiotics, maybe a tetanus booster."

"I don't have enough money for a doctor, and if they call my parents, my mother will freak out and come get me."

"Well, I don't think you're going on. Not for a while, anyway."

"I'm not quitting. Are you nuts? I've walked a thousand miles, for Christ's sake."

"You could have a scratch on the cornea. It's not something to play around with. Your vision could be permanently impaired."

Hank sat quietly for a moment, both eyes shut, head bowed down.

"Could be or is?" he finally asked.

"I don't know. An ophthalmologist might be able to repair the damage, if there is any."

"I'll be fine. It was just a branch whipping across my face. I'll get some ointment at the drugstore."

Snake and Medicine Man looked at each other, then glanced ahead at the trail. "Well, let's all just get going toward town," Snake said. "We can try to talk sense into him on the way. If he wants to lose an eye, that's his problem."

Hank stood up and stepped roughly forward, trying to keep his focus on the trail.

"Here, grab on to my pack," Medicine Man said. "That'll be faster."

They began to pass houses along the trail. A dog barked and rushed out toward them, baring its teeth, heading straight for Hank before stopping at the end of the leash. Going for the weakest member, Hank thought bitterly.

"You know you can easily finish the trail next summer. It won't take you long. You'll probably be doing twenty-five-mile days by then. After all, we're not doing it all at once."

Not the same, Hank thought contemptuously. *I'll finish it this time. It's just another trial.*

"It's awesome that you've done all this by yourself." Bones' voice had a tone of finality to it. Hank could imagine how he'd sound when he told someone he had cancer—professional, caring, but not too much. After all, it wasn't his body that had betrayed him. He got to play the hero. "It takes a different kind of guts to change plans and ride it out, even get help when you need it. Grace under pressure and all that. I know you'll be back one day."

Hank tripped on a root and almost fell into the dirt. He could hear the traffic up ahead.

Satin Covered

THIS BUTTON, covered in royal blue satin, came from a dress Gail wore when she graduated from high school. She kept it through college, then gave it to me to wear for my graduation. The silk felt so rich—cool and smooth, like a heavy gold necklace.

I remember her graduation clearly. Mom thought we should go because Gail didn't have many other family members, other than Claire and her grandfather, to be there. I had never been to a Catholic school before, and it seemed so alien to me, all the statues and crucifixes and nuns.

In a way, it's ironic. In my gut, I had always thought I had at least one thing over Gail: she's Catholic. She'll never really be one of us. Right? The Tilghmans have been Protestant a few hundred years before they ever set foot in the New World. I know of at least three country churches bearing the family name. Then what do I do but marry a Hindu. Suddenly, being Catholic's not so different after all. Suddenly, I'm the one who is outside the fold, not Gail.

The thing is, I always *was* the different one. Marrying Rishi just made it impossible to ignore.

I remember the button seller at the flea market and how the cameo buttons weren't her style. They're not my style either, but suddenly I want to look at them again. I want to see if they are the way I remember them. I walk upstairs to my office and retrieve them from a drawer. Delicate ovals of sculpted pearly white—identical except for the tiniest details—reflect the light coming in through the window.

Elegant.

Poised.

Feminine.

Like my mother. Like Gail. For a few minutes, I sit at my desk staring at them, trying to discern what this realization makes me feel.

Jealousy? Yes, but something else, too.

Wistfulness? Maybe.

I tuck the cameos back in the drawer, go back downstairs, and pick up the blue silk button. It's really not my style, either, but I feel a connection to it as I hold it in my hand.

Wistfulness . . . yes.

It's true. I miss my cousin.

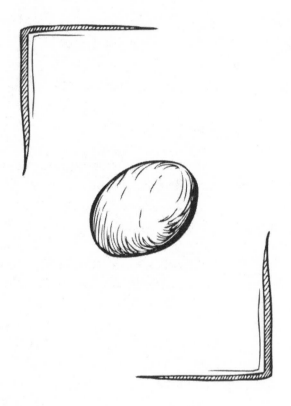

Commencement Exercise

Saint Mary's School, near Savannah, 1976

IN THE BACK OF THE LINE, someone had a bottle of champagne they passed along whenever Sister Ellen stepped away. Mary Cochran took a swig and gave the bottle to Gail. "Time to celebrate!" she whispered. Gail passed it on to Kathleen without drinking any. She hadn't had anything for breakfast, and she'd found that since she'd gone on the pill two weeks ago, she felt nauseated in the morning if she didn't eat anything. Just thinking about champagne right now was enough to turn her stomach.

Must be something like being pregnant, Gail thought, feeling the shadowy guilt that seemed to creep down her neck whenever she remembered the pink ring of tablets she'd hidden in a zippered pocket in one of her stuffed animals. She hadn't told anyone about them, not even Renée, her best friend. Certainly not her roommate, Margaret Evans, who claimed to be as worldly as anyone but was shocked way too easily and had a big mouth on top of that. Gail hadn't told anyone even though she knew that several girls, including some of the most popular, were on the pill. One or two were quite open about it, among their friends, at least. "Well, maybe it is a sin, but it has to be better than getting an abortion," Cindy Jones whispered one day in the locker room. Cindy was a Protestant.

Sister Ellen came back into the room, and everyone got very quiet. She went down the line, helping pin on the white caps that didn't seem to fit anyone, handing out tissues to the girls who'd put on too much makeup. When she came to Gail, she touched her face gently, with cool, dry fingers. "Perfect as always, my dear," she whispered. Gail felt the guilt creeping deeper and deeper.

A buzz of muted giggles broke out up the line, and Gail saw Cindy jerk the green champagne bottle under her gown. Sister Ellen didn't look in that direction, but she clapped her hands together and said, "Now girls," in a loud voice. "Sister Therese will be here momentarily to distribute the honor cords. I'm sure you all want to take one last moment to take a deep breath and remember the significance of this occasion." She pulled a trashcan out from the corner and set it in the middle of the room. "I will check on you again in exactly three minutes." And she slipped noiselessly out the door.

Cindy ran over to the trashcan and dropped the bottle in. Three more girls from the back threw theirs away as well. "Damn! How does she do that?" one of them whispered on the way back to the line.

How does she know? Gail wondered. She shuddered. What else does she know?

It wasn't my idea, she wanted to explain.

It was her mother's.

Gail had gone home for Easter break, just as she did every year. As always, she and her mother and grandfather had gone to Mass together at Holy Family on the outskirts of the city. Gail savored the procession of banners, the incense, the light coming through the stained glass windows as the gospel was read. It always gave her an odd combination of sensations. In many ways, going to High Mass—for Christmas or Easter—was what it meant to come home, to be with her mother and Judge Brennan, her grandfather. It had that returning familiarity of ritual, and she always felt close to the Holy, but not touched by it. After Mass, they had dinner together at Judge Brennan's.

As always, Lucille wore a starched white apron as she served ham, scalloped potatoes, asparagus au gratin, fresh strawberries, and coconut cake with French roast coffee.

As always, Judge Brennan had presented both Claire and Gail with porcelain egg-shaped boxes painted in delicate pastels. Lucille brought them out on a silver tray after the table was cleared. Gail's contained a set of pearl and gold earrings, Claire's a diamond pendant.

As always, Claire had nodded to Gail, who then kissed Judge Brennan on the cheek and said, "They're beautiful, Grandfather. Thank you." During the afternoon, Gail helped Lucille do the dishes, listening to her sing gospel songs as her hands—black on the top and softly pink underneath—dipped into the sudsy water and came out with a gold-rimmed teacup, a perfectly round plate, a stem of crystal. When the kitchen was clean and the dining room tidied, Lucille put on her coat and took the containers of leftovers Gail had helped her pack. At the back door, she hugged Gail hard, then stood back and looked at her intently. "Goodbye, you pretty thing. I'm going home to my family now. We'll have Easter tonight."

As always, Gail wondered what it would be like to go with her.

Everything had played itself out as in years past, right down to the moments Gail spent walking around Judge Brennan's house, watching the late afternoon sunlight stream into the paneled study as Judge Brennan talked on the phone, sitting down briefly in the den with her mother, looking at the polished mahogany shelves lined with pictures of her and Claire and the two black-and-white portraits of her deceased Grandmother Maureen. Everything had been the same until that evening, when Gail and Claire walked into their townhouse and Claire said, "I've made several appointments for you this week."

That in itself wasn't unusual. Gail usually spent Easter break getting her hair done, having manicures, going to the dentist and doctor.

Claire hesitated for a moment while she hung up her coat. "Tomorrow morning, I'm going to take you to Dr. Boyers. You'll be going to college in the fall, and I think it would be a good idea for you to be on the pill."

Gail literally felt too stunned to speak, and when she finally recovered, she said the wrong thing.

"But the sisters will never allow that!" she blurted out. Claire smiled and held out her hand for her daughter's coat, which Gail had been grasping as if it were a shield of some sort.

"You're a senior now. I'm sure you know all the safe hiding places. Besides, you've always been a good student. They aren't going to come snooping around your room."

Claire went through the downstairs, turning on lamps. Gail followed her, not saying anything.

Finally, Claire sat down on the leather couch in the den. Gail slumped down in a green wing-back chair.

For the last year or two, Gail had felt that she and her mother had an understanding when it came to sex. Gail didn't know how her mother knew she wasn't a virgin. They certainly never discussed it; Gail just somehow knew it to be true. She also felt that her mother didn't disapprove, although how she could be a good Catholic and not, Gail had sometimes wondered.

Going on the pill, though, that was another matter altogether. It implied that having sex wasn't something that just happened in the heat of the moment. That you were planning to sin all along. That you were trying to thwart God's will.

"Stop frowning, Gail, you're going to get wrinkles."

Gail stared at her mother. Claire's wrinkles—tiny lines around the corners of her eyes—almost seemed to enhance her beauty, to give her an air of wisdom and experience. She seemed impenetrable, but Gail gathered herself up to speak.

"I don't think I want to do it," she said, almost whispering.

Claire flipped through a magazine a few moments before she responded.

"Going to the gynecologist is nobody's idea of fun, Gail."

"It's not just that. I can't be Catholic and be on birth control pills."

"Oh yes, you can."

"I don't see how. Am I supposed to confess it? Then what do I do when the priest says to throw them away? How does that work?"

Claire put down the magazine and stared at Gail. Despite the awkwardness of the situation, Gail felt a closeness to her mother that she had rarely experienced. Or, if not a closeness, an uncloaking of sorts.

"At some point, Gail, you will decide which traditions and ideas you keep and which you let go. Right now, I'm doing it for you."

"I just don't like the idea of taking a pill every day. It isn't natural."

"That's true," Claire said, kicking off her brocade shoes and stretching her long, slender toes as she placed her feet on top of the ottoman. "Take a look around nature. What's natural is for females to get pregnant before they're even grown, to keep getting pregnant until they're old and worn out. That's what is natural."

Gail felt a messy flood of emotions running through her—anger mixed with surprise at being in an argument with her mother. Everyone else seemed to argue with their parents constantly, but she never had.

"I'm not a rabbit, Mother."

Claire stared at Gail, a bit of a smile on the corners of her lips.

"It isn't funny!" Gail was surprised at the intensity of her indignation.

"No, but it isn't the end of the world, either." Claire pulled her feet to her side and leaned her head back into the soft leather. "God! I'm exhausted. Would you get me a gin and tonic, Gail? Make one for yourself if you like."

For a moment, Gail thought about refusing, but the prospect of just sitting there with her mother was more than she could face.

When Gail came back with her mother's drink, Claire was looking at an art book. John William Waterhouse—one of a series of art books that Gail had given her for Christmas over the years. Claire had stopped on the portrait of St. Cecilia, sleeping in a Mediterranean garden, hymnbook in her lap, two angels on their knees before her.

"This angel reminds me of you, Gail," Claire said as she took the drink. "With her dark hair and her ivory skin and that serious expression. The other angel is staring at the saint, but this one looks completely enraptured by the beauty of the music."

Gail looked at the angel's face for a moment. It looked sad to her.

Claire stared at her daughter. "Don't worry, Gail. I'll take responsibility." She turned the page of the book to The Magic Circle, a Medusa-like woman drawing a circle of smoke in the sand. "That one's certainly different."

Gail didn't say anything. Claire closed the book and sighed.

"Look, Gail. Do you know how old I was when you were born? Twenty. I had only been out of St. Mary's two years. I didn't know anything about the world. Your father was twenty-three."

"So I totally messed up your life, is that what you're saying?"

A lot of mothers would have gotten mad, but Claire didn't.

"No, not at all," she said, shaking her head. "Things were different then. The year I graduated from high school, my mother went into a mental institution. Half the time when we visited her, she yelled and screamed at us. The other times, she didn't say anything. Judge Brennan worked twelve hours a day or more. So much for home life. I missed school. I missed the order, the peace, the beauty that surrounded us. I took classes at Agnes Scott during the day, but it wasn't the same. Back then most women who went to college weren't really planning for a career. When I met your father, I just let whatever happened become my life. It could have been a lot worse. I could have let the circumstances talk me into becoming a nun, although I do think I have more sense than that. I could have married some Irish Catholic son of Judge Brennan's friend who wanted ten children and a shrine in the front yard."

"My father was Catholic. He converted."

Claire stared at Gail intently, then spoke with unmistakable clarity. "Nobody really converts, Gail. Not all the way. You're always going to hear that whisper of who you really are echoing around your head. And believe me, your father didn't have a Catholic bone in his body. He never felt comfortable with it. He didn't see it as beautiful the way you or I do. To him, it was just strange."

Claire stood up. "I'm going to get a bath and go to bed." In the light of the lamp, her face seemed to soften. "Let me do this for you, Gail," she said quietly. "I know I don't sew dresses for you. I haven't taught you to cook or all those things Emma does. But this is something I can do, something I need to do."

Then she was gone. The moment was over. Gail sat alone, staring at the cover of the Waterhouse book. It was a cutout from The Lady of Shalott, her hair flowing about her shoulders, her eyes looking down the river's dim expanse.

* * * *

That was four weeks ago. The day after the last day of her last period, Gail had pushed the first pill out of the bubble pack and swallowed it with a big gulp of water, imagining she could feel it travel down her esophagus and land in her stomach. She stared in the mirror and wondered why she always did what her mother asked her to do, usually without question. Usually, without even thinking of questioning. It wasn't normal, she knew that.

She wasn't normal. Swallowing that pill every morning for four weeks reminded her of that fact. She wasn't normal, but she still pretended she was, until here she was now in cap and gown, ready to process but not ready at all. She didn't want to leave the school, where life danced before a backdrop of hushed reverence, where the scent of Sister Ellen's lavender and the sound of vespers infused her thoughts, where she went to sleep to the murmuring of whispered giggles and the knowledge that someone was watching all night. She wasn't ready, but she had to go along all the same. Judge Brennan and her mother would be there, and so would Aunt Emma and her family. Gail wondered what they would think about being here. It would seem strange to them—the statues, the nuns in their habits, Father Michael's strong accent.

Sister Therese came in and said some words, but Gail hardly heard. Then they were marching, walking into the auditorium, sitting in rows of hard metal chairs at the front. It was hot. She wasn't ready. She felt sick. She heard Mary's name called out and watched her walk up to the platform and take the diploma from Sister Therese. Barbara Green gave her a shove and whispered,

"Go on, Gail," and then she was walking up the stairs herself, shaking Sister Therese's delicate hand, taking the leather case that held her diploma.

She turned around and stared at the mass of faces in front of her, searching for something familiar as she walked back to her chair. There was polite clapping and then a flash, and she saw Uncle Charles with his camera. Another flash, and he put the camera aside, smiling broadly. Aunt Emma sat beside him, looking happy and a little uncomfortable in a new navy suit with a pillbox hat. Gail cringed slightly as she saw Hank and then Caroline sitting beside Judge Brennan, but they seemed to be okay.

As she walked forward, she realized that she knew without even looking where her mother was. Sitting at the end of the aisle, encircled by something Gail couldn't name but knew very well, something that kept Gail separate and yet was always there, an arm's length away, calling her.

She glanced at the ground for a moment before seeking out her mother's face.

The Button from Mom's Old Robe

FROM TIME TO TIME, when I was a teenager, my mother would retreat from the world for a while. It would start out with something subtle—like skipping her circle meeting or sending one of us to the grocery store. Then she'd miss church because she was too tired, she'd quit getting up for breakfast, and she'd stop ironing my dad's shirts. When it was really bad, she'd even quit working in her garden, and she'd stay in the guest bedroom wearing this awful quilted robe with light blue squares.

It didn't happen often, and nobody talks about it. At the time, my dad just said she wasn't feeling well.

Knowing what I know today, that there was another cancer growing in my mother's body, those episodes appear as omens, but at the time I just felt bewildered, wondering why nothing I did seemed to make her feel better. It was as if I didn't exist, had never been born. Everywhere I turned there were hollow punch-in-the-stomach unsafe feelings. The wolves were just showing up in my soul, but I didn't know what they were yet.

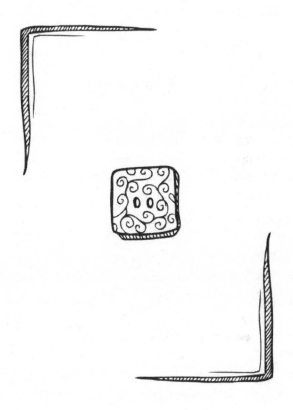

Bed of Violets

Ashton Mill, N.C. 1979

THE PHONE RANG TWICE and woke Emma, making her heart race and beads of sweat break out on her forehead. The rudest way to wake up, she thought, pulling a pillow over her head. When does anybody call in the middle of the night with good news?

Only it wasn't the middle of the night. It was . . . it was three o'clock in the afternoon, Emma finally saw, squinting at the clock across the room. It seemed as if it should be at least six. She doubted she could go back to sleep.

She could hear Caroline's muted voice, talking to Charles. Emma could recognize the tone—a little playful, a touch defiant, but mainly Daddy's girl. Caroline never used that tone when she spoke to her. She pulled the pillow tighter.

"Yes, she's still in bed! What is going on? She's usually up before seven!"

Emma could hear every word. If you're going to talk about someone behind her back, you should at least have the decency to make sure she can't hear you. Caroline should know that much. She was fifteen, for crying out loud.

"I already tried that, Daddy. I made eggs and toast and took it up at ten o'clock . . . Yes, I made eggs, and they were good, too. I can cook just fine, thank you, despite rumors to the contrary. Anyway, she wouldn't touch it. She said to leave her alone, and I will. It's creepy in there. The shades are drawn and the windows are shut tight, but she won't let me turn on the air conditioning."

Caroline was quiet for a while. Charles was no doubt cajoling her to have patience, everything would be just fine, it will just take a little time, gray skies are gonna clear up, put on a happy face . . . Charles never seemed to recognize that there actually were times when it was appropriate to worry.

An image came before her, a picture of Charles' stricken face, sun-burned and sandy, in the beach house at Kitty Hawk. His mouth opened to speak, and the words almost visibly poured out, one by one, in immutable slow motion.

Emma threw off the pillow and sat up. She could hear Caroline laughing. How predictable. Charles had told a joke, one from his endless repertoire of corn, probably a church sign saying—he had a whole notebook of those in the glove compartment of his car.

"*Daddy!* That's terrible." There was silence. "Okay, I promise. Love you too."

The phone receiver went down with a thud. A few seconds later, the stereo blurted on, and some cacophonic noise that passed for music found its way into the room. Emma jumped out of bed and started for the door, but stopped a few feet short. No, she told herself, I'm not leaving this room. She went over to the window and peeked out. The bright June sun made her squint, and she crawled back in bed.

If Gail were here, it would be different, she thought. Gail would never turn up the radio like that. She'd put on some soft, classical music, something to inspire pleasant thoughts, banish the horrid ones back to the dark recesses where they belonged. If Gail were here, Emma knew that when she did decide to venture out of the tiny guest room that she had claimed as her own, the house would be sparkling, beds made, furniture polished, a slight hint of lemon oil lingering in the air. There wouldn't be clothes—not quite dirty but not exactly clean—strewn in bedroom corners. The garbage in the kitchen wouldn't be overflowing. Empty glasses wouldn't sit in forgotten clusters throughout the house.

She didn't know where she had gone wrong with Caroline. Even Hank was a much better housekeeper, but he was in summer school at NC State. Gail would be coming for the weekend in a couple of weeks. Emma clung to the thought like a life preserver.

How could it be that Gail is Claire's daughter and Caroline is mine? Is that God's idea of a joke?

Emma tossed over to her side and prayed for forgiveness. She loved Caroline, she told herself firmly. She didn't understand her, but she did love her. She had done her best.

Still, Claire doesn't deserve Gail, that's for sure.

The horrid thoughts had first started about a year after the mastectomy, and it had taken Emma a while to put the two events together. Then she began having a recurring dream, or, if not a dream, an image that crept into her consciousness just this side of sleep. She was a little girl again, in the woods behind her grandparents' farm. There, on the forest floor, a patch of violets magically appeared every spring. A perfectly shaped rectangle, like a quilt on her Grandmother's feather bed. Emma would crawl into the bed and lie surrounded by their cool beauty, the sun filtered by the towering trees, the birds singing, a soft breeze blowing.

Then she realized that the corner of the violets was being overcome with wilt. The flowers shriveled and turned brown.

She couldn't get up, and the decay was spreading, withering the violets, row upon row, and heading her way.

The image always came just as she was going to sleep, waking her with a jolt and keeping her awake till the dead of night. For several years, she had forced herself to get up with the sun anyway, and things were generally fine in the morning light. But now she was tired, very tired. She felt that she could sleep a week without problem, could sleep a month, or even a year.

Charles had insisted she go to the doctor. She'd had a mammogram on her one remaining breast, its sagging accentuated by being all alone. "Clean as a whistle," her gynecologist had chirped. "I'd say you've got this thing licked, although we'll keep a close eye on you, just to be safe."

She kept having the dream. Before, when they'd told her the lump was malignant, she had been genuinely shocked. She didn't believe it, in fact, until she woke up in the hospital and felt the raw pain of missing flesh. Then, for a while, she was euphoric. She had dodged the bullet, had been given a second chance to finish raising her family, to plant another garden, to refinish her grandmother's dining room set. The euphoria passed and life went on until, very subtly at first, the horrid thoughts crept in. The odd thing was how they mutated themselves, cascading from disturbing image to disturbing image—a surgeon cutting into her while she was awake, Hank falling on a chain saw, baby birds abandoned in their nest—till they came to rest, over and over again, with the bed of violets in the woods.

The dream probably had nothing to do with a new invader in her body, Emma told herself. Probably nothing at all. Probably, it was that the whole experience—the violence of surgery, the nausea of chemotherapy, the ceaseless vigilance of watching for signs—had simply slapped her with the reality of her limited life span. Maybe it was nothing more than one of those mid-life crises she used to read about in her magazines.

There was a sound of clattering in the kitchen, and then the stereo became louder still. Emma felt a surge of adrenaline spread through her body, flushing her cheeks, quickening her breaths.

There before her was Caroline as a four-year-old. Her Sunday dress already wrinkled, straight brown hair falling in her face, running insanely around a room full of funeral guests, oblivious to the hushed decorum and the fine china. Emma looked for Charles, but didn't see him. Couldn't he control his own daughter for just one hour? Emma looked across the room and saw Claire, watching, with an unreadable expression on her face. She turned around and saw, with horror, her dead father, hunched with pain, confusion, and anger, reaching out to her, his eyes begging for help. He began to scream as something pulled him from behind.

Emma tried to calm her breathing, but the stereo blared into her mind, dispelling any peace. She stood up, pulled on her faded bathrobe, then, peeking out the door, snuck into the bathroom.

The cold water on her face felt good. Someone had put out new soap and towels. There was even a Mason jar filled with daisies. Emma sat on the edge of the tub and tried to gather herself together. She realized that the music had stopped. She heard footsteps, then a knocking on the door.

"Mom, are you okay?"

Emma pulled her bathrobe closer. "I'm fine."

"I'm going outside for a minute. I was noticing that vine on the mailbox is getting all in the bushes, so I'm going to cut it back."

Vine . . . vine. What vine? For a moment, Emma could barely picture the mailbox.

She stood up quickly.

"Caroline, that's clematis. It's just about to bloom."

No response.

"Caroline?"

Emma opened the door, buttoned the top three buttons of her robe, and slowly walked down the dark, quiet hall. When she got to the family room, shafts of light streamed through the picture window and made rectangles of brightness along the walls. She saw Caroline walking toward the end of the driveway with the shears in her hand.

Emma tapped on the window, trying to hide behind the curtain in case Opal Kinston was out. She would never live down being seen in her bathrobe at midday.

Caroline kept going, oblivious. Just let her go, Emma thought. Who cares about that vine except me? Besides, surely she'll see the flower buds and realize what they are.

Caroline reached the end of the driveway and Emma sighed with relief as she put down the shears. At the mailbox, with the afternoon sun shining behind her, Caroline looked more delicate than usual. Emma couldn't think why this should be, except perhaps the distance and the light let her see her daughter in a different way. Caroline's brown hair was loose and glinted in the sunshine as she walked around the mailbox examining the bushes. Her figure was slender and slightly boyish, but now it struck Emma as young and graceful rather than ungainly.

She remembered with shame a horrid thought that had jolted her on more than one occasion: the specter of Caroline going off to college and then coming home with a lesbian lover. In her vision, the most disturbing thing was the matter-of-fact way Caroline acted about the whole thing. As if it were perfectly natural.

Why she should imagine such a thing, Emma didn't know, except that it was the sort of thing Caroline would do just for shock value. She had a way of . . . of confounding things, of doing the exact opposite of what Emma hoped and dreamed she would do.

Emma closed her eyes and prayed for forgiveness from her daughter. When she opened them again, she saw Caroline holding the shears with one hand and gathering the clematis vines with the other, preparing to lop them all off.

"Caroline, stop!" Emma cracked open the storm door and tried to yell, but she found her voice uncooperative, producing only a muffled squawk. She cleared her throat, stepped out on the stoop. "Caroline! Don't!" She waved her arms. "Caroline!"

Caroline glanced up and hesitated. She walked part of the way down the drive with a questioning look on her face.

"What is it?"

"Those vines are clematis. You know, the big purple flowers that cover the mailbox every summer, the ones everyone makes over."

Caroline was silent.

"They're about to bloom. They need to be tied up, not cut."

"Tied up? With what?"

"There's some string in the cabinet in the garage. Use that."

"I don't know how. You do it."

Emma felt adrenaline flow through her body again. She couldn't speak, but looked down and gestured at her robe. Caroline simply stood there.

"I can't go out like this! Just get the string and tie them to the mailbox. Sort of drape them around as you go up."

"Drape them?"

"Never mind that. Just tie them up. It will only take a minute."

Caroline slid her sunglasses back on and trudged off to the garage. Gingerly, like a grandmother wading in the lake, Emma inched further onto the porch. Then, holding the rail, eased herself to sit on the step. She found that a part of her was attracted to the sunny day even as another part shrank back from it. The shade from the massive holly bush surrounding the porch protected her and let her look around. She breathed in slowly, noting all the nuances of smells—the fertile aroma of holly pollen, a hint of roses, the moist smell of the earth itself. Down the street, someone cranked up a lawnmower, and Emma imagined the strong sweet smell of cut grass wafting toward her.

At the end of the drive, Caroline quickly tied the clematis up one side of the mailbox and walked back to Emma.

"Well," she said, peering over her sunglasses, "I'm glad you decided to join the land of the living."

"Very funny," Emma said, looking away.

Caroline smiled. "You should have known that line would come back to haunt you."

Caroline sat in the sunshine on the other end of the steps. She looked out toward the street, chewing a piece of grass. "Are the vines sufficiently draped?"

"They're not draped at all, but that's okay. A lot of people tie them up like that."

They sat together silently for a few moments, feeling the breeze on their faces, listening to the bees hovering around the holly.

"Want some lemonade?" Caroline asked.

"You made lemonade?"

"Well, it's from a mix. It's pretty good."

"That's okay." Emma stood up. "I need to get back inside."

"Mother! You just got out here, for Christ's sake!"

Emma paused briefly. Usually she would have said, "Watch your mouth, young lady." But she didn't have the energy.

"Mom, come on. Stay outside for a little while. Look, it's a glorious day. Isn't that what you always used to say?"

Caroline had pushed her sunglasses up, and her eyes had red marks around the corners.

Emma sighed. "Caroline, I can't stay out here like this. You know that."

"Well, let's go in the backyard. You haven't seen the garden in a while. We'll just slip around the corner real quick, and if Mrs. Kinston sees us, she's just an old bat anyway."

Caroline grabbed her mother's hand and began walking. Emma didn't know why, but she let herself be led. The cool greenness of the grass tickled her feet, sunlight darted at her through the trees, and a bird startled her with an impromptu song. She felt bewildered and enlivened at the same time, as if the world had been reconfigured and she was a child again.

"Dad's been watering the tomatoes and squash," Caroline said as they stepped into the back yard. "I think some birds got the sunflowers again, though."

How odd, how perplexing for Caroline to be opening the gate to Emma's own garden, her refuge, her holy place. She couldn't say anything, but looked around, noting the weeds, the piles of leaves, the disorder. Suddenly she was tired again.

"Caroline, I really want to go in."

"Here, you can have the chaise lounge," Caroline said, leading her to the patio. "I was using it earlier to get a tan, but now it's in the shade. And here's my spritzer if you get hot. You can rest out here, okay? Sit down and I'll get the lemonade."

Emma held Caroline's hands as she sat down on the chaise lounge, feeling the plastic slats give way slightly, fighting back a hint of panic that rose in her throat. Caroline disappeared inside and came back with two plastic cups. She pulled up an aging aluminum chair and sat down.

"Cheers!" She handed Emma one of the cups. It was cold and sweet and wet.

"I like the kick after you swallow it," Caroline said. "Kind of like a whiskey sour."

Emma said nothing.

Caroline stared at her mother. "Jeez, Mom. I just can't get a rise out of you today. You're a lot worse off than I thought."

Emma remained silent. Caroline leaned back in the chair and sipped the drink. After a while, she began laughing softly.

"So, tell me, did you really think I was going to cut those flowers?"

A surge of shock ran along Emma's spine. When it passed, she dropped her cup, spilling the cold pale liquid all over her robe. Her throat constricted, and strange noises squeaked out as she finally took in a breath.

Caroline jumped up and started to reach out to Emma, then stopped.

"Mom?" she said. "Mom? Are you all right?"

Emma was shaking, holding her face in her hands. She had never felt quite like this before. It took several minutes to realize that she was laughing. It was absurd, but true. The whole world was absurdly true. She wondered why it had taken her so long to figure it out.

Finally she looked up at Caroline. "I'm fine. I just got my robe wet."

Caroline sat back down. Emma wiped her eyes with the sleeve of her robe. The sun made her relax, as if she were indeed drinking a whiskey sour.

Caroline rolled up the bottoms of her shorts and tank top. "Mom, you must be burning up. Why don't you take off that nasty robe? Nobody can see. Sometimes I lie out here naked."

"I assume that's another joke."

"Come on," Caroline said, tugging on the robe. "Take it off. I know you have a very proper gown on, anyway."

Emma slid her arms out of the robe and undraped it a bit in the front. Caroline was right. She did feel better. She sighed deeply and looked around the garden. Despite the weeds and untidiness, everything seemed healthy.

She stood up slowly and began walking among the rows, feeling the soft dirt crumble under her feet and the edge of her gown catch on the leaves. The squash plants had almost tripled in size since she'd last seen them, and the tomatoes had soft yellow flowers. The beans edged their way up the string lines, and the straight corn stalks swayed slightly in the wind. Usually Emma planted flowers amidst the vegetables so that the garden resembled a patchwork quilt, but she hadn't gotten around to it this year. Still, there were some perennials in bloom—lilies, primrose, oxalis. And there, in the corner, was a splash of purple and yellow Emma had never noticed before. She walked closer, keeping her eyes on them. In the hard clay where nothing seemed to grow, the violets raised themselves above the weeds and stretched bravely, obstinately toward the sun.

Part Four

Mending

IN EARLY JANUARY, my dad gave me a few bulbs from Mom's garden—irises, hyacinths, tulips.

"Do you remember how she'd get them to bloom inside during the winter?" he asked me. "I started thinking about that and wondering how she did it, so I looked it up on the internet. I dug them up in October and kept them cold all during the fall so they're ready to bloom."

He gave me three pots—the green tips already peeking out of the soil mixture. At home, I put them on the windowsill behind the kitchen sink. The next morning, the sun shone on them brightly, and even though the bulbs weren't blooming yet, they added a cheerful energy to the room. It seemed right to put the jar of buttons beside them, too.

So now the buttons are in the kitchen, "the heart of the home," my mom used to say. I see them all the time—when I get coffee, when I rinse a glass, when I water the bulbs.

Serious, Yet Modern

ONE OF THE GAIL BUTTONS sits midway down the outer edge of the jar. It's an angular wooden button that came from a leather blazer so sophisticated that it seemed out of place in our small town. I remember it because she told me it was the first thing she bought with her own money, a pittance really, that she earned while working for a small newspaper in Maryland, the kind of paper that comes out a couple times a week, where the same people write the stories, take the pictures, do the layout. It sounded kind of interesting to me, but it seemed a little grubby for Gail. I visited her there once and stayed in the small apartment she had over somebody's garage. You'd think that living like that would have loosened her up a little, but she was always the same—neat and stylish, perfect hair, perfect nails. She had a degree in photography from Syracuse, and her mother could have gotten her a job in a museum easily, but there she was, out in the real world.

Often, I wonder why it happens that I always notice the Gail buttons out of all the other buttons in the jar? It could be because her clothes had more style elements than the rest of ours, more distinction. Or could it be that there's some sort of force guiding me toward these and not others? Maybe it's because ever since I bought that card of cameo buttons, I've been thinking about her more and more and trying to figure out how Gail, of all the unlikely people on this earth, came to be a rival.

The first time I saw her as my adversary was in the hospital. It was Mom's last hospital stay, but we didn't know it yet. I drove down to Charlotte on Thursday night and planned to be there the whole weekend. At seven o'clock in the evening, it was just starting to get dark, and the hospital complex cast everything in deep shadow while the lights glared out above the last remaining daylight.

I could feel my shoulders tense up more with each step I took, going through the revolving door, getting a pass, going in the elevator to the ICU, but the worst thing was walking down the hallway, not knowing what to expect. That morning on the phone, my dad told me Mom had been in isolation earlier and her oxygen was up to six liters. I didn't really know what that meant, but it sounded ominous that she needed more.

I found the room number and pushed the door open. For a few seconds, I watched her before she knew I was there. She wasn't asleep, but her eyes were closed.

I could tell it was bad.

Maybe I'd known for a long time, but that was the first time I saw just how sick she was face to face. My whole gut twisted into an unnatural shape, and I felt short of breath. I just stood there, wondering what to do, trying to be quiet, when she opened her eyes.

I walked over to the bed and grabbed her hand. "Hi, Mom," I said, trying to sound cheerful. She closed her eyes again. "It's good to see you," I whispered.

She just lay there, breathing hard, the oxygen mask leaving marks on her face. I sat while the room turned dark. A nurse came in and turned on the fluorescent light over the sink. She smiled at me, but her eyes had pity in them.

"You must be the daughter," she said. "Your dad said you were coming."

"Yeah. I told him to take a day or two off. He's going to wear himself out."

"He's really been faithful. I see him almost every day I'm here."

She walked over to the bed and touched my mother's arm. "Mrs. Tilghman. I have your pills for you."

Mom opened her eyes and looked at me. "Your daughter's here," the nurse said. I tried to smile. The nurse put the pills in her mouth and gave her some water. She coughed violently. I felt like looking away, but I didn't.

"She's been having a hard time swallowing lately," the nurse said, smoothing back Mom's hair. "We give as much as we can through the IV, but there are a few pills she still has to take."

The nurse rearranged the pillows, then turned to me. "Do you want anything to eat?"

"No, thanks," I whispered. I knew then it was even worse than I'd thought. Hospital workers never offered visitors something to eat when the patient was going to get better. You can just hop on down to the cafeteria, no big deal, stay out of our way, we have more critical problems to attend to. But now, the nurse was going out of her way to be nice, to show some charity.

That night I stayed until eleven, just sitting there. Sometimes I'd try to talk. I'd think for five minutes about something to say, something just right that would get her interest and make her feel better—about Rishi trimming the azaleas right before they were supposed to bloom, about the new bakery on the corner that made the best cinnamon rolls (other than hers, of course), about how our cat loved to sleep in the clean clothes basket. I meant for these stories to put her in touch with the world outside the hospital, but they all sounded hollow. After a while, I gave up. When it was time to leave, I touched her arm. "Good-bye, Mom," I said, forcing a smile. "I'll be back first thing in the morning."

She looked at me intently, desperately, perhaps. "I hope you sleep well," I said. "I'm staying right across the street. I'll be here first thing."

She closed her eyes. I thought about spending the night, and I guess I should have. I didn't get any sleep.

The next morning, things were different. There was another nurse, young and energetic. The sun was shining, and a bird was singing its heart out on a blossoming willow branch just outside the window. Mom woke up as soon as I came in the room.

"Hi, Sweetie," she said. Her voice was thin and tired, but basically the same as always. I felt an immense flood of relief.

"Hi, Mom. I'm glad you're feeling better today." I sat down in the chair.

"Have you eaten?" she asked.

"I had something at the hotel. They have a breakfast bar."

"Oh . . . a breakfast bar." She shut her eyes and drifted to sleep. I looked at a magazine. Eventually, the nurse came back in.

"I don't want to disturb her. I'm just changing the IV," she said, hooking up a plastic bag. "My name's Cindy. I don't think I've met you."

"I'm Caroline. Her daughter."

"I didn't know she had another daughter," the nurse said. "I've met your sister."

"I don't have a sister."

"Oh . . . she has black hair. Came last weekend when I worked."

"Gail."

"That's it."

"She's my cousin," I said.

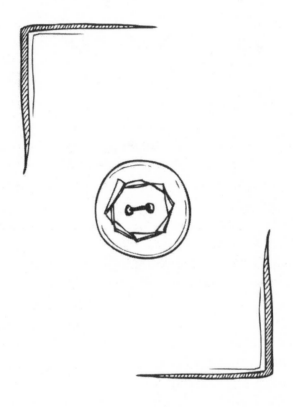

Still Water

Eastern Shore of Maryland, 1980

THROUGH THE FRAME OF THE CAMERA, the water looked like
Daubigny's paintings of the river Oise. Darkly smooth, with
spots of evening light and yellowing grass along the edge. From
some angles, it could even be Monet. There was water like this
all over the peninsula, wetlands hugging the roadsides, marshes
among the farmers' fields, peaceful ponds beside the houses. It
was a land of water unlike anything Gail had known before.

Funny, she had never thought that the water might be deep.

Gail adjusted the zoom and stared through the camera again,
this time including the banged-up white diving boat with its
middle-aged driver. The photo should look sinister, she thought,
like Doré's illustrations for *Rime of the Ancient Mariner*, but no
matter how many adjustments she made, the water still seemed
beautiful. She looked at her watch. She needed to finish here
and drive to Henson to write the story. There was never enough
time for the photos.

She focused again and forced herself to click the shutter. She
took two more and turned abruptly away. The tow trucks and
policemen were still there, lights flashing, radios squawking in
and out, diesel engines spewing fumes into the air. Beyond

them, Sandra Davis, the woman whose car had slid into the swamp, was standing with her husband, biting her nails.

Gail heard a sharp clank and saw the dripping hulk of a rusted car being pulled onto the tow truck. The mud on the cars gave off an offensive odor that mingled with the swampy smell and almost choked her. She felt a coldness travel down her body, turned away quickly, and walked toward the police. Her stomach knotted up at the thought of interrupting them. This was the part of the job she didn't like. Taking the pictures was great, writing the stories she didn't mind, doing feature interviews was kind of interesting. But talking to firemen, going to the courts, interrupting policemen . . . those things she never felt comfortable doing.

She noticed one of the three policemen looking at her as she walked. He was probably twenty-four, about her age, with hair so closely cropped she could barely tell it had a hint of red to it. Even though it was still cool, he wore short sleeves, which showed the outlines of his arm muscles. He stood straight and silent, his strength reaching out and touching something inside her.

The other two stopped talking when she got near and waited for her to speak. She always hesitated a moment before asking a question. She didn't know why she did this. Mike, the other reporter, didn't do it. He just started asking without a, "hello" or, "excuse me" or anything. She'd tried doing that, but it never seemed to work for her.

She pulled out her pen and forced some words from her mouth. "I'm Gail Sommers with the *Star* . . . if you have a few minutes, I'd like to go over a couple of things."

She'd met the oldest man, Deputy Welsh, a couple of times before. He nodded his head. The other two watched.

"Okay . . . let me just verify what I have." She hesitated again, but they didn't say anything. "Three days ago, Sandra Davis lost control of her car on the curve back there and went into the water. She got out without being hurt, but when the tow truck went to pull her car out, they got another one instead."

"Right," Deputy Welsh said. "They pulled out three cars before they got hers, so we called in some divers to see what else is down there. We now know there's at least three more."

"Do you think they're from previous accidents?"

"Don't know yet. I'd say from the looks of the first two, somebody just dumped them here. The wife probably got tired of looking at them in the yard, so they disappeared in the middle of the night. Convenient spot for a lot of folks around here who don't feel like making it to the dump."

"Right." Gail wrote quickly, feeling a little disappointed. She'd probably overreacted when she called Mr. DeKay in Henson to tell him about the story. She felt this was her chance to prove herself to him.

Why she'd taken this job she didn't know. Maybe because it let her take pictures. Real pictures, not some artificial collage of images. Maybe because it enabled her to be on her own for once. A chance to try and figure out what she wanted. Maybe some of both, but whatever the reason, the last six months had been harder than she'd expected. She and Mike ran the *Star*, a tiny Manaset County weekly owned by a larger paper, the *Chronicle-News*, in Henson, about an hour away. The two of them did everything except sell advertising, and she was very, very tired. Every Tuesday, they went to Henson to finish stories, help the copy desk with the layout, and proof everything. Gail had to borrow a desk and always felt as if she were intruding on everyone else's territory. Occasionally, though, she'd get lucky and a story or picture would be significant or good enough to run in the *Chronicle-News* itself. So far, these stories had always run on the inside.

"Talk to the police and the towing people," Mr. DeKay had told her over the phone. "Ask them how those cars got in the water without anybody knowing about it. See if they might be involved in any crimes in the area. And don't forget to talk to some of the local people who drive on that road. If the police don't want to talk, tell them it's a matter of public record. Okay? And try to get over here by six so you'll have plenty of time."

Mike, who'd been at the paper for two years and had the title of Editor, was on vacation, or he would have been the one covering this story. Gail tended to get the stories Mike didn't want or didn't have time for—the recipe contests, quilting bees, 4-H projects and other minutiae of rural life. Secretly, these things fascinated Gail. The way people shared their domesticity so openly, told her their stories, let her camera into their homes . . . it was all humbling in a way she couldn't explain. She had once shot three whole rolls of film photographing jars of canned vegetables sitting on the shelves in Mrs. Sarah Eblen's carport. She became lost among the colors of the corn, beans, pickles, chow chow, peas, and beets, topped with cheerful fabric and lit from behind by the dusty afternoon sun. When she finally packed her bags and made it back to the office, Mike hit the roof. And she'd told him about only one roll.

Gail tried to think of something else to ask Deputy Welsh when one of the divers surfaced and waved his hand. "Excuse me," Deputy Welsh said without looking at her. Gail watched the three men walk closer to the water, sensing that something was happening, but not knowing what to do about it.

She flipped a page in her notebook and walked over to the Davises, a skinny couple in their late forties.

"I'm Gail with the *Star*," she said, holding out her hand. "Sorry about your accident. How are you feeling?"

"I'm fine." Mrs. Davis' voice was shaky and her eyes were bloodshot. "I just scraped my side a bit getting out."

Her husband was staring at the diving operation. "I wonder what they're so excited about."

The divers got back in the boat and rode closer to shore. Gail watched them talk intently with Deputy Welsh, pointing and drawing diagrams with their hands. She sensed a heaviness spreading out from them, a foreboding creeping toward her. The Davises were silent as they watched. Gradually, Gail realized Mrs. Davis was crying. Tears oozed out of the corners of her eyes and under her glass rims till she brushed them away with the palm of her hand.

"Here," Gail said, handing her a tissue pack from her purse.

Mrs. Davis took a tissue and wiped her face, but the tears kept coming.

"You can't imagine how fast the water can pour into a car," she said in a thin, forced voice. "The door wouldn't open until it was almost full, and it was so cold. I barely got out. That could be me down there."

"We don't know there's anybody down there," her husband said, not taking his gaze off the water.

"Look at them! They've found something besides another car. You know they have."

The three of them stood silently, watching as the boat went back to the middle of the water, then stopped and waited while a diver made adjustments on his suit. What's taking them so long? Gail thought, twirling the button on her jacket, fighting back an urge to squirm or run or do anything but just stand there watching. The sun, which had been shining across the water, set quickly, leaving everything in a twilight gray.

Finally, the diver sat on the edge of the boat and simply fell backward into the water. Gail sensed the presence of an unnamable and shapeless being creeping up behind her. She knew that when she turned around, she wouldn't see anything, but the sense of it was so close she couldn't help but look. Forcing herself to move slowly, she turned around and stared at the road, where there was nothing. On the horizon, shafts of rosy warmth spread across the sky. She breathed in and out, sending her breath upward, feeling calm return.

"Look!" Mr. Davis said. "He's back up already."

Gail turned back to the water. The diver had climbed back in the boat, and the driver started up the engine and revved to shore. The men huddled with the police and the tow truck driver. Gail talked to Mrs. Davis, writing notes carefully in her notebook, watching the men out of the corner of her eye. Finally, as darkness and cold began to take over, Deputy Welsh walked over.

"Well, we're going to wrap it up here for today," he said in an authoritative voice. "It's too dark to continue."

"What'd they find?" Mr. Davis asked.

Deputy Welsh was quiet for a moment, looking at Gail directly. "Well, it looks as if there were nine cars down there total. Like I said before, most of them were probably dumped, but we won't know for sure till tomorrow."

Mr. Davis seemed to get angry. "That curve is a hazard. There's no guardrail, no signs. No telling how many accidents have happened here."

Deputy Welsh remained calm. "I agree it is dangerous. We've asked for guardrails for here and other places that are just as bad. I'll call the county in the morning, and in the meantime, we'll have flares up and Deputy Morrow will stay here overnight. The towing company is taking your car in now, so there's nothing else to do at the moment."

"Well, I think it's a sad state of affairs when my wife has to go in the water before we get guard rails up on a hairpin curve."

"Come on, Tommy. I want to go." Mrs. Davis started walking toward the truck, then stopped and looked at her husband. "Come on. It's cold."

Mr. Davis hesitated a few seconds, then walked to the truck. Deputy Welsh turned toward Gail. They stood silently a few moments before he finally asked, "Now, is there anything else you need?"

Gail fumbled through her notes and went over the details, the questions Mr. DeKay had told her to ask. She tried to sound professional, got all the facts and names and times, but she couldn't make herself ask the one obvious question. Welsh wouldn't answer at this point, of course, but she knew she should ask anyway.

Finally, she closed her notebook and looked around. It was almost completely dark now, with spots of light coming from the flares on the road and the flashlights and police car head-lights. The unvoiced question surrounded them.

Deputy Welsh answered it, surprising Gail with the gentle-ness in his voice. "It was really too dark for them to know any-thing for sure, but I'm going to go back and check old missing persons reports. We'll all just have to wait until morning."

"Thank you," Gail said quietly, shaking his hand.

She got in her car and drove, cautiously, to Henson, parking in a gravel lot behind the two-story brick building with the old-fashioned masthead sign. The *Chronicle-News*, it declared, making passersby take notice. She walked up the dusty stairwell and stepped into the noisy confusion of a newsroom three hours before deadline.

Gail left her camera in the photography department, then sat at the TV editor's desk and began writing.

MANASET—Still water runs deep, the people of this rural community have discovered after Sandra Davis's Ford Fairmont went off a curve on Route 12 and slid into the surrounding wetlands.

All around her, people were coming in from assignments and settling down to write. Energy seemed to rise out of the floor and into the air to be inhaled along with stale cigarette smoke and burned coffee. It smelled good. She lost herself in the story, immersed in following the path of the words leading a luminescent green trail across the computer monitor. Her cheeks flushed, and she became oblivious to the particulars of what was going on around her, in tune only with the general atmosphere. When Robert Brackett touched her on the shoulder, she jumped.

"Sorry, Gail," he said, with a little smile. "I've been trying to get your attention. I've got the negatives ready if you want to see them."

Robert was a tall, skinny kid a year or two out of college who had been a photographer at the *Chronicle-News* a few months longer than Gail had been working there. She liked him because he seemed to enjoy what he did without being overly impressed with himself, and he often praised her photographs with obvious honesty. She'd never gotten any feedback from Mike, just silent nods or, at most, "Okay."

She followed Robert back to the photography department, went through the light trap and walked into the darkroom. She always felt privileged when she was invited here, as if she were entering some private club where important decisions were made and deals cut. The red light made her think of prostitutes in feather boas, an image furthered by the cheesecake pictures that were tacked to the wall along with the other pictures. Negatives hung from a clothesline like nylons drying in the fresh air.

Robert opened up the little refrigerator where they kept film and pulled out two Cokes.

"Think fast!" he said. He tossed her one, which she was able to catch with one hand.

"Thanks. How did the photos come out?"

"Pretty good, I think. Have a look."

Gail picked up the loupe and bent over the light table. The first set of negatives were close-ups of the three cars that had been pulled out of the water and then stacked against each other in the mud. The reversed black-and-white images had an other-worldly quality to them, as if they were from an unknown moon of an unknown planet.

"Those are kind of interesting," Gail said.

She turned to the second set of negatives, which were overall shots of the scene—the divers, the sheriff, onlookers, cars. The final set were close-ups of the divers. In one, a diver was stand-ing in water about chest deep, pulling his mask away from his face to let the water drain out. Behind him was a clump of sea grass and the three mangled cars, which, from the angle, ap-peared larger than life. As Gail stared at the photo, she felt the shapeless thing forming behind her again. She felt her breath come faster and faster and tried to focus on the picture. Robert had walked over to the other bench and was hanging some more photos on the line, softly humming Eric Clapton tunes as he worked.

Gail stood up, deliberately putting the loupe down, trying not to look behind her toward the light trap. She crossed her arms around her tightly.

Robert stopped humming and looked at her. "Did you see the one of the diver in front of the cars? That's my pick. It has that nice swamp-monster quality. Creature from the Black La-goon. You do good work, if I do say so myself."

Gail didn't say anything, hoping Robert's spoken words would banish the shapeless thing. He looked at her for a mo-ment, hung another picture—school children holding a giant replica of a check—then turned around.

"Are you okay?"

Gail tried to smile, nodded her head slowly. "Yeah . . . sorry. It's been a long day."

"'Cause you were really zoned out there for a minute." He continued to look at her. "Wrecks aren't my favorite thing to cover, either."

"No. No. It's not that," she began. Robert said nothing, continuing to pull black-and-white photos out of the liquid—a speaker at a civic club, a little boy leading a goat, the raising of the new flagpole at city hall. Gradually, as she watched the normal, mundane parade of images, Gail felt the formless thing retreat. Robert picked up a towel and wiped off his hands.

"I remember this one wreck out beyond Milkins," he said, grabbing a package of Oreos from a darkened shelf. "I couldn't sleep for three nights. Still happens to me sometimes. Here, have a cookie. You shouldn't skip supper, you know."

Gail smiled, taking a cookie and sitting on a stool. "Thanks for looking out for me. I've got to get back soon."

"Yeah, I know, nose to the grindstone and all that. Do you have a preference for the photo? Not that it really matters, but I like to make suggestions when I turn them over to Kathy."

"Actually, I think the diver with the cars is the best, too. Has an interesting focus."

She got off the stool to leave, turning toward the light trap.

"The wreck isn't what bothered me," she said without looking at Robert. "My father died in a diving accident when I was eight, and it was a little weird looking at those pictures, especially in black and white. It makes them look older, you know what I mean?"

The room was silent except for the electric hum of the clock.

"I'm sorry," Robert said. "That's a totally unfair thing to happen to a kid."

"It is, but I can honestly say I never thought life was going to be fair." Gail laughed, sneaking a sideways glance at him. "I guess I can thank my mother for that bit of wisdom. You know how it's so hard for kids to finally realize they're not the center of the universe? Well, I never had that problem. Oh well, I guess I should be thankful I had a safe childhood, nobody ever tried to hurt me, I always had a house to go to over the holidays. You follow a few court cases and you realize how lucky you are."

"That's true," Robert said softly.

"Well, I've got to go . . . back to the cold, cruel world."

"Take it easy, Gail."

She entered the light again, blinking a few seconds before heading back to the newsroom, trying to pick up the rhythm of her story.

> Deputy Welsh would not comment on the possibility that there were bodies in some of the cars; however, he did note that the Sheriff's Department would be checking missing persons reports from around the country and would be looking into local cases as well.
>
> "We're not ruling anything out," Welsh said.
>
> Helen Craft, who lives a few miles from where the cars were found, said she has had trouble driving around the curve herself.
>
> "It gets real slick when it's wet," Mrs. Craft said. "I've skidded on that curve a lot, and I know I'm not the only one. There'll be fresh tire marks there every few days."
>
> Welsh said there were no previous reports about accidents at that particular spot.
>
> "In our area there are a lot of curves like this where the water is close to the road," he said.

"People should keep in mind that often the water is deeper than it appears."

Somehow, Gail couldn't connect to the energy in the room anymore. The words no longer formed a path, but darted here and there without connection to one another, as if skittish of something on the horizon. Gail sighed, realizing she was not only tired but hungry. The Coke and Oreo hadn't helped, and the aroma of microwave popcorn coming from the sports desk was almost nauseating. If she could get done with this story soon, maybe she could sneak out for supper at the cafeteria across the street before it closed. What she really wanted was something embarrassingly old-fashioned, like the meat loaf and mashed potatoes with green peas and carrots her Aunt Emmy used to make. The cafeteria wasn't nearly that good, but it was the best she could do at the moment. She tried to tie down the remaining pieces:

"There are still five cars down there, but it's getting too dark to finish examining them under water, so we'll wait until tomorrow to finish up and retrieve them," Deputy Welsh said. "The divers will be back at 7:00 a.m. and we'll have a patrol on the site until then."

Jay Myers, one of the divers from Henson Aquatics, said the water was too dark to make out much about the remaining cars.

"There is a deeper section of water very close to the road and most of them are in that area," he said. "Beyond that, it's too dark to see a whole lot."

Meanwhile, Mrs. Craft said she might have

trouble sleeping tonight.

"I think of all those times I drove around that curve and could have gone in too," she said. "And to think of those cars down there without anybody knowing about it . . . that just gives me the creeps."

Gail read the story carefully, not knowing whether it was good or bad, just glad that it was over. She turned it over to the *Chronicle-News* copy desk and went out for supper. When she came back, she helped lay out the *Star*, sizing bride's photographs and writing headlines. She was no longer hungry, and she'd reconciled herself to the tiredness.

She left about ten thirty. The night was perfectly still, with an almost-full moon. Did that mean it was time to plant or not? The farmers here followed some sort of rule, but she couldn't remember it.

She stopped at the bend in the road where the deputies had placed flares and a barricade. The same deputy she'd noticed in the afternoon got out of his car and walked toward her, his silhouette hinting of power.

Gail got out of her car, driven by something she couldn't name. "Hi. I just wanted to look at the scene in the dark, if that's okay with you."

Deputy Morrow stood close, staring at her. She stared back, sensing the shapeless being and something else surrounding her. Finally, he stepped aside. "Be my guest," he said, continuing to watch her closely.

Gail walked to the edge of the road. Light from the moon highlighted faint ripples that slowly traveled across the surface until they touched the tall grass and disappeared. The only sound was the rhythmic tones of the frogs and insects. She slowly breathed in the briny air and closed her eyes. It was all so peaceful, like a lullaby on a summer evening.

She opened her eyes again and stared at the black water in the moonlight. It spread out in all directions below the road. It was shapeless, but beautiful too. A quiet blackness reflecting the moon. A soft wetness like a puddle after a spring rain.

Gail glanced at the three cars that had been pulled from the water and now seemed to cower in the shadows. What else was on the bottom, waiting for morning to be pulled from the water, to have all its secrets exposed in the sunlight? Maybe there were people who had been murdered lying down there, stuffed into a car trunk as she had been imagining all afternoon. But no, now that she was here in the darkness she couldn't believe it. Surely there would be some sign, an uneasiness about the place, but there was nothing. Everything was calm, beautiful.

More likely, there were lost family members who had been given up long ago. People who had ventured off the interstate for a scenic route through the tidewater county to see the marshlands, the wide fields and old wooden homes. They weren't used to the narrow roads and the water so near and quietly slipped off the asphalt and sank before anyone went by. The expanding circles of water had long since erased the panic of their last moments and now they rested in the soft cradle of the muddy bottom.

"Hey! What are you doing?" A sharp voice broke into her thoughts. Deputy Morrow ran down to the water and grabbed Gail's arm. She looked down and realized she had stepped into the water and was walking out into the blackness.

"God, I'm sorry. I . . ." She didn't know what to say, really. "I thought I might have seen something, but I was wrong." He was looking at her strangely. "I'll just get out of your way now."

Gail hurried back toward her car, feeling her face burn with embarrassment, her arm hurt from his strong grasp. Deputy Morrow went back to his patrol car. She hoped he hadn't gotten wet.

She started the car and drove off, watching the headlights cut through the gathering fog, listening to the engine run. She drove without thinking along the flat curving roads, glancing from time to time at the moon. What was it you were supposed to do? Look over your left shoulder and make a wish? She couldn't remember, but the calmness she had felt earlier slowly returned.

The water still glowed in the moonlight. It was unfathomable, she thought. Yes, that was the right word. Unfathomable— the peace, the hidden depths, the dark water lapping softly all around. She felt that the mystery itself was here, a palpable presence in the air. She wished it could stay that way.

Driving home, the moon seemed to follow her, appearing in the mirror every time she glanced back, then coming up above the road as she rounded a curve. The newspaper was forgotten. She had no thoughts of tomorrow. Instead, words she had memorized many years ago filled her mind, their rhymes echoing above the silence of the dark, narrow road:

Full fathom five thy father lies,
Of his bones are coral made:
Those are pearls that were his eyes:
Nothing of him that doth fade,
But doth suffer a sea-change
Into something rich and strange.

My Favorite from College

I PUT DOWN GAIL'S BUTTON and search for one of my own. I smile when I find the blue-gray button with the crackled lines.

In college, I had a dusty blue silk blouse that I loved. I wore it on those occasions when I needed all the confidence I could get, when everything had to be just right. Not too formal, not too preppy, not too sloppy, not too dowdy, not too big or little, not too anything. It felt great, and it worked with jeans or with a tight black skirt. Mom liked it, too—it was one of the few pieces of clothing we agreed on. That's why I wore it to see her during that last hospital stay.

Sitting by her bed as the clock moved slowly toward noon, I discovered that the morning improvement didn't last long. Around ten o'clock, she started to get restless. I got a paper towel from the sink and put it on her forehead. It smelled like wet cardboard. She opened her eyes. "Does that feel good?" I asked.

She pulled the oxygen mask aside and looked at me. "Caroline," she whispered. "I need something."

I rang for Cindy. "She needs something for pain," I said. I felt out of breath.

Cindy frowned and looked at the chart. "According to the doctor's orders, I can't give her anything until eleven o'clock.

214

Let's try to turn her. Sometimes that helps. You get on the other side."

Willing to do anything that might make Mom feel better, I helped Cindy roll Mom's tiny, birdlike body. Cindy rearranged the pillows and pulled the covers up. "There. We'll see if that helps."

"Is that any better?" I asked.

Mom didn't open her eyes, but whispered. "Maybe. A little bit." I knew it wasn't. I looked at the clock. Forty minutes until eleven o'clock. I walked around the room.

"Do you want me to wipe your face again?"

She shook her head. Her teeth were clenched. Thirty-five minutes.

"How about I rub your back?"

"No."

"I can see what's on TV."

She opened her eyes and looked at me. "Caroline," she said in the strongest voice I'd heard yet. "Please just leave me alone."

I knew better than to have my feelings hurt, but I felt as if I'd been punched in the stomach. I sat down, dazed, and watched the clock inch its way toward eleven. I wondered how my earlier optimism could have vanished so completely. At five till, I called Cindy again.

She injected something into the IV, a disconcerted look on her face. "It always makes people so sleepy," she whispered. "I hate knocking out patients like that. It takes a while for it to kick in, though, so you should have some more visiting time."

Right, as if we were having tea or walking in the park. It took thirty minutes longer before I noticed any change.

"Here's lunch," a chirpy voice called out. A young aide wearing scrubs with a wild tropical bird pattern came in the room. "Where do you want it?" she asked.

I cleared a place on the bed stand for her. She set it down and left.

"Mom, do you want lunch now, or would you like to wait a few minutes?"

Quiet. She was out of it, finally. I lifted up the tray and stared at the contents: meat loaf, potatoes drowning in brown, waxy gravy, mushy carrots, a misshapen white roll, a brownie for dessert. An unbidden joke came to mind: never eat meat loaf unless your mom made it. At first I laughed inside but after a second or two I could feel the gears switch and I was crying inside. And then I was actually crying, standing there staring at that pathetic meat loaf with tears spilling over the corners of my eyes and my nose seeping. It's funny what will set you off sometimes.

"Caroline."

My dad's voice. Wouldn't you know the one time I lose it, someone walks in and catches me? I rubbed my face and then made a show about cutting up the meat loaf.

"Hey, Dad," I said, trying to sound chirpy like the aide who'd brought the tray. "She's not hungry now, but I thought I'd cut the food up in case she changes her mind."

He walked over and squeezed my shoulder, then he leaned over Mom, took her hand and kissed it. "Hello, precious one," he whispered. She didn't say anything, but I swore I could see her relax and kind of turn toward him the least bit. I could feel my throat tightening up again. I went to the sink and drank a cup of water, took a deep breath, stared in the mirror for a few seconds.

"Dad, you should have stayed home and rested," I said, pulling up the other chair. "I'm here for the weekend. You need a break."

"I rested last night. Did you have a good visit?"

"She was kind of out of it last night, but this morning we talked a little. She ate breakfast, I think."

"Early morning is usually the best. The medication makes her a little loopy, but she's fairly alert till that second dose at eleven."

He was speaking mechanically, as if reciting something memorized as a child.

"Then she sleeps most of the afternoon. Late afternoon is the worst. Sometimes you have to get them to call the doctors to approve an extra dose for break-through pain, but if she gets that and the eight o'clock dose, she'll usually sleep through the night and have a decent morning."

"God, Dad. How long has this been going on?"

"But I think they're going to start her on a pump today, and maybe that will help."

His voice had a strange flatness to it I had never heard before. He wasn't looking at me. He was staring at her.

"What about when she goes home?"

Then he did look at me, a look I hadn't seen in a long time, full of some knowledge that was beyond me. He smiled. "You know what? She's going to sleep for a while now. Why don't we go out for a bit?"

Walking out the doors to the courtyard, I felt the spring breeze cool on my face. I'd only been in the hospital a few hours, but already it was hard to believe the world outside was still carrying on with spring. Flowers opening. Birds singing. Bees buzzing.

We found a bench in the sunlight and sat down.

"You know," he began, then stopped. That's always a bad sign, when someone starts out that way. No one ever says, "You know . . . things are going so swimmingly that at this rate all our problems should be solved within a month."

And besides, I did know. I just didn't want to hear it out loud.

He squeezed my knee. "You know, this last chemo session didn't go very well. It was really, really rough. Dr. Ellis spoke to me and said he feels that it's not providing any benefit at this point. That it's detrimental, in fact. So we're not going to do it anymore."

"What are they going to do then? Radiation again?"

He was quiet. A squirrel ran by and jumped into a dogwood tree.

"Right now, Caroline, we're just going to do everything we can to make her comfortable. There aren't any more treatment options."

He took a deep breath, then spoke in a definite voice. "Dr. Ellis thinks she might make it another few weeks, but she has to stabilize a little more before we can take her home. I don't want to move her if we can't keep her comfortable."

I was surprisingly dry-eyed. I wondered if Dad thought I was callous.

"Have you told Hank?" I asked.

"I called him last night. I knew I'd be seeing you today or else I would have called you. I called Gail, too. She's been coming a lot."

"So I hear."

"Sorry I didn't make it last night to meet you." His voice was beginning to tighten up. "I just couldn't right then. Making those phone calls was all I could do."

He looked away. I thought about my dad sitting in the house alone, watching it get dark outside. I felt a heaviness settle over me. We sat there a little longer, that weight getting heavier and heavier.

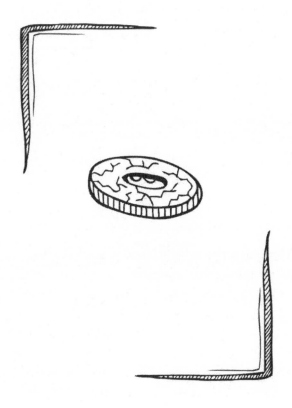

Truth or Dare

Ashton Mill, N.C. 1983

"OKAY, CAROLINE, YOUR TURN."

I watched tiny bubbles rising in the crystal champagne flute in my hand. They reflected the light from the massive chandelier in the Holladays' dining room, creating hundreds of sparkling spheres. I took a sip, even though I could feel the pleasant light-headedness starting to intensify.

"Caroline . . ." Lauren nudged me with her foot. It struck me as odd that we were the only two people in this gorgeous—and I mean *gorgeous*—mansion on New Year's Eve, sipping Dom Pérignon over re-heated shrimp scampi, listening to rhythm and blues piping over the stereo. The combination of circumstances—the light, the champagne, the stereo—seemed so strange that I resolved to tell the truth.

"Well . . . mine is kind of unconventional." I took another sip of champagne.

"Come on, Caroline. I told you, didn't I?"

"I know, but this is different." I hadn't played Truth or Dare since I was in middle school. Even then, it had seemed like a stupid game to play, and I couldn't understand why I felt compelled to make this confession all of a sudden. But I did. I set

220

the champagne glass down and took a breath. "Okay, okay. Here goes. About a year and a half ago, our neighbor died. I had known him since I was three years old. Our families grew up together—you might know his son, Bill Allen? He was a friend of my brother's. Anyway, Mr. Allen got cancer. I saw him once before he died when I took over a casserole my mom had made—he was so thin and frail, like a skeleton, but he still smiled when he saw me. He said, 'So, have you been fishing lately?' He used to take me and my brother and Bill fishing down at Jackson Pond. He loved doing things like that. It was like he would be the last person you'd think of dying."

I stopped for a minute and took another sip of champagne. I couldn't tell what Lauren was thinking, but then, I didn't really know her that well. We'd had a few classes together in high school but that was about it. She had been one of the golden girls I pretended to despise, with shining auburn hair and clothes that made you think, in spite of yourself, "It would be nice to have a jacket like that." Or a pair of pants. Or boots. Or a blouse. Not that they were at all opulent. They were simply perfect.

"It made me sad to see him suffering, but I didn't really think about it that much. I had a summer job during the day, and I'd go running in the evening, hang out at night. I just put it out of my head until suddenly he was dead and we were at the funeral home."

I could really feel the champagne. I was passing through that wonderfully relaxed, floating sensation where everything seemed brighter and bigger than it really was. In this case, it was hard to tell—the Holladays' house really was bigger and brighter. At least it was bigger and brighter than any house I'd ever been in.

"Yeah?" Lauren seemed bored. But then, she must get bored easily, I thought. The rest of her family had left the day after Christmas to go skiing at their ranch in Wyoming, but she was tired of doing that every year. She'd explained it to me when we ran into each other at the gym: "Every Christmas we're rushing around getting ready and then we're there for ten days, and it is totally beautiful and everything, but I mean, how many times do you want to ski? And the only other thing is to go into Yellowstone and snowshoe or maybe look for elk. So I decided to stick around here and see what was going on."

Not a whole lot, I thought as I drained my glass, then tried to hold in a burp that immediately rose to the back of my throat.

"So . . . my parents and I went to the visitation at the funeral home. A lot of people were there—everybody liked him a lot. I hadn't been to a funeral since I was a kid, so I was checking it all out. Kind of like the first time you go to a wedding shower you notice every little thing—the napkins, the cake, the gifts that people bring. So I noticed the greeters when we came to the building and the burgundy guest book we signed and how there were several different parlors so they put the names of the dead people up on one of those black signs with removable letters. It said, 'Jones . . . the Maple Room; Allen . . . the Magnolia Room.' Like you were at a hotel convention or something. The Convention for Dead People and Their Friends."

I started laughing at the thought. Lauren laughed, too. She had a nice, easygoing laugh that made you feel comfortable. I'd discovered this over the past couple of weeks that we'd been hanging around together. It was unlikely for us to be friends, I admit. I mean, here I was majoring in computer science at Georgia Tech, a geek, basically, while she was studying international marketing at Vanderbilt. I guess it was just one of those things you do when you're home from college, trying to figure out who you are. I guess Lauren was doing the same thing.

"We went into the room . . . the Magnolia Room . . . and I got a little panicky all of a sudden. I never know what to do when someone's really upset. I mean, what can you do? We were waiting in line to see the family and I looked around and there was a little side room with the casket in it. And my dad said, "Let's go say goodbye to Joseph." My mom was crying in a Kleenex—they actually had boxes of Kleenex set out on the furniture—and my dad put one arm around her and one around me and walked us over to the casket."

"Wait a second, Caroline," Lauren poured the last two or three drops of champagne. "Time for reinforcements." She grabbed another bottle we had retrieved from a wine rack in the basement, shook it up, and, aiming at the far wall, folded back the wire and released the cork.

"Whoa! That was great," she said after the cork had popped ten feet or more, spewing a comet's tail of bubbles onto the lace tablecloth, the Persian carpet, the silk upholstered chairs. Lauren was laughing again. "Oh no . . . Olga's going to kill me." She made futile dabs at the eruption with her linen napkin. "That's the maid. I told her there wouldn't be much of a mess this week since everybody's gone. Oh well, maybe I can clean some of it up tomorrow. It's not like this is the first time champagne's been spilled in this room."

She sat back down and refilled the glasses. "I'm sorry," she said, trying not to laugh. "Go on. Please."

I didn't feel like going on, but it was too late now.

"Well, we walked over to the coffin, and it was really bizarre. I had never seen a dead person before. And here was Mr. Allen who had been alive just days ago, and now he was dead."

Lauren laughed. "That's not terribly profound, Caroline."

"I know." Now the irony of using her as my confessor somehow gave me momentum, an urge to keep talking. "I can't explain it exactly. He was laying there, his body completely wasted. I mean, the flesh had just fallen off his bones, and he had been so vibrant before. But anyway, I was trying to act respectful and somber and everything and trying to ignore the fact that he looked terrible, and I was wondering why he'd wanted to have an open casket. He'd helped plan the service—I heard my mom talking about it. I mean, why would you do something like that?"

Lauren stared at her glass for a moment. She seemed to have lost interest.

"Then we were all standing there looking at him, not saying anything. What are you supposed to say, anyway? Are you supposed to touch them? Pat their hands? Say goodbye? But we didn't say anything, except my mom whispered, 'Poor Joseph.' And suddenly it was like I was possessed or something."

I stopped. I wasn't saying what I meant.

"What did you do?"

"It was as if there was another person inside me. I got this unbearable urge to laugh out loud, to poke my dad in the ribs and say, 'Yikes! He moved.' You know, make a big joke out of it all. I know that doesn't sound like a big deal, but what was so odd was that I really felt a battle going on inside me. I mean physically—I could feel my lips starting to smile, my hand going out to poke my dad.

"One part of me was saying, 'Stay cool. Stay cool.' And the other part was screaming, 'He doesn't care. He's dead. Have a little fun, for Christ's sake.' And I honestly didn't know which side would win, it was so close. Then my dad took my arm and we turned around, and I saw Mrs. Allen staring right at me and I thought, 'Oh my God, she knows. There's no way I can face her.'"

I finished the glass. I was starting to feel a little queasy, but I felt better, too. At least I'd tried to explain.

"So then what did you do?"

"Well, I realized she didn't really know. I don't think I had a smirk on my face or anything, but I was almost shaking because I'd come so close to losing it. We waited in line for a few more minutes, then we shook hands with Mrs. Allen and all the family. I didn't say much, but they were all very gracious."

We sat silently for a few minutes. Lauren stared at me, then started laughing.

"You bitch," she finally said.

"What?"

"I told you about shoplifting a hundred-dollar bottle of perfume from Keller's Pharmacy, and you tell me about something you didn't even do? Something you just thought about doing?"

"I knew you wouldn't understand, but that's it. Total honesty. My true confession."

I don't know why I felt a need to interpret for her. "The thing is, I had no control over it. It was pure luck that I didn't jump up on top of the coffin and start telling dirty jokes or something. It was terrifying. I mean, what if there's something wrong with me? Something that hasn't come out completely, but is just waiting for the right moment?"

I stopped for a minute, trying to clear my head. "You know, my mom tells this story about when my grandfather died. I was about four or five years old. Anyway, the day of the funeral I was a holy terror, running around the house, breaking things, getting in fights. That's not normal, is it?"

"Oh, come on. A lot of people laugh when they're uncomfortable. My sister does it all the time. And funerals are about as uncomfortable as it gets. Tell me something real, something really shameful."

"Well, I suppose I could tell you about the time I did it with Jimmy Barnett when my parents were out of town, and I didn't even like him."

"You mean *the* Jimmy Barnett?"

"Jimmy Barnett, yeah, the one who went to McGregor High."

"Jimmy Barnett, the basketball captain, the president of the Key Club, the most gorgeous guy in school?"

"I guess."

"*Tell me.*"

"There's really nothing to tell, and besides, I don't feel bad about it. Well, a little bit, maybe. We were working on this history project together and . . . I don't know. I didn't dislike him. I mean, he seemed reasonably intelligent and he wasn't too snobbish. We both just let things happen. It was kind of an experiment, I guess you could call it."

"Oh my God. I can't believe this. I had a crush on Jimmy Barnett since third grade, and he never paid any attention to me."

"Well, that's all there was to it. I haven't even thought about it much, but I can't forget that look on Mrs. Allen's face. Every time I see her, I think about how I could have ruined her last memory of her husband. For no reason! Just by being stupid. Stupid. *Stupid!*"

"Caroline, get over it." Lauren was clearly done with the game. "So you almost laughed during a funeral. It's just like when you're a kid at church and you have a giggle fit."

"This is beyond that. This is something sinister, some demon that pipes up, and I never know when it's going to surface or where it comes from or what it's going to tell me to do."

I knew I was babbling, but I couldn't stop.

"It's like you suddenly realize how much power you have . . . drive over the center line, kill a vanload of people. Drop the baby, maim it for life. Laugh during a funeral, break the hearts of an entire family and mortify everyone you know."

I finished my glass. "It's not that one incident, that's what I'm trying to say. The funeral thing . . . that's just a metaphor. The real thing is that I'm always getting this urge to do something outrageous. My mother might say, 'Caroline, why don't you get a perm in your hair to make your face look a little softer,' and instead of getting a perm, I dye it pink, just because she was trying to make me into something I didn't want to be, trying to make me into a new, improved version of herself."

"You dyed your hair pink? Like a punker?"

"It was fairly close to burgundy. Besides, it was wash-out dye—gone in six weeks. I did it right before my cousin Gail came for Thanksgiving." I laughed, remembering the expression on Gail's face. "She's the anti-Caroline. She does everything my mom loves—shopping, wearing the right clothes, dreaming about her future wedding and children. Gag. Gag. Gag."

I was surprised by the ferocity that came out with the words.

Lauren stared at me for a moment, then poured out the rest of the bottle. "It's almost midnight," she said. "Let's turn on the TV."

We went into the den, with its cathedral ceiling and window walls, and turned on the television. Throngs of people in parkas clapped and blew horns and jumped up and down, trying to stay warm.

We were both quiet.

"Right about now my dad is making a toast," Lauren said. "He always ends up by saying, 'And now . . . to the love of my life, my blushing bride, my guardian angel . . . please don't leave me till the kids are grown.' Then, when it's midnight, he picks her up and kisses her. It used to be so embarrassing, but now it seems kind of cool."

Then the ball was falling . . . four . . . three . . . two . . . one . . . The people on television threw confetti and jumped even more enthusiastically. They looked just like the people last year. Maybe they were the same people, gathered together again for this strange ritual.

"Well," I said, raising my glass. "I'm not much for toasts, but happy New Year anyway."

We chinked glasses. "Happy New Year," Lauren said. "May all your demons be exorcised."

Standing up seemed to have made all the bubbles from the champagne rise up inside me. I could feel a wave of nausea following close behind.

"Oh my God, I'm going to be sick."

Lauren grabbed my arm and dragged me toward the bathroom. "Here, here . . . don't do it on the new rug, or Olga really will kill me."

I went in and shut the door—there was no way I was letting Lauren watch me throw up—and I barely got the seat up in time. Then I knelt down and let myself retch everything up into the Holladays' sparkling toilet. Every errant thought. Every stupid impulse. Every mistaken idea . . . like the idea that I could be friends with Lauren Holladay, someone so glossy she could steal from sweet Mr. Keller and think it was just a story to tell. She could just wipe it away, like I was wiping a drop off the burnished Spanish floor tiles, and everything would be as good as new.

Some vomit splattered on my blouse. I tried to blot it out, then I dropped the tissue in the toilet and stared at my watery shadow, lurking like a hurt dog behind the bushes.

I went over to the sink—dark green ceramic with brass hardware. I washed my face with cold water, patted it dry with the monogrammed towels, then sat down on the toilet to stop my head from spinning.

It was completely quiet except for the sound of the heat coming through the shiny air vent. I wondered what Lauren was doing. Watching TV? Talking on the phone? For all I knew, she had left the house.

I put my head in my hands and willed it to be still, but it didn't obey. Instead, it danced maniacally to a song of questions that kept popping into my mind: *What are you doing here? Just who do you think you are? What's wrong with you?*

I didn't have the energy to get up, so I decided I might as well stay put until I figured some things out. I just sat there, listening to those questions, and I kept seeing Lauren's face staring at me, her thick hair curling under just so, her makeup perfect, her cashmere turtleneck bringing out the blue in her eyes. I didn't want to see her, but that's what was in my mind. After a while, her face started to change. The hair turned darker and the cheekbones more defined, and there I was, looking straight at Gail.

It seemed so pathetic that I would've started laughing and crying at the same time except for the fact that my head was pounding. And the really pathetic part was that Lauren and Gail weren't alike at all. Not really. Since this was the night for confessions, I had to admit that.

Gail was elegant and poised, but she also had a basic goodness and decent instincts that I envied. She never blurted out things without thinking, never hurt people's feelings. She was too eager to please, especially with the guys, but deep down I could understand, a little. It wasn't her fault she was like that.

God, it was even possible that Lauren wasn't the devil incarnate either, but I didn't want to think about that. My mind was messed up enough already.

I stood up, washed my face again. Now I could hear the TV blaring—one of the late-night shows with the brash one-liners and prompted laughter. I was relieved, knowing I could walk out of the room and just watch a stupid show for a bit, then leave without losing too much face. Maybe I'd get off easy and never see Lauren again.

I started to open the door, but as I grabbed the shiny knob, I glanced at my reflection. In old movies, doing that always prompted some life-changing revelation, so I thought it might work for me. Couldn't hurt. I stood there in front of the mirror for several minutes, staring at my pale face and bloodshot eyes. Green around the gills, as my friends at Tech would say.

Oh well, I figured, opening the door. Who wants to gain enlightenment in a rich girl's bathroom, anyway?

The Sophisticate

I PLUNGE MY FINGERS IN THE JAR and select a button blindly: it's another one of Gail's. Shiny and black, with a whorl of gold in the center, a single side button from a pair of sleek black pants. She can wear black like nobody I know, except maybe her mother. In those pants, she seemed so slender and yet powerful, too. Confident, even privileged, able to handle anything.

I remember how she often knew exactly what to do when Mom was in the hospital, even when everyone else was floundering. There was one weekend when she and I had both come up, about a week before Mom died. We were taking turns sitting with her, and it was my turn when Mom started squirming and twitching in the bed. I knew the pain—the active, living kind— had taken over again. I couldn't think of anything but the discomfort possessing her like an angry spirit, filling the room, swirling around like a sandstorm.

At that point, I knew enough to call the nurse, to insist on medication right away, to push the limits, but even then, the pain was still there. The nurse, an older woman with an exasperated look on her face, had finally had it with me. "I've called the doctor three times," she said, looking at Mom with a steely expression. "He said he'd review her meds when he does rounds. That's it." And she walked out.

I was too angry to do anything but stand at the foot of the bed, seething. My anger joined the pain and they danced around the room, spinning a web around us both, strangling any good feeling that was left. I forced myself to take slow, deep breaths and then I sat down beside her.

"Mom," I whispered. "I'm still here." I looked out the window. "It's beautiful outside. There's a row of azaleas in full bloom. I bet yours are blooming, too."

She didn't say anything. I turned on the CD Gail had brought—Pachelbel's Canon with nature sounds. I smoothed the covers. I sat down again, and she was staring at me.

"Mom," I said holding her hand. "Do you want me to do anything?"

I didn't expect an answer. To be honest, she hadn't said anything that didn't relate to pain relief in several days, but she looked at me so intently I knew there was something else she wanted.

"I love you, Mom," I said. She nodded, squeezed my hand. That wasn't it.

"Do you want to see Dad?" I asked. She shook her head. "Hank?" She kept staring at me and somehow, even though she didn't speak, I knew what she wanted.

I stood up and went to find Gail.

That was the first time I felt that maniacal collision of anger, jealousy, and panic—a total and overpowering shock that almost exiled sanity from my soul. I was a child in the forest, wandering lost and alone. I knew better. I knew my father and brother were walking with me, but I couldn't sense them in the thick wilderness. I wandered around and around, getting more and more lost, finally giving up and sitting down in the deepest, blackest part, letting the wolves of rage and despair consume me.

After I sent Gail to Mom's room, I went to my car in the parking lot. I sat there in the stale heat and after a while, the tears stopped coming. The wolves retreated into the shadows, and I could wipe my face dry, go back inside. To be honest, I didn't think about it much at the time. I forgave my mom. It's easy to do when someone you love is dying. I was totally okay with her.

But I didn't forgive Gail.

Every time I saw her, the wolves came back.

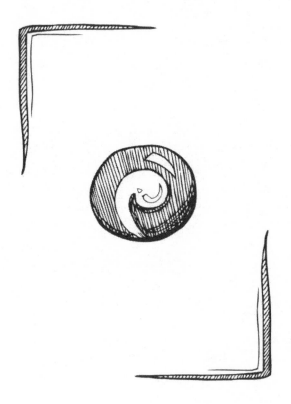

The Crazy Quilt Lady

Greenville County, S.C. 1982

. . . AND THEN I SEEN THE KING in all his glory. He was dressed in white from head to toe and there was a light a shinin' on him and he kindly shimmered all over. He held out his hand to me and said, "It's all right. Don't be scared. Ain't nothing gonna hurt you."

See, I been scared of the dark ever since I was a child. And it was dark . . . Law, yes. Pitch black. The kinda dark that like to take your breath away. Why, you couldn't a seen your own hand if you held it right in front of your eyes, it was that dark.

And I was scared. Oh, Law. The fear run through me when them lights went out. I was frozen, just like a little ole rabbit. Now I ain't never drowned, 'course, but that's what I 'spect it would be like. The water moving in on you and the more you try to fight it, the more it covers you up. Gets in your nose and mouth and ears and you go under. That's what it was like. The darkness was a drowning me.

All's I could do was to hold on to that stair rail and pray, "Jesus please help me!" And then I seen him.

Gail looked down at the tape player. Through the plastic cover, she could see the two wheels turning slowly as Ida Wilson's story transformed itself from a silent code on the translucent brown film into the hard-edged accents of her cigarette

235

voice. Beyond her cubicle, Gail heard the door open and the mumbled greeting of the receptionist. She switched off the tape player, and the wheels stopped.

She didn't have to work on this story just yet. It wasn't scheduled to run in the magazine, *Carolina Visions*, for two months. The upcoming issue's cover story was about a retiree who had played the trombone in Glenn Miller's Air Force band and now directed a local group called the Swing Time Pops. It was the only swing band in the Piedmont made up exclusively of people who had been in World War II, and they had developed quite a reputation among the retiree communities throughout the region.

Actually, Gail had come in early to get caught up with her other assignments. It was her turn to do the calendar, and she liked to get that out of the way so she could tackle her list of other things to do—photo shoots to set up, interviews to arrange, sources to contact, facts to check. Things she had to finish before she could even think about writing. Each week, she could feel the growing current of tasks to accomplish trying to push her back, cause her to slip behind. But she was holding fast. She was determined not to miss a deadline.

So she had come in early, but when she saw the tape of her interview with Mrs. Wilson, commonly known as, "The Crazy Quilt Lady," she felt as if she had to listen to it again, to see if it clicked with her memory's version of the late afternoon meeting at the small brick ranch house. But now that other people were beginning to come in, it didn't feel right to listen to the tape. The morning's fresh quietness had been broken, and she slipped the cassette into her satchel to take home and listen to at night.

She had gone to Mrs. Wilson's yesterday. She had to use her map to find the crowded neighborhood of small square homes. Some had been added on to over the years, breaking up the uniformity. But you could still tell that these homes were designed to be built fast—they were solid and sturdy but had little thought for aesthetics. There wasn't much that was pretty about them, but a lot of the families took pride in them anyway, setting out flowers and manicuring hedges on the tiny lawns. Some painted their trim in unusual colors to distinguish them from their neighbors, bright splashes of aqua or salmon in a sea of white and tan and black.

Gail pulled up to No. 104. It was an especially plain house, with a thin and weedy lawn and just a few misshapen shrubs placed irregularly along the foundation. There were no shutters to add interest to the solid brick front. Just plain windows and a torn screen door. She got out of the car and walked up the cracked sidewalk, trying to suppress the prejudice that kept rapping at her mind. And, even with a perfectly clear perspective, it was difficult to see how this could be a story worth telling, how anything extraordinary could happen here. Gail pictured Mrs. Wilson as just another dumpy grandma working on her quilts for the church bazaar, a little delusional perhaps, but not at all interesting.

The doorbell was broken, so Gail tapped on the aluminum part of the screen door. A yappy dog began barking and running toward the door, scraping its nails on the hardwood floor.

"Muffin, Muffin, you hesh up, now. Just hesh up!" Mrs. Wilson came into the front room, and the dog switched from frantic barking to a low growl, its lips pulled back and its eyes bugging out.

"Don't you pay him no mind," Mrs. Wilson told Gail as she opened the door. "He just gets a bit excited when someone comes to visit, don't you Muffin?" The dog continued growling and put its wet whiskers on Gail's legs as she walked into the room. "You just wait right here while I put him in his room so's he won't be a botherin' us." Mrs. Wilson scooped up the dog and went down a hallway.

Gail looked around the room and felt her stomach tighten up. Every inch of the small space was filled. There were armchairs in faded yellow upholstery, a floral couch that leaned to one side, a coffee table overflowing with old issues of *TV Guide*, black velvet pictures on the walls, brightly-colored needlepoint hangings, rumpled pillows, used glasses and mugs, a collection of dying houseplants, a TV with gangly rabbit ears spread out above it, and huge orange ashtrays that hadn't been emptied in quite some time.

God, how do I keep getting stuck with these assignments? Gail wondered. It would probably take a week to get the cigarette smell out of the new black pants she was wearing.

Mrs. Wilson came back in the room. "Now then, you must be the young lady who called from the paper."

"Yes, ma'am," Gail said, holding out her hand. "I'm Gail Sommers with *Carolina Visions*, and we're interested in your quilts for a piece in our July issue."

"Why, honey, you don't hardly look old enough to be outta school. I declare! Let me get you some iced tea."

"Oh, no thank you, really. I just had a soda before I left."

"Well, then, I reckon you want to see my quilts. They're in the basement. That's where I had my vision, you see."

"That would be a good place to start, then."

Mrs. Wilson led Gail to a scratched door, and they went down a creaky set of steps that had been covered in green shag carpet. "Right here on these stairs is where it happened," Mrs. Wilson whispered, "but I'll tell you about that later."

The basement was unfinished, but the cinderblock was painted white, and bright fluorescent lights hung from the ceiling. In the middle of the room, there was a long, wide table covered with white material. A pegboard filled with spools of thread was nailed to the wall next to bins filled with cloth. A sewing machine was placed between the wall and the table. "I'm working on the back for one of 'um now, but I'll show you how it'll come out. But come this way now."

They walked around the back of the stairs to another area. "Here are my quilts," Mrs. Wilson said. "Leastways, these is the ones I've been told to keep or haven't been told what to do with just yet."

Gail felt her lungs fill up with delight. All of the walls had been covered with magnificent, large quilts, mounted on burnished brass rods, their complex designs looking more like fine Chinese carpets or medieval tapestries than any quilts she had ever seen. High rectangular windows let in the late afternoon sun in broad prismatic beams that converged in the center of the room on a single quilt that lay on a plain oak table.

"They're absolutely gorgeous," Gail said. "I don't know what to say. They're exquisite."

"That one there on the table, that was the first I did after I had my vision," Mrs. Wilson explained.

Gail went up to the table and looked more closely at the quilt. Its intricate pattern swept and swirled in spirals of subtly changing hues that modulated from deep blues to greens and yellows and reds and purples and back again.

Mrs. Wilson chuckled. "You wanta know something funny? The Smithsonian Museum of Washington, D.C. offered me $10,000 for that quilt, and I betcha I didn't put more than fifty dollars worth of material in it."

"But your time! You must have spent months working on this. The pieces are so tiny."

"Oh, not so long, I 'spect. I don't really keep track of time. I just do what I'm told to do and the time goes by real fast."

"It's fabulous," Gail said. "Oh, do you mind if I turn on my tape recorder while we talk? That way I can take photographs while you're explaining things."

Mrs. Wilson cracked a smile. "You go right ahead and suit yourself. It don't matter to me."

Gail switched on her tape and began setting up her camera. "You know, when I first heard about your visions and the quilts you had made, I assumed that you were making quilts *of* Elvis. This is nothing like what I expected."

Mrs. Wilson was laughing again. "Law, everybody seems to think that. They come up to me in town and says, 'You the lady who makes the Elvis quilts? You the Crazy Quilt Lady?' But no, the quilts ain't pictures of Elvis, and they ain't crazy quilts neither. They's just pictures of what he tells me to make, what he tells me in the visions, you see."

"And he tells you what to do with them, too?"

"Yes, ma'am. He does. They's a plan for each one, you know. They's a few I'm told to keep, like that 'un the Smithsonian wants so bad. Some of them I give away to somebody who might be needin' something special. Some of them I sell. Get a right good price for them, too. You might be surprised."

"What's the highest price you've gotten for a quilt?"

"Well, I don't know as I should say, but they's museums out there and lots of rich people who don't have nothing better to do with their money. I ain't got $10,000, but I come close enough. 'Course, I don't keep any profit. That wouldn't be right, now would it? It's a gift been given me."

"You don't keep any money?"

"Just enough to buy the material and thread, keep my sewing machine up, things like that. I don't need nothing more—I live off mine and my husband's pension."

"What do you do with the money, then?"

"Why, whatever he tells me to do. I might give it to the church or a family that's needing it. You know them bells down at the old Episcopalian church? I paid for those to be fixed with the quilt money. That took several quilts to pay for. You wouldn't a thought bells could cost so much money. I declare."

"Is that your church?"

"Law, no, chile. I'm Baptist like everone else in my family. Go down here to the Bedrock Independent Baptist Church. But he told me that old Episcopalian church needed their bells fixed. Hadn't played in five years or more. Said the town needed to hear them bells. They is pretty, don't you think?"

Gail nodded as she focused her lens on the quilts. She realized that they looked different depending on the angle. From some places, you could see a picture emerge—a landscape or silhouette. From other places, the geometry of the pattern was the most striking aspect, the unending symmetry and depth creating an almost hypnotic effect.

"How many quilts have you made so far?" Gail asked.

"This one I'm working on now will be number one hundred one. I been making quilts five years now. 'Spect I'll keep on doing it till he tells me to stop."

"And did you make quilts before?"

"Law, no . . . I sewed. Made my own clothes and curtains and things like that. But I ain't never made a quilt before my vision. 'Course, I kindly knew how to do it from watchin' my granny when I was a chile. It all came to me when I started."

"So what did you do before the vision?"

"Worked down at the mill, same as most people round these parts. Worked there thirty-five years before I retired. My husband worked there thirty years before he had his heart attack."

Gail snapped a picture of a quilt with a sunburst of orange in the center.

"So you make about twenty quilts a year," she said. "You must spend an awful lot of time down here."

"Oh, I don't know 'bout that. It don't seem like a long time. 'Course I have my dog to keep me company."

Gail glanced around at the quilts again. Standing there, surrounded by the coolness and color and light, reminded her of the time she had visited St. Patrick's Cathedral with her senior class in high school. A hush had fallen over her as the group left the noisy street and stared up into the soaring ceiling. She remembered the peaceful feeling that had filled her from head to toe, a feeling that everything would somehow work out . . . that she would be happy one day.

"Could you show me around your work area?" Gail asked.

"Ain't much to show," Mrs. Wilson said when they walked over to the table and sewing machine. "I keep my thread over there. 'Course, I got to have every color they make 'cause I never know what color I'll need. Same thing with the cloth. I buy a lot of the cloth, but sometimes he tells me to ask so-an-so if they have any old fabric. People know 'bout my quilts, so they don't mind giving me an old dress or something. I get lots of unusual cloth that way. Sometimes it don't look like anything special at all till I cut it up and put it in the quilt."

Gail looked at the pieces of fabric spread around the sewing machine. Mrs. Wilson was right—they didn't seem special, just some old fading fabric cut into narrow strips. "Now, what will this quilt you're working on look like when it's done?"

"Well, it's kindly hard to describe. Here's some of the pieces, but they don't really let you know what it'll look like. I can see it in my mind, but I don't know how to describe it."

"So this pattern was described to you in a vision?"

"Why, yes. Ever single one of 'um was."

"Could you describe the first vision you had for me?"

"Well, like I said, it was on that staircase right there. I had come down here to tie up some old newspapers—back then I kept all sorts of things down here—and I was going back upstairs and the lights went out."

Mrs. Wilson closed her eyes and seemed to be watching something take place in her head. "And then I seen the King in all his glory. He was dressed in white from head to toe and there was a light a shinin' on him and he kindly shimmered all over. He held out his hand to me and said, 'It's all right. Don't be scared. Ain't nothing gonna hurt you.'

"See, I been scared of the dark ever since I was a child. And it was dark . . . Law, yes. Pitch black. The kinda dark that like to take your breath away. Why, you couldn't a seen your own hand if you held it right in front of your eyes, it was that dark.

"And I was scared. Oh, Law. The fear run through me when them lights went out. I was frozen, just like a little ole rabbit. Now I ain't never drowned, 'course, but that's what I 'spect it would be like. The water moving in on you, and the more you try to fight it, the more it covers you up. Gets in your nose and mouth and ears and you go under. That's what it was like. The darkness was a drowning me.

"All's I could do was to hold on to that stair rail and pray, 'Jesus please help me!' And then I seen him. Jesus done sent him to me to put me at ease. He held out his hand and touched my arm and all the fear poured outta me. I wasn't scared at all. I was just as calm and peaceful as you can imagine. Then—this is the part that's hard to explain—he told me what I was supposed to do with the rest of my life. He told me to make these quilts right here in this basement, but the thing is, he didn't say it so's you could hear anything. He just told me in my heart."

"And since then, how do you get the visions for the quilts?"

"Well, that's kindly hard to explain too. It's kinda like when I get to a point where I have to decide what to do—what color to use, what shape to cut—he shows me in my heart, you know? I don't see him in person anymore like I done that first time, but I know it's him all the same. I can feel him down here in the basement. I never get scared no more."

Gail looked at Mrs. Wilson, who was wearing a cotton housedress and bedroom slippers. Her graying hair straggled about her face, and her fingernails had turned yellow from cigarettes.

"I'm curious," Gail said. "Were you a big fan of Elvis before the vision?"

"No, ma'am. No, I wasn't. I never did like that rock an' roll. I liked gospel singin' better. 'Course, now I know he did sing gospel music, too. He'd sing, 'How Great Thou Art' and it woulda sent shivers down your spine to hear it. My neighbor played that record for me once. He'd gone to hear him back when he was young. Said it was the most moving experience of his life."

"You know," Gail said, trying to choose her words carefully. "Some people don't believe Elvis ever died. What do you think about that?"

Mrs. Wilson laughed. "Child, child. It don't matter. We're just a passing through this world anyway. Our loved ones is on the other side, waiting for us. They still watch over us like they done when they was here. It's the same with Elvis, whether he's here like you and me or over on the other side. Lots of people love him, and he loves them back. I figure that's why he asked me to make these quilts."

". . . As an expression of love?"

"Why, yes," Mrs. Wilson said. She gazed at the crucifix around Gail's neck. "You ain't Baptist, are you?"

"No, ma'am, I'm not."

"Well, maybe you can't see it the way I do, but I know I'm telling you the truth. And the proof is right over there in that room. You know it is. Do you think I coulda' made all them quilts by myself?" Mrs. Wilson laughed again. "Law, law. People is funny sometimes. Now come on upstairs, and I'll get you some tea. Lookin' at quilts always makes me thirsty."

Gail had gone upstairs and accepted a glass of tea—she couldn't say no again without being rude—and then she got in her car and drove away.

Ever since then, she had been filled with an unbearable sense of yearning. All day long, her work was interrupted by images that popped into her mind. Images of Mrs. Wilson surrounded by the rich colors of her quilts. Images of geometric patterns spreading out in all directions. Images of pieces of cloth magically coming together to make a whole.

She left right at six o'clock. As she parked her car in front of No. 104, she kept telling herself that she just needed to ask a few more questions for her story.

Mrs. Wilson was in the middle of cooking supper. The smell of frying meat mingled with the cigarette odor. As she tapped on the door, Muffin began yapping and running to the front.

Mrs. Wilson came to the door, looking a little surprised.

"I'm so, so sorry to disturb you, Mrs. Wilson," Gail began. She didn't know exactly what she wanted to say. "I just had one more quick question to ask you, and I was on my way home anyway. I hope I'm not putting you out."

Mrs. Wilson opened the door. "Well, come on in, child. Let me go pull the pan off the stove so it don't burn. You wanna have supper with me?"

"Oh, no ma'am. I wouldn't dream of it," Gail said, raising her voice as Mrs. Wilson went through to the kitchen. She tried to be as assertive as she could. "It's rude enough of me to stop by uninvited, without calling or anything. I would feel terrible if I imposed on you anymore."

Gail looked about the room with its yellowing, flat paint and the clutter that seemed to have a life of its own, growing and recreating right under her eyes. In the kitchen, she could hear Mrs. Wilson singing along with some gospel music on the radio. "I'll be right with you," she yelled to Gail. Muffin sat in the doorway to the kitchen growling whenever Gail turned her head that way.

"Well, then, what would you like to know?" Mrs. Wilson asked when she came back into the room.

A flush ran over Gail. What was she going to ask anyway? She stood silent for a second, and then the words came out of her mouth. She had no idea where they came from.

"I just wanted to know how you knew it was the right thing to do? I mean, I know you saw a vision of Elvis and then you felt that you had to make these quilts, but how did you know you could do it? How did you know they would be beautiful and inspiring and not ugly or ordinary or tacky? How did you know that this is what you're supposed to do?"

Mrs. Wilson looked puzzled. "Honey, I just felt it in my heart like I told you before. When you feel something like that, you have to act. Like the song says, 'I'm gonna move when the spirit says move.' Sometimes messages come to you but they ain't in words. You just gotta listen."

Gail thanked Mrs. Wilson and said goodbye. As she got in her car, the heat from the sun wrapped around her like a blanket woven out of sadness and regret. She rolled down the windows and drove through the countryside for an hour or more, trying to calm down. After a while, the late spring sun began to set. She stopped her car by a pond in the middle of a field. Cows were looking for morsels of sweet clover among the grass. A hill rose up behind them, and on top stood an old deserted house starkly silhouetted by the setting sun. Shafts of red light pierced through the house's windows and traveled on to glint on the pond's surface. A dark forest framed the entire scene, its black green sometimes broken by pinpoints of light.

Gail felt the painful yearning she had felt when she was a child back at St. Mary's. She shut her eyes and could hear the voice of Sister Bernadette, the skinny young nun from Chicago who taught Gail's third grade art class.

"You have a gift, Gail," Sister Bernadette had said. "I can clearly see it. You see the light in the colors, the pattern in the shapes. God has given you something special, and now it's up to you."

Sister Bernadette had been so earnest in her dealings with the girls, so passionate when she spoke of Monet or Wyeth or Michelangelo. Gail had liked her immensely, but some of the others had laughed at her behind her back, mocking the way she clasped her hands together and raised up on her toes when someone's work especially pleased her.

Gail could see her face before her now—so sincere and determined. "Remember the parable of the talents, Gail?" she had said. "And the lesson from the parable? Those to whom much is given, much is expected. We're not to bury our talents in the ground. We're not to sell our birthright."

Even so, the last time Gail had touched a paintbrush outside of school was the day her father died.

Gail opened her eyes. The cows continued their steady grazing. It was the time of evening when everything was still—the day creatures were settling down, the night creatures were still quiet. The only sound was that of the cows ripping up their clover.

Then . . . very softly at first, another sound broke the stillness of the damp, cooling air. The cows looked up momentarily, then returned to their grazing.

Gail got out of the car and was leaning against the fence post. And she was weeping, crying inconsolably for the picture she saw in front of her . . . and for all the other pictures that were not and never would be.

The Eagle

I SPIN A BUTTON on the countertop, where it twirls like Vishnu's disk. It's one I recognize easily, from Hank's dress uniform.

After college, he served in the army for two years as an aerospace engineer. He investigated plane crashes all over the world. I never saw the appeal of military life, but in many ways it suited Hank well. The order and discipline meshed with his serious personality. At least that's what I thought until I saw him in the hospital with Mom.

She never did go home. Three weeks in the hospital. Three weeks of driving from Raleigh to Charlotte every few days, memorizing every exit, every billboard, every field I passed. Three weeks of tensing up every time the phone rang, of being summoned because this might be it. Three weeks of not sleeping at night unless I slipped out of bed and did the crossword while I drank glasses of wine and finally curled up on the futon in the den.

I saw a lot of my family during that time. My mother's last days brought out strange things in all of us, but especially in Hank. Unexpectedly, he would try to joke about things. He had some stupid running commentary about the catheter and apple juice, and every time a new nurse came in the room he'd say, "Do you know the name of the designer of these hospital gowns? Seymore Hiney." I thought I would deck him except I knew that inside he was feeling the same way I felt.

I remember one time I came to the room when Mom was asleep. The door was ajar and I peeked in. Hank was standing by the bed—he didn't know I was there. It was one of those moments when I could sense something—a presence or a power or a communication—something I couldn't quite name but I knew it was there all the same. I don't know if he was praying or silently speaking to Mom or what, but I knew I should step away quietly and let the two of them be together in the stillness.

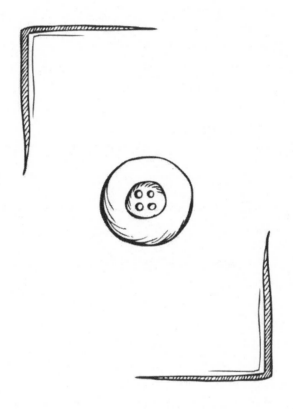

The High Untrespassed

HANK WOULD HAVE BEEN OKAY if it weren't for the Christmas presents. Some were wrapped in shiny red foil with curly golden ribbons falling off the edges like a little girl's hair pulled back in a ponytail. Others were unwrapped—a doll peering out from her cellophane window in a crushed cardboard box, her frozen smile now appearing like an expression of horror, a multi-colored basketball smashed into shapelessness, a broken perfume bottle sending a sweet smell into the air to mix with the odor of burnt fuel, rubber, and something worse.

Hank broke into a sweat even though the temperature was well below freezing. Come on, he told himself. He took a deep breath. You've seen it all before. This is no different. It's not like they're civilians. He forced his mind to ignore it all— the obscene bits of red and green, the little pieces of broken candy canes, the stained Santa hats. It was a question of will, of course, since the holiday gaiety intermingled with the telltale bits of evidence—ripped metal, distressed solder joints, and worn screws, yellow tape marking where bodies had been, burned trees, and scarred earth. They were all pieces in a giant jigsaw puzzle. Hank just needed to put them back together.

He heard a crunching sound and looked up. Two members of the Canadian Aviation Safety Board were walking toward him. Hank looked at his watch and realized it was almost one o'clock in the afternoon. Three hours had gone by. The analytical part of his mind had triumphed again.

"Find anything interesting?" one of the Canadians asked, his breath rising like a smoke signal.

"There are some things, but I wouldn't want to make a guess yet. You?"

"'Bout the same. I hope we can get this finished soon, though. It's not the kind of thing I still want to be doing come Christmas Eve, if you know what I mean."

"Right." Hank looked over the scene again. The shredded uniforms and crushed boots didn't bother him. He was used to these. It was those Christmas presents. The irrational part of his brain wanted them to be taken away, to simply be gone, but this wasn't possible yet. Nothing could be moved until the initial investigation was over.

"Kind of makes your stomach go bad, doesn't it?" the other Canadian said.

Hank drew his eyes away from the scene and looked at the Canadians. He ordered his mind to behave. "What do you guys do for lunch around here?"

"Come on over to the tent. We've got some good hot chowder to warm you up."

After sunset, Hank went back to the hotel and forced himself to eat a sandwich in the café. The others were there, too, but nobody was talking much. He wanted a couple of good stiff drinks, but he had to be up early tomorrow, his mind ready to sort through the tiniest pieces of evidence, so he settled for a glass of milk.

Back in his room, Hank took a hot shower and went to bed. He kept thinking of his own flights home from Europe; the last time was only a few months ago. Like an old friend, a thrill of excitement had filled him as the plane lifted off the runway and burst into the air. He rested his head so that it was easy to see out of the window and sat, transfixed. Below, the coastline of France appeared, then the green pastureland of the British Isles, followed by a vast expanse of blue sky broken by gauzy pieces of white. The sun, glaring through the windows, seemed so close, its strength heating the glass and giving everything a cheerful brightness. The smell of coffee filled the air and the stewardesses smiled. Up there at 30,000 feet, everything was good.

Hank was always surprised how soon the jagged edges of Canada appeared below. North America already. Tundra and rocky cliffs jutting into the water, reaching toward the Old World. Bits of land in a cold brutal ocean, a landing site for crusty old fishermen, beautiful in a barren sort of way, but not the kind of place most people would choose to live.

Or die, Hank thought. He was just too tired to fight his mind anymore. He couldn't help but wonder what it had been like for them. Stationed in the Sinai for six months, away from their families in an alien country filled with hostility. A helpless feeling overcame Hank as his mind traveled to Egypt. The land of the Pharaohs. Pyramids and mummies. Noisy open markets. Heady perfume oils filling the air. Silent women with eyes lined in black. Smooth dark skin glistening in the heat. Ancient curses rising through the sands of time and pulling you down, down, down to your fate.

Stop it, Hank told himself.

Just stop.

But he couldn't. It was the beginning of a long night, and there was no work to divert his thoughts. He wanted to get up and review the notes he had taken, try to sort out a theory, but he was too tired. He hadn't realized how the cold could make you tired just like the heat. Could leave you all muddled so that your own mind played tricks on you.

Even now he could see them, going home at last, after so many months. In time for Christmas, for turkey with cranberry sauce and sweet potato soufflé. All their favorites spread out in front of them. Parents and wives and children crowding around. "Do you want anything else, honey?"

Joking with each other, they get on the plane. Uncontrolled happiness spreading from one face to another. Someone buying beer all around.

In Germany, the plane stops to refuel and they get off. It isn't the States, but after being in Egypt for six months, it's close enough. Uniforms filling the shops in the airport, buying whatever catches their eyes. They have souvenirs from Egypt, of course, but Amy would love that doll with the blond hair and it's really time Justin learned to shoot a basketball . . . and Karen always did like Chanel No. 5. Yes, please do wrap it. I won't have time when I get back.

Canada is the last stop. They file into the airport lounge, exuberant, disrupting the pre-dawn quiet with Christmas songs and horseplay, waiting for the plane to come off the refueling blocks and take them home.

Hank forced himself to get up and turn on the light. He wasn't going through the rest of it.

* * * *

Two days later, Hank got a phone call.

"The Canadians feel they have the situation under control," Col. White said. "Of course, we'll keep some men around, but we want you to go to Fort Campbell and work with the public affairs office."

"I've never done anything with public affairs," Hank said. "I've only done field work."

"Well, this is an unusual situation. Two hundred and forty-eight servicemen and women from the same post—it's shaken up things quite a bit and there are swarms of media people there. We need a technical person on site who can answer questions."

"With all due respect, sir, I believe I could be more effective here."

"Most of the work has been done here, Lieutenant, and this isn't our turf. We need you at Fort Campbell tomorrow morning. There will be a debriefing session for family members at 1300 hours."

Col. White hung up. Hank's stomach tightened again. After that one bad night, he had managed to get down to business and had even begun to enjoy his work. Like his other investigations, it had become a quest—finding an overall message in the bits of debris, an answer to the riddle that would set things right again.

Leaving the site wasn't good, Hank was sure about that. What use was it? Especially that part about him meeting the families. Families were like Christmas presents—they just got in the way, made things difficult. It was hard to see the message when families were in the picture.

Hank sighed. There was nothing he could do except hope his time at Fort Campbell would be brief. He pulled his suitcase out of the closet and began throwing in the few items he had scattered about the room. He grabbed a bottle of Rolaids and popped two in his mouth before he left the room to go down to the bar.

* * * *

The flight to Tennessee was disappointing. A layer of impenetrable gray hid the ground, blocking the view of Newfoundland's desolate shoreline, the gleaming towers of Manhattan, the neat squares of the heartland. The captain's voice was expressionless when he explained about the turbulence they hit as soon as they became aloft. The plane dipped abruptly, and someone near the back gasped.

Hank remembered the disdain he used to feel for people afraid to fly. There was a time when he never felt more at peace than when he was flying. It was such a victory—technology defying the bonds that had held man on the ground for so long. A silver piece of metal transporting people from sunrise to sunset and back in a few short hours. The ability to look down on the continent and see earth as God saw it.

And if something did happen, what better way was there to die? In a car, for God's sake, stuck on the ground? In a hospital surrounded by the old and sick? No, no . . . that Greek boy—Icarus—had been right to fly close to the sun. To die young, soaring through the air—that was the best a person could hope for.

Hank wondered about the dead soldiers. Had they felt this joy of flight? Were they filled with exhilaration when they died? Or had they come to the point he had reached and realized it wasn't worth it after all?

In Nashville, Hank rented a car and drove to Fort Campbell. As he came into town, the sky's dreariness seemed to sink and cover everything. Streetlights burned even though it was midday. Christmas decorations hung limply from soggy creosoted poles. Flags flew at half-staff. Even the store signs had abandoned their commercialism and succumbed to grief: "Our prayers are with the 101st," "God will provide," and, "Blessed are the Peacekeepers."

Once on post, Hank went to the conference for family members, held in a nondescript building in a sea of nondescript buildings. The post commander was there with other high-ranking officers, but all Hank could see was the mass of faces in front of him. Young faces, yet old. A twenty-year-old mother clutching two toddlers as if they were lifejackets. A teenage boy looking around the room, searching for something he could not find. A baby crying inconsolably.

As the commander began to speak, a high-pitched sound filled Hank's ears, softly at first, then gaining in intensity so that everything else became muted and distant. He looked around and realized that a fog had filled the building, blurring his vision so that he could see only one person at a time. He shifted his eyes to clear his sight, but as he passed from one face to another, he felt each person's sadness enter him and settle deep inside.

Someone tapped him on the shoulder, and he realized it was time for him to speak. Through the fog and the noise, he felt himself step up to the podium and go through the litany he had been told to say . . . a thorough investigation is underway, many agencies are cooperating, we will discover the cause of this tragedy so it will never happen again.

Finally, it was over. The fog and noise left the room and Hank felt a breeze blow in from the open door.

"You are as white as a sheet," the woman next to him said. She was from the public affairs office and had coordinated his trip to the post. "Why don't you get something to eat before you pass out? I have enough problems on my hands without dealing with fainting soldiers."

But Hank wasn't hungry. He went to the room he had been given and lay down on the bed, staring at the ceiling. Why couldn't they just let him do his job? Now he was helpless while the riddle was still out there waiting for an answer. He had known that coming here would be a mistake.

The next days were no better. Even when the winter sun shone clear, an icy fog seemed to hover over the Tennessee-Kentucky border, covering the post and area towns in gray. Hank continued to work with the public affairs office, helping decipher reports coming in from Canada, participating in press conferences, even talking to family members. He was always surprised to hear words come out of his mouth; his body felt as frozen as the Newfoundland tundra.

A few days before Christmas, Col. White told him he could leave. "Go on home and see your folks for a few days before you come back to Washington," he said over the phone. "God knows we all need a break from this mess." But Hank didn't want to go to his family. He had seen them all right here—his mother's eyes filling with tears as she shook her head, gray streaks of hair falling around her face. His dad sitting silently amid his own clumsy grief. His sister's voice asking over and over, "Did he feel any pain?"

The wives were the worst. Most of them were young, like Jennifer. He wondered for the first time ever if he really should marry Jennifer. Did he really want a bond like that? Maybe it would be better to stay free, unencumbered, although in his mind he'd been married to her for years. They were just waiting for him to finish with the army and for her to finish graduate school. He was supposed to meet her at home for the holidays, but he couldn't. He would call and explain that he couldn't make it this year with the crash still under investigation. His family would understand. Jennifer might not, but he was willing to take that risk.

He went back to Washington. The office was deserted and he worked day after day from before sunrise until well past dusk, trying to put the pieces together, but it was a mission without meaning. Icing had been identified as the cause, and Hank's work was merely backup. All the usual rituals he went through—the sorting of piece after piece, the examination of the flight recorder, the interviews with witnesses—they were futile now.

On Christmas Day, he walked through the city's empty squares, sat by monuments, stared into the blue sky mirrored in the reflecting pond. He walked by the National Air and Space Museum and gazed at the outlines of Skylab through the tall, shining windows. He felt nothing, not even the cold.

January wore on, one day the same as another, until one morning Col. White came into Hank's office and shut the door. A smile spread across his face.

"Guess what I have in my possession, Lieutenant."

"I have no idea, sir."

"Passes. Passes for something you will like."

"What's that, sir?"

"Oh, come on, Lieutenant. You should be able to guess. What happens in five days?"

"I really haven't been keeping up, sir."

"I know you haven't. You haven't been the same since we got back from Canada, but this will do the trick."

He pulled out two slips of paper and gave one to Hank: **VIP pass, Cape Canaveral**.

Hank looked at the slip of paper and then at Col. White. He had never noticed before how much the older man looked like his father, especially now, as he waited for Hank's reaction.

"Well, what do you think?"

"Really, sir, this is too much. I have a lot of work to do here. Lieutenant Graham deserves it more."

"Oh, come off it, Hank. I know you've wanted to see a launch for years, and this will be up close and personal. You're in a funk, now. That's understandable. We all go through it sometimes, but it's time to pull out of it. You and I will be flying to Florida on Thursday."

As Col. White shut the door behind him, Hank didn't know what to feel. After a few moments of just sitting, he pulled an old notebook out of his bottom drawer. He had kept it since he was eleven. It was tan colored and on the front was written, in uneven sixth-grade script, *Diary of American Space Travel*.

He glanced at the first entry, which included crude attempts at technical drawings as well as a short paragraph in thick, blurred pencil:

> Today Neil Armstrong, Edwin Aldrin and Lt. Michael Collins launched off on the first mission to the moon. I watched it on TV. There was a lot of fire and smoke when the rocket lifted off into the sky. I held my breath until they were out of sight.

Hank flipped through the pages. The entries gradually became longer and included detailed drawings. He remembered how he'd found the notebook during a visit home while he was in college. He took it back to campus and kept it in his desk as a type of talisman. From time to time, he would add things to it, like the first launch of the Columbia shuttle:

> April 12, 1981. America sends a crew into orbit on the anniversary of Vostok 1, first human spaceflight.

The last remaining entries were sparse dates with cryptic abbreviations followed by empty pages. He put the notebook back in the desk and returned to work.

* * * *

Five days later, in his hotel room in Florida, Hank pulled out the notebook again. He had packed it on the spur of the moment, in spite of himself. Now he felt compelled to add one more entry. He uncapped a pen and turned to a blank page.

January 28, 1986

It was colder in Florida than I thought it would be, but the sun was brilliant and the sky was so blue it hurt. Everyone was excited, especially Col. White. He kept looking over at me, with that grin on his face, slapping me on the back and saying, "This is it, my boy. What we all dream about back in the office. Blast Off!" He winked and showed me a flask in his coat. "1976 Chivas Regal," he said. "To toast a successful launch." I had never seen him like this before.

There was a boy, 10 or 11 years old, a few rows in front of us. He was watching the television monitor and kept giving the rest of us updates from time to time. "They're checking the fuel tanks. They're opening the hatch."

Finally, a roar went through the crowd as the crew came out of the holding area and walked toward the space shuttle. America's best and brightest: seven men and women, white, black and Asian, smiling and waving to us all. "There's Christa McAuliffe," the boy in front yelled.

They waved one last time and crawled through the door, and then it was sealed shut. It seemed like the countdown would never end, but finally the last few seconds were ticked off: four . . . three . . . two . . . one. Then a tremendous blast seemed to shatter the air itself. The slender white vessel rose, propelled by furious orange flames. Silence fell over us all, even the kid in front. It rose gracefully for a full minute or more and then there was a flash and a billow of white smoke. The trail of smoke changed course, spiraling toward the earth like a shooting star.

For a fraction of a second, everyone stood motionless as we witnessed it all: the glorious explosion, the cleansing fire, the rising smoke of the sacrifice. The breeze blew, and I lifted my hand to feel a warm mist, like a blessing descending upon us all.

A Silver Heart-Shaped Button

MATERNITY CLOTHES ALWAYS LOOK TOO CUTE, with pastel colors and flowers and little hearts, like this button from one of Gail's blouses. It's so sweet, I'm not sure why a grown woman would wear it at all, especially Gail, who always dressed well. I guess having a baby does crazy things to you. I think my mom got the shirt from Gail, hoping I would wear it someday. She never did give up.

I remember a conversation we had not very long after Rishi and I got married. He had already entrenched himself as the easy, agreeable one. "I can see why Rishi wouldn't want to start another family," Mother had told me on the way back from a Christmas gathering. "He has the little girl to support already, but I really think you could talk him into it. He seems to enjoy children so much." She looked at me conspiratorially. I resisted a groan.

It went on like that all the time, that persistent whisper in my ear: be like me, be like me, be like me. I can still hear that wistful tone in her voice on the telephone. "Is anything new with you?" Her real question screamed out at me, "Are you pregnant yet?" I told her about the new program I was working on, about my business trip, and the more I talked, the more I felt like a kindergartener showing off my latest drawing.

"I saw Brooke Stevens the other day with her new baby," my mom said once. "She said she's never been happier."

"That's good, Mom."

"He's real cute. Looks just like his daddy. You know she's thirty-five, and this is her first baby?"

"Yeah. That's great."

"Did I tell you how happy she is?"

Years later, I can still feel the muffled scream rising up my throat, feel my arm start to throw the phone down, feel my blood pressure soar as I struggled to keep my voice level.

"Yeah, Mom, you did. I'm glad for her."

It was moments like these when I realized a fundamental truth: I had a different source code than my mother. I was her blood daughter, but Gail was her spirit daughter, and there was always a bond between them that I could never even understand. Mom not only loved Gail, she *was* Gail.

So I find it very odd that this button doesn't make me angry or jealous or uncomfortable.

It should.

Gail was at the hospital with Mom a lot. She said Claire was keeping the kids, which I find hard to imagine. One Sunday morning, Dad and I were there together. Without saying so, we were both trying to find some magic solution to brighten the darkness we kept slipping into as Mom continued slipping away. We had turned on a church service on television because we didn't know what else to do. It was a small TV, and the sound wasn't very good, which made it all seem that much farther away. We were watching hundreds of tiny people in choir robes, opening their mouths, making muffled music, but at least it was something.

And then Gail was there. Dad brightened up. He leaned over my mom and said, "Look who's here." She opened her eyes and smiled.

Gail put down her bag and walked to the bed. She quietly hugged and kissed my mom, held her hand, and they stared into each other's eyes. "Hi, Emmy," she whispered. "I'm giving you hugs from Miranda and John and Eric. We all love you so much."

"Here, Gail, sit here," Dad said, getting out of his chair. Gail sat down, still holding Mom's hand.

The whole atmosphere in the room changed. Changed for the better. Right then, all I could feel was relief.

Now I stare at the heart-shaped button, trying to figure out exactly what it is that it makes me feel. And it surprises me.

Because of all things, I feel happy.

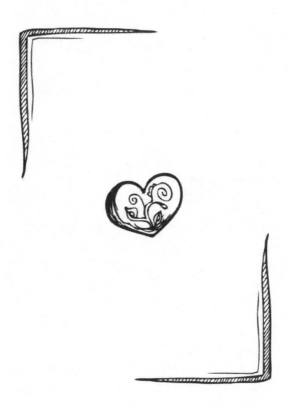

The Doula

Atlanta, 1989

THROUGH THE WINDOW, Gail could see Eric digging a ditch for a drainpipe. The pipe had been sitting on top of the ground for the past two months, ever since they had to redo the downspout. Old houses always required maintenance, Eric had said. The drainpipe hadn't seemed to worry him much until today, and now he was digging as if he were a POW and this was his last chance out. The ferocity of his movements was impressive. He was getting dirty and sweaty, even though it was fairly chilly for an October morning in Atlanta.

Gail wished she were out there, too.

She wanted to lie down, but before long she would have to sit back up, and it still took at least five minutes for her to sit up by herself. She'd never even thought about the act of sitting up before her abdomen had been sliced open like one of Eric's rainbow trout. Now it seemed almost impossible—her muscles wouldn't cooperate and the pain was truly shocking. By the time she did manage to get up and walk to the nursery, the baby would be frantic and she probably couldn't nurse.

The baby. The baby. Why couldn't she call her Miranda? She'd picked that name out months ago—Miranda Nicole Rollins. It had seemed so sure, so full of possibility and beauty. The name looked perfect on the birth announcement—a lavender card with delicate white lilies framing the dark purple print and the wonderful quote from Shakespeare. But Gail was having a hard time calling her Miranda. She'd even called her Emily twice, which was the name of her best friend's daughter.

She stared out the window at Eric's industry and wondered what project he would pick out for tomorrow. He'd taken two weeks off from work for when the baby came and he might as well get something done, right? To be fair, he didn't stay out there all day. He would come in and help—rock the baby while Gail took a shower, change the baby, get lunch together. His eyes were full of wonder as he looked at his tiny daughter, at her perfect hands and feet, her dark head of hair, her face that looked exactly like an angel's. But along with the wonder was an undercurrent of panic. Before long, he'd go back out and attack the ditch.

Gail had noticed that the people who came by—the neighbors and friends and work colleagues—fell into two categories. Those who cooed and ahhed and said how envious they were, how there's nothing so special as a brand-new baby in your life, a perfectly innocent being to love and hold. And those who also cooed and ahhed but then looked you straight in the eye and told you not to worry, things will get better.

Gail had always assumed she belonged with the first category of people, but now she was taking comfort from the second.

And then there was her mother who, as usual, defied category. Three months ago, she had taken Gail to lunch at Calhoun Corners. During dessert, the waiter had brought out a canvas covered in brown paper. "Here's something for the nursery," Claire had said without ceremony. "I hope it goes with your things."

Gail carefully tore off the paper and revealed a reproduction of a John Singer Sargent painting, a portrait of four sisters in a high-ceilinged room. The youngest sat on an Oriental rug holding a doll, while the middle one stood off to one side, and the oldest two leaned against a large Japanese vase near the shadowy background. The white of their dresses caught the light, and their faces shone with an almost unearthly quality. Gail felt her eyes fill with tears, but knew better than to let her mother see them. She stared at the painting until she felt calm enough to look up and speak. "It's beautiful, Mother. Absolutely perfect."

"I'm putting together an exhibit of work by American impressionists. A lot of them are depictions of children, and I thought you might like that one. It has a nice, moody undercurrent."

Her mother put out her cigarette and called for the check. Lunch was over.

When Miranda was born, Claire stopped by the hospital briefly with a delicate vase of flowers. She'd brought bagels by on their first morning home, a sunny Saturday. Eric had made coffee and the three of them sat together at the breakfast table, watching people walk by as if it weren't a new world at all. Gail had only had about three hours of sleep at a time since Wednesday, the day before she went into the hospital. She was still taking Percocet for pain and looked about her with a sense of unreality and fragility. She noticed that her mother and Eric were staring at her.

"Feel okay, Hon?" Eric asked.

"I'm fine."

"Why don't you go back to bed? I'll take care of the kitchen."

"No, I'm tired of being in bed."

"But you need to rest. You need to sleep when the baby sleeps, remember?"

"I don't want to go to bed, okay?"

Eric was silent. Claire got up and gathered her keys and purse. "Gail, why don't I get a doula to help out for a few weeks."

"What's a doula?" Eric asked.

"You know, a woman who helps new mothers. She helps with taking care of the baby, getting up at night, keeping up with the housework. Sometimes they help with the birth too, but they don't have to."

Eric looked enthusiastically at Gail. "That sounds great," he said.

"No," Gail said deliberately. "I don't think so."

Claire was silent while she pulled on a tailored navy jacket. "The idea is that a doula is experienced with all this and knows exactly what you need."

Most people's mothers do that, Gail thought. "We'll be fine, Mother," she said.

Eric still looked hopeful. "It might be nice to have a little help for a while."

"I do *not* want a stranger in my house, okay Eric? Especially not now."

Over the table, Eric and Claire exchanged a look. Gail couldn't believe their nerve. She wanted to storm out of the room, but she was too tired. She wanted to put her head on the table and cry, but she still had a tiny reservoir of pride that wouldn't let her. She just sat there, watching a twenty-year-old with well-defined legs jog by in gray shorts and a black sports bra.

Claire walked across the hardwood floor, her heels tapping out an elegant cadence. "Okay, then. I'll see you soon." She opened the heavy wooden door and walked into the sunshine. Gail couldn't decide if she was relieved or panic-stricken. She wanted Emma.

Despite herself, Gail had felt hurt when Emma couldn't come. Her mind understood—Emma had to take care of herself now, had to save her strength for what lay ahead—but deep down, she still felt abandoned.

Now Miranda was ten days old and Eric thought it was time to get back to normal. As if they could.

Across the hall, the baby began to thrash about and make little grunting noises. Gail felt even more tired.

She went into the nursery and stared at Miranda. Black hair framed her seashell-like ears, and her dark eyelashes made perfect arcs over her pink skin. Miranda opened her deep blue eyes and stared straight at Gail.

"Hello, baby," Gail whispered, running her finger along Miranda's mottled skin. "Are you hungry already?" Miranda began flailing her arms about and opening her mouth, showing pink gums and a tiny tongue. Gail reached in and picked up the baby, cradling her against her chest, feeling her breasts tightening. Once again, she felt the responsibility she had toward this child surround her very being and harden like cement.

She heard the door open, and Eric yelled up the stairs. "Gail, look who's here!"

"Now don't wake the baby, Eric," a familiar voice rang out along the wooden floors of the foyer. "That's the first rule."

Holding Miranda carefully, Gail hurried down the stairs, feeling a stab of surprise when she saw not only Emma, but Caroline as well.

"Hey, Gail . . . nice place," Caroline said, looking around the foyer over her sunglasses. "I like that stained glass. Did you steal it from your church?"

Gail stared at them for several seconds, not sure how she felt now that her savior had actually arrived. Emma looked tired, but pretty much the same as usual, Gail thought. Caroline was wearing clogs, jeans, and a mustard-colored turtleneck, but there was a new air about her, a sense of sophistication she hadn't had before.

"I had some comp days to use up," Caroline said, breaking the silence. "So Mom and I thought we'd come down and check out the new cousin, the new house, see how the parenthood thing is doing."

"Oh, it's doing, all right," Eric said. He and Caroline hadn't known each other that long, but they always seemed to speak the same language.

"Gail, honey, I hope we're not disrupting your routine, but I had some casseroles in the freezer, so when Caroline said she had some days off, it just seemed like the thing to do. I couldn't get you on the phone, so I talked to Claire and she thought you wouldn't mind."

"Yeah, we had the phone off the hook for awhile," Eric said. "It was crazy enough without all that ringing."

Miranda began crying and Gail bounced her gently.

"Whoa. Got a good set of lungs," Caroline said.

"Here, let me see my new niece. Oh . . . Caroline, look at her. Isn't she beautiful? Gail, she looks just like you did when you were born."

Gail held Miranda out a bit, pulling the receiving blanket back from her face.

"You have the right to remain silent," Caroline said, peering straight at the baby. "Anything you say can and will be used against you."

Emma seemed embarrassed. "Caroline, what on earth are you doing?"

"Well, her name's Miranda, isn't it? I'm just mirandizing her. I thought that name was a little strange at first, but you know, it's really good advice to start life out with. Anything you say *can* and *will* be used against you. It took me years to figure that out."

"Caroline, I don't know what gets into you sometimes. Miranda is from Shakespeare. You remember the birth announcement. It's a beautiful name. I love it. Now, let me hold her."

Gail gave Miranda, now crying fully, to Emma's stretched-out hands. "I think she's getting hungry, even though I nursed her an hour ago."

"Oh, she's fine. I'm used to crying babies. Caroline cried her whole first year of life."

For a moment, Miranda quieted down. Emma's face wore a mixture of happiness and something else Gail couldn't quite place.

Caroline looked at Emma. "Okay, Mom, you can't adopt her, you know. Better give her back to Gail."

"Here, you hold her. I want to give Gail a hug." Emma gave the baby to Caroline and embraced Gail. "We're so happy for you," she whispered.

Gail stepped back. Emma felt so frail and birdlike. "Aren't you tired? There's a nice sofa in the sunroom. I used to go to sleep out there when I was pregnant."

Miranda was squirming and crying. Caroline gave her back to Gail.

"Yeah, Mom. You go rest. Gail's got to do the nursing thing. Geez—she looks like Dolly Parton. I'm going to see where Eric hid our bags."

"Here, the sunroom is just around here. I'll sit in the rocker and you put your legs up for awhile."

"Really, I feel fine Gail, but I will rest for a bit. Caroline will get on to me if I don't. She can be such a drill sergeant sometimes."

Gail unbuttoned her shirt and tried to guide Miranda's searching mouth to her nipple, feeling a hint of panic when she couldn't get her on right away.

"I'm still having a little trouble with the breastfeeding. I always thought that would be like instinct, but it isn't."

"The baby has to learn, too. Before long, it will be so easy you won't even think about it."

"And they say if you do it right, it shouldn't hurt. Well, I'm doing just like they showed me and it still hurts."

"Oh, yes. I remember that. It does hurt at first, even if you do it exactly right. That gets better, too. In a few more days it won't hurt at all."

Miranda finally settled on Gail's breast and began sucking. Emma smiled, then leaned her head back and closed her eyes. Her face was more wrinkled than Gail remembered it.

After a few minutes, Gail switched Miranda to her other breast, feeling relieved when the baby latched on easily. Gail's breathing slowed dramatically, and her eyes began to shut. She felt as if she were turning to liquid and could be poured into a mold. The image pleased her as her mind wandered among the shadowy dreams of half-sleep. She watched her self reshape into a river, a tree, a bird. In front of her was the deep forest of sleep Emma had entered so quickly and easily, but for now Gail was content to remain where she could still feel the baby sucking, wedged securely on the tapestry pillow in the rocker. She could feel a ray of sun warm her shoulder. In the kitchen, she could hear the clank of dishes and the smooth sound of water running. She smelled the lemon scent of dishwashing liquid and the rich aroma of freshly brewed tea. Beyond the windows came the repetitive thud of shovel on dirt.

Gail floated from liquid image to liquid image, feeling exquisite pleasure from each. If I stay here long enough, she thought, I could emerge as something altogether different. Rested. Serene. A Madonna.

She sensed a presence at the edge of the room, then heard soft footsteps cross the tiled floor. The presence knelt beside her, gently took Miranda, put Gail's feet on a footstool and covered her with an afghan. Gail fluttered her eyes open and briefly saw Caroline tiptoe away. Gail smiled and followed Emma into the deep.

* * * *

A delicious smell of baking meat nudged Gail out of her sleep. She felt the confident beat of a reggae song emanate from the kitchen stereo and saw the shadows of Eric dancing with Miranda in the den. She glanced over at the sofa and saw that Emma was gone. She looked at the clock. It was one thirty.

She stood up, realizing the pain from her incision was much less.

"Look Eric, Sleeping Beauty is finally up," Caroline said when Gail walked into the kitchen. She was pulling a dish out of the oven, and the heat lifted the strands of hair framing her face. "Don't worry. I didn't make this. Mom had it in the freezer. Chicken and wild rice. Guaranteed to cure what ails you."

"Smells wonderful," Gail said, feeling unexplained tears come to her eyes. Eric came in the room with Miranda, who looked around the kitchen alertly.

"She's been awake this whole time and hasn't cried once," Eric said, pulling a chair out for Gail. "She likes that baby swing we got at the garage sale."

Gail sat down and looked around her. The warmth of her kitchen—the shining oak cabinets, the terra-cotta floor, the deep green plants, the hanging copper pots—wrapped around her. She felt hungry for the first time in weeks.

"I hope this trip isn't too much for Emma," she said, surprised to realize that she wasn't just trying to be polite.

"Dad was a little worried, but she really wanted to come. She'd been looking forward to it so much. She's made all these clothes, and you should see the freezer. All those casseroles neatly labeled and organized. Just like my apartment!"

"Oh! I forgot to ask you. How is the world of computer programming?"

"It's great. Eventually I want to get into game design, but I've been working on this big industrial project lately, for a plant out in Ohio. They're all such old farts. I think I'm the first woman programmer they've seen, but I showed them. Can you believe they tried to hire me?"

Two hours ago, Caroline's confidence would have dug right into Gail's soul, but now she felt genuinely happy for her.

"Well, it was very nice of you to bring her when you're so busy."

"No biggie. I think she's fine. They say she's responding to the chemo really well, and she's pretty much normal in between sessions. It's just something she has to get through, but she'll be okay."

"Where is she?" Gail asked.

"She's upstairs unpacking, looking at the nursery, probably snooping around your bedroom. By the way, did you know that those nursery monitors can be picked up by cellular phones? Better watch what you say."

Eric laughed. "Well, anyone eavesdropping on us would be pretty bored these days. Unless they're interested in the baby poop report."

"Yeah, that and the very exciting sore nipple status. There are probably people out on the interstate choking on their coffee as they drive by."

"Y'all are grossing me out. Do you mind?" Caroline took a salad bowl out of the refrigerator and put a foil-wrapped loaf in the oven. Gail noticed that the table had been cleared and set for the first time since they'd come home from the hospital.

"Eric, why don't you put Miranda in the swing and get the drinks. I'll go get Mom."

"Here, I'll take her," Gail said, holding out her arms. "I miss her." Miranda felt almost like a warm kitten in Gail's arms. Her navy blue eyes gazed about Gail's face for a moment before she started nuzzling.

"Uh oh. Should have let her be," Eric said.

"Good grief, she eats like a horse." Caroline pulled the bread out of the oven. "I brought this bread all the way from a real Jewish deli in Raleigh, so I hope you appreciate it."

"I didn't know there *was* a real Jewish deli in Raleigh," Eric said.

"Yeah, well, times are changing. Once we let you Catholics in, the whole South started to go."

"I hope you know how bad you sound," Gail said, feeling fully awake. "By the way, what does your mom think of your new boyfriend?"

Caroline slammed the oven door shut and stood straight up.

"What are you talking about?"

Gail started laughing, became lost in it, feeling its power travel from her lungs throughout her body.

"That look is priceless, Caroline. That's the best present you could have given me."

"So how do you know?"

"It was just a lucky guess. You seemed different somehow and I didn't think it was all the job."

"Well, tell us about him," Eric said.

"There's nothing to tell. He's just a good friend."

"Yeah right, that's why you almost dropped the bread. Come on," Gail said, leaning forward and whispering, "Is he black?"

Caroline was silent for a moment, as if considering something carefully. "Not exactly," she said. "Does it matter?"

"Not to me."

"Then why did you ask?"

"Because you can never do anything the easy way. I know you'd never get serious with some WASP your mother would like."

"I am *not* serious with anybody, for Christ's sake, he's just a friend I do stuff with sometimes."

Miranda began whimpering, and Gail unbuttoned her shirt.

"Gail, it's ready, can't you wait?"

"We can eat while I nurse. It's better than listening to her scream."

Caroline sighed and looked around. "Drinks," she said, heading for the cabinets.

"So . . . your mom will be down soon so you better hurry and tell us. What is he?"

Caroline rolled her eyes. "He's from India, okay? No big deal."

"So is he Muslim or something?"

"You know, we haven't talked about religion a lot, thanks, but I think his family is Hindu."

"How old is he?"

"Will you stop it?"

"Forty? Forty-five? What?"

"I don't know, maybe forty."

"Divorced?"

Caroline put the last glass of tea on the table and glared at Gail. "Okay, we're ready here. Go get situated. I'm getting Mom, and I think she's had enough excitement today, so if you two could just behave I'd appreciate it."

Caroline walked out of the room. Gail and Eric exchanged a look over the table, then began laughing.

* * * *

The sun shone through the glazed windows as they ate, casting a glow on the dishes and silver. They were silent for a long time, concentrating on the blend of flavors and smells before them. Even Miranda was silent, propped in her car seat, sleeping the all-consuming sleep of a newborn.

"It's wonderful," Gail finally said. "I can't believe how hungry I am."

"Nursing makes you hungry. You need to eat. All the casseroles are very mild, so they shouldn't upset Miranda. And be sure to drink a lot, too."

"Mom, I think she can figure out when she's thirsty."

"It's so she'll have plenty of milk. Did you put all the casseroles in the freezer?"

"I got in everything except the presents."

"You've done enough without bringing presents," Gail said. "This meal alone is worth more than words can say."

"Oh, there's that cake you made still in the car, too."

"Well, go get it, honey. We need to celebrate."

Caroline and Eric went to the car. Emma leaned back in her chair and stared at Miranda.

"She's just beautiful, Gail. That's one thing about a C-section baby. They're usually prettier."

Gail looked at Miranda. Her head leaned to one side and her breathing raised and lowered her whole body.

"She is pretty, isn't she?"

"Here's dessert," Caroline said, holding it in front of Gail. "Mom's special lemon pound cake with glazed frosting."

"Oh, Caroline, give her the presents first."

Caroline went out of the room and came back with a large box wrapped in lavender with a sheer bow around it.

"This is from Mom. I have something too, but it isn't really wrapped."

Gail slowly unwrapped the box and pulled back the tissue paper. There lay an ivory gown with neatly ironed pleats and lace edging. Gail lifted it up and held it in the sunlight, letting its long skirt billow out from the box.

"Your father was baptized in that," Emma said quietly. "I know there might be one in your side of the family, too, but I thought you might want it anyway."

"I love it," Gail said. "It's beautiful."

"It used to be white, but the ivory is kind of nice, I thought. I redid it a bit—put some new buttons on, that type of thing." Emma laughed. "I redid it before your dad was born, too. My mother almost killed me. She got so mad she went into labor right then and there, and I ended up delivering him."

"Mom, we've heard that story a thousand times."

"I know. I know. Hank and Jennifer are mailing something, and I have some other clothes, too. Oh—and an azalea that I rooted from our yard, but that's the main thing."

"Emmy, it's so precious. Thank you. She will definitely wear it when she's christened. I hope you can come back then."

"I'll certainly try. Caroline, go get your present."

Caroline went into the foyer and returned with a large newspaper-wrapped board. "Well, this isn't really like me, but I saw it and it reminded me of you."

Gail smiled at Caroline before tearing the paper. She turned the print over and drew her breath in.

"I can't believe it. Look, Eric. It's a John Singer Sargent, like the print Mom gave me."

Two girls in flowing white dresses stood in a garden of carnations and roses, intent on lighting Chinese lanterns. Their faces were full of innocent charm, unconscious of their beauty.

"Caroline, that's truly lovely," Emma said.

"It's called *Carnation, Lily, Lily, Rose.* Isn't that odd? But I found out that the artist used to call it *Damnation, Silly, Silly, Pose* and I thought that was great. Also, this guy—Sargent—he did a whole series of male nudes that hardly anyone knows about. When I found out about that, I knew it was the right picture."

"Honestly, Caroline!" Emma said, looking at the ceiling.

Caroline stared at the picture for a minute. "It's a little traditional for my taste, but my friend—you know, the one I told you about—my friend really liked it."

Gail set the picture on the chair and stared at it, finally allowing the tears to roll down her face. Emma patted her hand. She heard a car door shut outside and looked up to see her mother walking up the sidewalk.

Eric unwrapped the cake and cut into it, releasing a fresh, sweet smell into the air.

A Large Purple Button

BEFORE THAT LAST HOSPITAL STAY, there were some good times, like when we went to the beach again. Often when Mom was sick from the chemo, she told us she wanted to do that, needed to do it. She said she needed to hear the waves again, see the seagulls and pelicans in the air, watch the shrimp trawlers move across the horizon. We didn't know what to think, but she felt so bad then that we'd promise anything she wanted, anything to help her get better. When we were finally able to go, Claire special ordered a plum-colored swimsuit and matching cover-up that this button came from. Mom looked great in it.

We stayed right on the ocean so it wouldn't be too far for her to walk. In the morning, the sun would just pour into the condo and we could look out on the low tide as if everything had been remade the night before. We boiled shrimp and pan-fried flounder. We swam in the ocean during the day, walked on the beach in the evening, and played board games at night.

That last vacation has been a comforting memory for me, a safe spot in my mind to retreat to while I work things out. Since Mom's death I've read a lot on the internet about dying and grieving. I'm surprised by how much is meaningful to me, to Caroline the Cynic. The metaphor of the dying person as a traveler on a voyage, the concept of hospice as a haven for that voyager. The image of a ship passing out of our view only to arrive on another shore, greeted by rejoicing. These are the images I've clung to.

I've read other things too, that are sometimes helpful. Dying people often seek out those people with whom they have unfinished business. They have a need to say those things that have gone unspoken, to put to rest open issues. I suppose that could be true of my mother. Maybe she didn't leave me any last words because she felt all was right with us. That's what I like to believe.

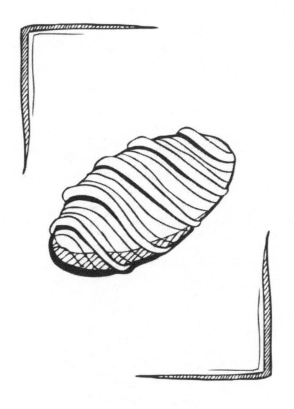

Kitty Hawk II

The North Carolina Outer Banks, 1996

EMMA PULLED HER COVER-UP around her as the ocean breeze picked up. She was sitting in front of the sand dunes entertaining Gail's baby boy, John, with a shovel and bucket. His chubby round face concentrated on the yellow plastic as he stabbed at the sand, lifted it abruptly, and let it pour back down to the earth. It was remarkable, Emma thought, how even amidst the tremendous change each decade brought, the rituals of childhood stayed the same. There was still that bright-eyed fascination with life itself, with the wonder of falling sand and sunshine.

Her family couldn't understand why she had wanted to come here again after all these years. Nobody had been here since the accident, as if they could forget about it by ignoring the place it had happened. Emma herself didn't understand why she wanted to be here again, but she knew it had something to do with the ocean itself, with its constant tearing down and building back up. Being here by the water, she had been able to cry for the first time since she'd found out she had ovarian cancer. After all those years of worrying about breast cancer, to be stricken with this had seemed like a bad joke. Everyone thought she could

285

fight it, too. After all, she'd done it before. But they weren't the ones who were cut open and sewed shut, subjected to a slow drip of toxic chemicals followed by surges of radiation. Not just for a time, but over and over again.

At first, in between sessions, she'd tried to block it all out and keep on going. There had even been a couple of times when she thought she had conquered it, but it always came back. After a while—what had it been? Two years? Three? After a while, she just stopped feeling. A grayness covered everything.

Then, lying in a reclining chair during a chemo session, an image of the ocean sprang into her head. It wasn't ominous and dark, as she had come to think of it. It was shining and clean and powerful. At that moment, she knew that if she could just see the ocean, things would be different.

They'd arrived at the beach in the evening. A storm had just blown by, and the sun was shooting through openings in the clouds. She took off her shoes and walked into the tide and began crying. Why was that? she thought. From the depths of her memory, she remembered an old spiritual she had heard as a tiny child:

By the waters of Babylon
Where we sat down
And where we wept
When we remembered Zion.

In her mind, Emma could see the Israelites sobbing, with their long hair trailing into the river, their tears falling into the water and silently disappearing. She wondered if they had felt relief.

The sun grew stronger, and Emma reached in the bag for some more sunscreen for her and the baby. Joe Keller, the druggist who worked in the downtown pharmacy before it had been forced out of business by Wal-Mart, had explained that one of her medications caused skin sensitivity to the sun. Not that she was worried about skin cancer at this point, but having a sunburn was one experience she could forgo.

Emma looked toward the ocean, where the rest of the family was playing in the surf. Charles was helping Hank and Jennifer's six-year-old twins, Drew and Danielle, ride waves. He would hold them on their brightly-colored floats until just the right wave came by, then give them a push in front of the white ridge. Their faces held a mixture of glee and terror as they rode into the foam. Charles watched them intently and then began clapping when they jumped up and ran back toward him. Emma couldn't hear him, but from the way Hank and Jennifer were laughing, she knew he was exhorting them with words of wisdom from a church sign. Something like, "God promises a safe landing, not a calm passage." Or, "Will Power—You give God your Will, He gives you the Power." During the past year, he had made friends with a young black engineer who was a part-time preacher at a Missionary Baptist Church. The two of them spent every Monday evening putting up a new message on the sign outside the tiny church in a run-down part of town. Charles even went to services there sometimes.

Caroline and her husband, Rishi, waved at Emma as they set off on a walk. Despite herself, Emma felt a little wave of shock at seeing Rishi's dark arm draped around her daughter's shoulders. She knew she shouldn't have that reaction—it wasn't right or nice or anything else. But she did, even though she'd grown quite fond of Rishi. He was from southern India, and he had a gentle sense of humor and manners that were slightly old-fashioned. Around him, Caroline seemed to be a much nicer person, less stormy.

Victoria, Rishi's eight-year-old daughter from a previous marriage, had come to the beach with them. Her skin was lighter than Rishi's—a rich almond color—and her fine features were set off by perfect waves of jet-black hair. Emma looked at her and seven-year-old Miranda, building a drip castle on the beach. Both girls had a heartbreaking innocence in their coral-colored swimsuits, their skin covered in sand and saltwater, their hair tangled by the wind. This is how I'll always remember them, Emma thought. Like lilies in May.

Emma stared at them all. It was hard to believe her little family had grown so big. Things had changed so much. Looking up and down the beach, Emma had a hard time recognizing anything familiar. Shiny new houses and condos overwhelmed the remaining old homes, which seemed to cower in front of the massive construction cranes that dotted the horizon. The big green house they used to stay in was long gone, but Charles had found a small condo complex near the quieter end of the beach. It was nice to be right on the beach, where she could see the waves glowing in the moonlight all night long. And the place had a screened porch and a pool with comfortable lounge chairs where she could watch the children play, glistening with the water in the sun.

Emma gathered up the baby and their bags to go get lunch. As she stood up, a gentle wave of dizziness went over her for a moment. She stood still with her face to the sun, listened to the surf crashing, felt the baby's soft tender skin against her own, regained her steadiness, and headed through the sea grass and down the trail.

* * * *

Sitting by the open French door in the condo's master bedroom, Emma flipped through a beach magazine and saw an ad: "Orville and Wilbur were right—Experience the thrill of flight—Hang glide with Kitty Hawk Kites." Something about it made her stop and look more closely. There was a man about Hank's age running down a huge sand dune with a bright green glider on his back. He stared straight ahead in concentration. She fumbled through her sewing kit for scissors, then cut out the ad to give to Hank. Not long ago, she had instinctively steered away from anything that could present the slightest danger to members of her family. It had always been a struggle just to let Caroline and Hank go to the lake or ride their bikes downtown. Now she felt differently.

She remembered Hank's intense desire to fly, his dreams of space when he was a boy. He had never laughed easily, like some, but you could tell when he was engrossed in something he loved. Lately she'd seen a mild expression of that when he was playing with the twins or talking to Jennifer. That was as it should be, but Emma knew there were other things inside him, too.

That night, after supper was over and the kids were in bed, she showed the ad to Hank. He looked at it for a moment, then made a grandfatherly sound like, "hmph" and put it down. "Do you want to go hang gliding, Mom?"

The others looked at her quizzically. They're really wondering about me, she thought. They don't know what I'll do next.

"No, Hank," she said. "I don't want to go hang gliding, but I want you to. It looks like fun."

Hank picked up the ad and looked at it again before shaking his head.

"I don't think so, Mom. This probably costs about $100 and there's no way you could go very far as a beginner."

"I'll pay for it. Go as often as you like. It's a present."

Jennifer came over and looked at the ad. "Hank, you should do it," she said. "What a great chance."

"I thought you wanted me to help with the boys, remember?"

Emma and Jennifer looked at each other and smiled.

"Are you scared?" Jennifer asked.

"Very funny."

"Scared of what?" Caroline asked, walking in from the kitchen with a Popsicle.

"I'm not scared of anything," Hank said. "Mom wants to throw her money away on this hang gliding operation, that's all."

Caroline looked at the ad. "That is so cool. Rishi, come check this out. Hank's going hang gliding."

Rishi came over and looked at the ad. "'Ahh . . . to soar with the birds,'" he read the text. "'No sound but the wind above and the ocean below. Just you and the sky and the flight.' These people must be Hindu. Sounds very Vedic."

"What does that mean?" Jennifer asked.

"Family secret," Rishi said, holding his face in a serious pose before dodging a pillow thrown by Jennifer.

The door opened and Charles came in from his nightly walk.

"It's beautiful out there," he said. "There's heat lightning, and I saw some fox fire wash up from the tide."

"Hank's going hang gliding," Caroline said.

"Oh, God," Hank said.

"Really," said Charles. "When?"

"How about tomorrow?" Emma asked. "I'll call first thing."

They all looked at Hank.

"Okay, okay," he said, looking at Emma. "I give up."

* * * *

Just after dawn, the tide began to recede, leaving unmarked sand glistening in the new day. Other than the surf, the beach was quiet—there were just a few early morning walkers out looking for shells along with sandpipers skirting the foam at the water's edge.

Gail and Emma came down the path through the sand dunes. They didn't speak, neither one wanting to break the fragile golden haze that covered everything about them. The two women found a spot on the beach and set up the umbrella. For several minutes they simply sat there watching the ocean gracefully withdraw.

Finally, Gail opened her bag and pulled out a box. She looked up at Emma.

"It's a nice gift," she said, fingering a set of paints and a sketchpad. Emma noticed her hands were shaking.

"I never forgot how you loved to paint," Emma said, her eyes hidden behind dark glasses. "I wanted to know that you hadn't forgotten either."

Gail ran the new bristles of the paintbrush over the palm of her hand. "I don't know," she whispered. "It's probably too late."

Emma looked straight at the ocean. "It's something you do for yourself," she said. "The rest doesn't matter."

Gail looked up and down the beach, at the sea grass and sand dunes, the silent figures walking in the distance, the sun beginning to burn away the haze. Then she looked at Emma sitting in the shade of the umbrella. A cool spot of lavender, a center for all the rest.

"I remember painting your picture," Gail said.

Behind her dark glasses, Emma smiled. "I remember that too."

"If you don't mind, I'd like to try again."

Gail walked around the umbrella and found a spot where the angle of light was just right. She spread a blanket on the sand and sat down. Then, with steady hands, she turned to the first blank sheet, squeezed some color onto her palette, and plunged the brush in.

* * * *

During the heat of the day, Charles gathered the grandchildren

291

inside the air-conditioned condo. "I'm trying to pick out next week's sign message," he told them. "Tell me which of these you like the best."

Emma could hear them as she lay on her bed resting, their voices floating in and out of her half-dreams.

"Here's a good one that seems to relate to our time here at the beach," he said. "'Be fishers of men: You catch 'em, he'll clean 'em.' I like that. What do you think?"

In the silence, Emma could picture the children's faces as they stared at Charles, not old enough to grasp the point. She knew he would go on, undeterred.

"Okay, here's another one," Charles said. "'If you go against God's grains, you'll get splinters.'"

There was a notable silence in the condo. Finally, Miranda said, "I don't get it."

"Hmmm . . . All right, how about this: 'Don't give up. Moses was once a basket case.'"

Emma laughed and floated into sleep.

* * * *

In the midst of a dream, the door opened and footsteps came down the hall.

"Hank," Charles said. "How was it?"

Emma opened her eyes and listened.

"You should have seen him," Jennifer said. "He was a natural. He went twice as far as anybody else."

"Is Mom awake?" Hank asked.

"I'm in here," Emma called out.

Hank came in the room and sat down in the wicker chair by the bed. His hair was blown and his face was sunburned, but his eyes had that look she'd wanted to see. Proud. Content. Exuberant in a controlled, Hank-like way.

"Well . . ." she prompted.

"It wasn't like what I thought," Hank said. "There were all these college kids in my group, and I remember thinking this is really a waste of time. But then we got out to Jockey's Ridge and everything changed. It's 138 feet high, the tallest sand dune on the east coast, and the winds were strong.

"We got five turns and on my first time, I started running down the hill and I didn't know if anything at all would happen. All the other guys had gone about 40 yards or so. Nothing great, but they'd gone a ways. I kept running, and then the wind took over and it lifted me up. I could look out over the ocean and the clouds and everything else.

"I was really flying."

* * * *

Cool, salty air blew through the screened-in porch where Emma sat with a pile of her family's clothes. "Remember to bring any clothes that need mending," she had told them before the trip. This was one thing she could still do. They wouldn't let her do laundry or cook or anything else, but she could sit on the porch, watch the waves, listen to the seagulls, and sew. She remembered how Mary Reed had sat on the screened porch of her house, knitting hour after hour, watching the neighborhood children play.

Of course, the children were adults now and could take care of themselves, but sometimes little things went undone. Rips, hems, missing buttons—things that were easy enough to fix during these lazy afternoons at the beach. Her own mother had done the same thing for her when Emma was so busy with a young household. Now she understood why. It made her feel good to still be able to make things right for her children.

Like this blouse of Caroline's. Emma didn't know how to describe it—a pale green cotton dyed over in an exotic pattern of bright patches of color. Caroline had a lot of clothing like this, unusual things she bought at out-of-the-way shops or picked up during her visits to India. The blouse was beautiful in a unconventional way, but Caroline probably hadn't worn it in months because the button on the collar was missing. Good thing it's the only button on the blouse, Emma thought. It should be easy enough to find a replacement.

She opened up the glass jar she kept spare buttons in and began sorting through them. It was like handling bits and pieces of the past—buttons from loved ones' dresses and suits and coats carefully gathered up and saved for future use. She had inherited many of the buttons from her mother and grandmother, even her Great Aunt Maggie. Each woman adding to the collection, like curators of a family museum. Now what would happen to them? Emma wondered. Would people even use buttons in the future, or would everything have Velcro?

An image came into Emma's mind. Six-year-old Caroline, in a rare moment of quiet, sitting on the floor of the sewing room, sorting through the buttons as Emma sewed. Late afternoon sun poured through the windowpanes and glinted on Caroline's straight brown hair. From time to time, she'd pick out a special one and hold it, glittering, in the palm of her hand. "Look at this one," she whispered in Emma's ear. "It's from a wizard's cloak. He cast a spell and disappeared and this is all that's left." Emma could picture Caroline's eyes shining intently as she spoke, staring at the button, caught up in her own world.

Emma sighed. As much as Caroline had loved playing with the buttons, she probably wouldn't have any use for them at all now. She wasn't exactly the domestic sort. As far as Emma could tell, Rishi did most of the cooking that went on in their house. She couldn't imagine Caroline keeping a button collection.

Maybe I should give them to Gail, Emma thought. She remembered how Gail had always loved to help around the house when she came to stay in the summer. They'd spent hours together on sewing projects while Caroline was either outside or holed up in her room with a book. Plus, Gail had a daughter herself now, someone who might want the buttons one day.

Emma looked out to the beach and wondered—again—if Caroline would ever have children. It wasn't totally unreasonable, she thought. Caroline seemed to have fun with Victoria. A thought sprang into her mind—Caroline's daughter would be as beautiful as Victoria. It was followed by another thought, a thought she had only recently allowed herself to acknowledge: *Even if she has a daughter, I'll probably never see her.* It wasn't a horrid thought like the ones that used to haunt her. It didn't scare her or make her feel ashamed. It simply was.

In her mind, she had been preparing for months now. Getting her house in order. Returning to this beach. Trying to find little nuggets of meaning to pass along to her children. She felt good about what she'd given Gail and Hank, but there was still a looming question mark when she tried to think of just the right thing for Caroline. Sometimes at night, when it was hard to sleep, she worried about that.

Emma let a handful of buttons pour through her fingers, feeling their coolness caress her skin. Her mind drifted freely in and out of the past, and she felt a strong sense of calm. Here in the daylight, she knew the answer would come to her in time.

An opalescent oval caught Emma's eye. It was the button from a suit she had bought when she first started teaching. She'd been wearing it when she first met Charles at church. She wouldn't have guessed that the same button would work on an old suit and Caroline's blouse, but it did.

Emma plucked it from the mix and began sewing.

Victoria's Easter Button

I SHOULD KNOW BETTER, of course, but as I hold the egg-shaped button over the jar, I still expect something cosmic to happen. I keep thinking about a legend my college religion professor told. When Siddhārtha Gautama, the Buddha, finally decided to renounce all earthly riches, he threw a priceless golden platter into the river. As it sank into the water, the young prince heard an echoing chime ... the sound of the platter hitting a mountain of platters, platters which had been thrown in the river by all the Buddhas who had preceded him throughout eternity.

I have no idea why that story has stayed with me all these years, but it has. I can sense every detail of it: the way the wind kicks up the sand and stings the young Buddha's skin, the bright silk robes flowing about his body, the hot sun glaring on the water and reflecting on the golden platter as it flies across the surface, the moment of quiet before a single beautiful note rises from the depths, the final warm feeling of freedom and release. That experience has become part of me, one of many experiences I've claimed as my own. Like the Great Spirit pulsing out of the drum and filling the dancer. Or the Spirit of Love reaching out to turn the globes and create the music of the spheres.

They're all things that I don't exactly believe. Still, I like the comfort of their beauty, so I keep them close to my heart.

I found this button in the back of our closet, a lavender egg button that came off an Easter dress I bought Victoria when she was six. The day we bought it was the first day we spent alone together. I couldn't think what else to do with a six-year-old child, so we went to the mall. We looked at the frilly little girl dresses and declared them to be way too prissy. Near the end of our shopping, Victoria saw a white cotton dress with a yellow satin sash and a row of different-colored egg buttons. We both thought it was perfect.

Her mother never liked the dress, of course, and I'm afraid it probably came to a bad end. Still, when I found the button in the closet, the freshness of that moment came back to me. The button is tender and childlike, and as soon as I found it, I knew what to do with it. I brought it straight to the kitchen.

I hold the egg over the jar for a moment longer, then drop it in.

Nothing cosmic happens. No lily-white hand rises to take it. There isn't music. Just a quiet clink. I thought I might feel disappointed, but I don't. I decide that the button I dropped in was significant. Not in a cosmic way, perhaps, but significant nonetheless. Again I remember what Marie said: A button is a little thing, but it's a thing of use. Something to connect, to hold things together. Not perfectly—not strong and fast like a metal zipper—but holding them together still.

Feeling satisfied, I screw the lid on the jar and place it back on the windowsill. Then I walk upstairs and shuffle through my desk drawer until I find the card of Shakespeare buttons. I stare at it hard, daring those wolves to come.

And they do, but different than before. They are quiet, walking on the pads of their feet, putting their noses up in the air, trying to catch a scent. I watch them carefully to make sure they won't threaten or attack. They watch me back. We get tired of watching each other, and after a while, they lie down and go to sleep.

* * * *

I stand on the edge of Gail's sidewalk, the buttons buried deep inside my backpack. The walk is made of old brick, and it curves behind some bushes so that I can't quite see how it ends. I remember the last time I was here, when Miranda was born and I brought Mom down. That was a good time—everything in my life seemed clear, possible, new. I wonder why I haven't thought about that time in so long. About tiny Miranda, with her soft, wrinkled body. About the confidence I felt being on my own for the first time, the excitement of meeting Rishi, the good feeling I got from organizing the visit.

I stay there at the edge of the walk for a moment, looking around. The yard has changed a lot since then. Now there is jasmine growing up the downspout and a bank of azaleas behind the drive. A Saint Francis stands surrounded by heather, and I can hear a fountain close by. I walk slowly to the front door, which is made of weathered wood and has a big brass knocker shaped like a claddagh ring. I take a breath and knock. As I stand there waiting, I feel something cold touch my leg. A big, black dog is there, cautiously sniffing. It looks up and stares at me with bright, round eyes.

The door opens and there is Gail, looking more like Claire than ever. She hugs me briefly, then steps back and laughs.

"I see you've met Lupa," she says, leading me into the house.

* * * *

If this were a fairy tale, that would be it. The End. Forgiveness. Reunion. Happily Ever After. It isn't quite like that.

To be honest, I want to get out of Gail's house as soon as I can. We sit on the porch, watching John play with the dog in the yard, looking at Miranda's school pictures. I want to shake my foot, stand up and sit back down, do anything but sit there and visit. There are reminders all over Gail's house—the sewing basket in the back room, the lemon crisp cookies that were my mom's recipe, even a picture from our last vacation at the beach. I am on edge the whole two hours I'm here, but still feel as if I have something to complete.

Finally, I am leaving and we're at the door. I pick up my backpack and say, as offhandedly as I can, "Oh, I saw these the other day, and for some reason they reminded me of you." I hand her the card of buttons and wait to see how she will react.

It isn't fair, of course. There's no way she can know the enormity those things have grown to in my mind. I know that, and still, I wait to see.

She stares at them and then looks at me quizzically. She's either thinking, *How odd to give a present of buttons* or *I can't believe Caroline bought these.* Maybe both.

"I met this strange woman at a flea market," I begin to explain. "She collects buttons, and when she showed me these, I thought of you."

She continues to stare at them.

"It's nothing, really," I say, zipping the backpack shut. "Better go."

"No," Gail says, grabbing my arm. I look at her, wondering what she means.

"It isn't nothing. It means you'll come again," she says, looking straight at me.

"Sure," I shrug.

"No, I mean it. You're the closest thing to a sister I have. Promise you'll at least meet me somewhere. Sometime."

Something in me falls away, and I choose to let it go. I stand there for a moment, trying to find the words I need to say. "Okay," I finally manage. "That would be good."

Then I set off down the path.

* * * *

Six months later, Rishi massages my neck muscles and says, with his exaggerated accent that makes me laugh: "Ahh . . . Good. Very good. The karma is dropping away. You are making progress!" I don't know. Maybe. I think *maybe* we all are. Hank doesn't seem quite as driven as he used to be. He had laser surgery on his eyes and is building a glider in the basement just for the fun of it. My dad retired in June. I'm helping him do a website of church signs. Last week he got 896 hits.

I've seen Gail several more times. It's still awkward, but we're working on it. In a way, we're getting to know each other as real people, as adults, for the first time ever. I'd come to think of her as so much my mother's child that I never saw how different she really is. She's a photographer and a painter. She owns at least fifty pairs of shoes and has a weakness for mimosas. Lately, she's learning to weave. Last time I saw her, she told me her mother had taken up with a fifty-five-year-old sculptor she'd met at the museum. Gail seemed embarrassed, but for some reason I laughed, and soon she was laughing too. We were drinking Diet Coke and lying in the sun, so I raised my glass and said, "Here's to Claire, my coolest aunt, a woman who knows what she wants and isn't afraid to go after it." Gail looked at me as if she hadn't thought of that before. Sometimes it takes someone else's perspective before you can see your mother as a person in her own right.

My business is going well. Victoria has become my chief tester and quality control expert. Whenever she comes, we spend hours together, working on plot lines, perfecting the puzzles. Rishi is a little jealous, but he'll get over it.

The wolves still come, but they're not as ferocious as they used to be. They're restless sometimes, whining and pawing the ground as if looking for words. Usually they stay in the shadows, simply watching. And on rare occasions—like the other day when the cat was sprawled across the windowsill purring full throttle while Victoria and I were engrossed in a project and Rishi was downstairs filling the house with the aroma of tamarind, coriander, and cardamom—on rare moments like that, they leap and run through the snow, filled with purpose.

* * * *

I always thought I would have a dream of my mother. I don't know what exactly . . . a vision of her carrying a lantern through a dark forest, showing me the way to go, some sort of message from beyond. For years and years, it didn't happen. I dreamed of going to the grocery store, driving on the interstate, working on my computer, but not of her. I hoped, even, that I would have the opportunity to talk to her. I wanted to tell her we are all okay, even Dad. I wanted to tell her that Gail and I have embarked on something new. But first, I wanted to tell her that I, her daughter Caroline, have become a button collector.

And yet, whenever I dreamed, she was absent. I always felt an empty final feeling settle over me, a lostness.

Then, the other morning as I was waking up, an image stayed with me. It kept popping up through the day and followed me around. It was something other than a dream. I was walking down the hall of my parents' house, and it was dark and quiet and cool. It was late afternoon, and the sun was streaming through the den windows in the back. She was sitting in the armchair, her sewing kit by her side, reading glasses pushed down her nose, intent on pulling the needle down and through, down and through. She heard me walk in and looked up.

She was glad to see me.

QUESTIONS AND TOPICS FOR DISCUSSION

1. Do you feel Emma's relationship with Gail is a way of attempting to extend her relationship with her brother?

2. Is Caroline's anger at Gail misplaced, or do Gail's actions warrant some blame?

3. We collect family memories in many different forms. Does your family have a unique collection that reflects its history?

4. Through most of history, women have been limited to expressing their creativity, dreams, desires, and accomplishments through crafts. How much of this has carried on to influence today's hobbies of quilting, scrapbooking, knitting, and others?

5. For most of her life, Caroline feels she doesn't belong. Does that feeling encourage her to seek out others who may feel they are also outsiders? Does it impact her decision to marry Rishi?

6. What could Charles have done to help Caroline feel more accepted?

7. Does Gail's mother, Claire, have an inability to form close relationships, or does she express her feelings in unconventional ways? Why do you think she keeps her daughter at arms' length?

8. Did Gail become the mother she felt she never had?

9. What is the significance of the correlation of personality traits between Caroline and Claire?

ACKNOWLEDGMENTS

For that sweetest of gifts, encouragement, as well as the hard gifts of honesty and discernment, I thank all the Wordwrights and especially Katie, Elaine, Susan, Pat, and our fearless founder, Ted. And for their collective well of patience, I thank Miriam, Alicia, Lauren, and other friends who kept on giving whenever I asked for just a little more feedback.

High praise and appreciation to Ann for her shining example, inspiration, and support.

Much, much gratitude to Rebecca for her vision, guidance, supreme editing skills, and, most of all, for seeing possibilities I could not.

For their sparks of insight and infusions of creative energy, I thank Patrick and Laurel.

Finally, I will be forever grateful to Jeff for enabling my writing habit, believing in me, and being the coolest techie ever.

ABOUT THE AUTHOR

Elizabeth Jennings has worked as a features writer, copywriter, tutor, and adjunct instructor, but first and foremost, she is a reader on the hunt for the next great story. Her fiction has appeared in a variety of publications, including *Prime Number Magazine*, *Apalachee Review*, and the children's magazine *Ladybug*. A native of Clemson, South Carolina, she earned degrees in English from The University of North Carolina at Chapel Hill and The University of Delaware. She lives with her family in the Blue Ridge Mountains of North Carolina. You can contact Jennings through her website at www.elizabethjennings.com.

Now available from Cup of Tea Books

Another great book club selection!

BOBBI REED

almost always

Here's the way Eva sees it: if John is so concerned about her butting into strangers' lives, he shouldn't leave her sitting at a table in Bob Evans with nothing to occupy her time . . .

Enter Cecelia—a pregnant teenager who needs a family for her baby. Fate has placed her at the table behind Eva and John.

Now Eva has a chance—a chance to give her daughter, Shelly, the one thing Shelly desperately wants.

But nothing is ever as easy as it seems.

Because sometimes daughters are not born to us—they are gifted by desperate teenagers—or seated behind us at Bob Evans . . .

www.cupofteabooks.com

Something Yellow

By Laura Templeton

"Now, young lady, you're going to have to help your mama through this." My great-aunt, Eloise, crushed me to her side in a hug that defied her ninety-some years.

"Yes, ma'am," I said, not sure if she was referring to the cancer or to Cailey's disappearance. Or to both.

I still held the pan of macaroni and cheese as I carried on multiple conversations and accepted hugs from distant cousins. Between the McCanns and the Callahans, Mother's people, our family practically owned this corner of the county. Finally, Tina Lynn realized my predicament and headed my way to help.

Before she could reach me, I heard someone call my name. I turned to see Aunt Eloise moving toward me like a ship plowing through swells.

"Holly, look who's here."

When I realized who she was steering my way, my stomach dove to my feet. Houston Phelps.

Cailey was dead for sure.

Coming soon from Cup of Tea Books

Cup of Tea Books

An Imprint of PageSpring Publishing
www.cupofteabooks.com